Undone

Phil Warner

Author Notes

This novel is a work of fiction and although some of the names may exist, most of the characters are completely fictitious.

Note that Amp is the actual groundskeeper at Publix Field in Lakeland, Florida, his wife's name is Amanda, and he has five children. Beyond that, again, his character is pure fiction. Including Amp's character in this work is only meant to be a tribute to those who work diligently behind the scenes to ensure that our professional sports operate smoothly.

Yes, I did lose an elementary and secondary school friend, Mark Golding to a tragic accident as described early in this novel. Mark loved to drive and unfortunately his passion took his life.

Also, the owner of Antonino's Original Pizza is Joe Ciaravino and a dear lifelong friend who is very proud of his pizza and his parents who taught him their craft.

Lastly of course, references to Windsor/Detroit/Chicago NHL legend Bob Probert are non-fiction. I had the honour of playing high school football and minor hockey with Proby. The last time I saw him was over 25 years ago, but it was really nice to catch up with him. He met my very young son and Bob was expecting another child just days later. It never ceases to amaze me as to how gentle and kind he was off the ice. Please bless Bob's soul and his family.

Part One - Narrated by Roberta Hodgson

Chapter 1.1 – Securing the Scene

My name is Roberta Hodgson and I am a traffic cop with the city of Detroit. I am at the tail end of an overnight shift and it is just after 7 a.m. in mid-April. By any standards, we have been blessed with some beautiful weather here in the Motor City this spring. Even early in the day today, it is already 58 degrees and there is virtually no humidity. We are in a warm spell and I will enjoy it while I can. I dread July when we can get well into the 80's with humidity to match and thankfully, the snow and wind chills of our Michigan winter are a distant memory at this point.

I am patrolling in Southwest Detroit on this fine morning and in my rear view mirror, I can see the newly rising sun glistening off the Detroit River.

As I am coming up on a curve on Jefferson Avenue West and crossing the Rouge River, I catch a glimpse of something shiny in the peripheral vision of my right eye. I am not sure what, but there is something on the riverbank. Being a Sunday morning, there is not much traffic, but I still do not want to just hit the brakes. I coast over the bridge and find a safe location to make a U-turn. As I travel back over the bridge, there is no oncoming traffic, so I drive on the wrong side of the road to get a better look at what caught my eye.

While I pull to a stop, I put on my flashing lights and I pull over onto the shoulder facing against non-existent traffic. Sure enough, there is a vehicle on its roof. I exit my cruiser quickly in case the accident is fresh, but I suspect not. I do not see any smoke, steam, or spinning wheels. The presence of any of those might indicate that I will need to help someone out of the vehicle, but the vehicle appears to have come to rest, hours before.

I brace myself to either find an unconscious driver or worse, and I pray that there are no children on board. Throughout my career, I have seen far too many young souls lost in careless driving accidents. I silently hope that the driver found their way out of the vehicle and is safe and sound somewhere sleeping off this misadventure.

After approaching the passenger side of the vehicle, I break the window with my baton to allow me access to the door controls and I unlock the vehicle. I hustle around to the driver's side of the vehicle, but then my heart sinks. A black male is hanging upside down in the driver's seat still secured by his three-point safety belt. I suspect that he has been there for some time as his head is bloated and his eyes are open, bloodshot and bulging. His left arm hangs down below his head and is swollen, but his right arm is caught up in the steering wheel. It is obvious that the swelling is from the blood pooling in the inverted lower extremities. After opening the driver side door and checking for a pulse unsuccessfully and unsurprisingly, I survey the interior to determine that there is no other occupant in the vehicle and I return to lean on my cruiser fender. A deep breath helps calm my nerves and I curse the fact that there is no hope of any amount of CPR reviving this driver.

My first priority is to call in the license plate of the vehicle and request assistance. While I wait, I secure the area with traffic markers on the shoulder and I direct the next two officers and cruisers that arrive to set up and redirect potential traffic to the far lane.

As determined from the license plate and the ownership, it appears the deceased is a David Stone, who is only 24 years old. I am also informed of a documented warning for the driver from less than two weeks prior. After donning clean latex gloves, I enter the vehicle from the passenger side. I carefully open the glove box, anticipating random items to fall out, and I retrieve a plastic dealership packet that likely has the ownership and insurance information. The paperwork is also in the name of David Stone.

After crawling along the roof liner, I reach to feel each of the driver's four pants pockets and I find a wallet in the right back pocket. To myself, I silently hope that the name on the driver's license is also David Stone, but then I question myself as to why. I guess it will be simpler if all the names match. Sure enough, the driver appears to be David Stone as well, but with the condition of his face, I cannot confirm that it is one in the same from the DMV photo. I put the wallet back into the exact same location and orientation from which I took it and that is when I notice something that gives me chills.

I see an old English D tattooed on the inside of the left forearm. This old English D is the one you see on a Detroit Tigers hat. Even non-baseball fans might recognize the logo if they have ever watched Magnum PI, whether it was the eighties television series with Tom Selleck or the recent reboot version. The logo leads me to believe that this David Stone is likely the rookie shortstop for the Detroit Tigers. I quietly say to myself, "Shit," and then I feel guilty for somehow thinking that this lost life is any different than if it was some random 24-year old male. As an officer, I am always very cautious, but now I have a heightened awareness of everything I do, as this will be a tragic event for the city of Detroit and the media will scrutinize every move the Detroit Police Department makes.

Chapter 1.2 – Initial Investigation

Detroit Police Department policy is that whenever there is a fatality in a motor vehicle accident, a homicide crash investigator is assigned to document and investigate the scene. My superior indicates that they want a homicide detective on-site, in addition to a crash investigator, and I am told that we may have to secure the site for quite some time. While I wait for the investigator and detective to arrive, I tour the area and scribble in my department issued notepad.

I assume the vehicle was coming from the northeast and was heading southwest, but see no skid marks. The road is dry, but I do notice a puddle on the shoulder that appears dark in color. I am not sure if it is something from the vehicle or if it is just pooling dew, or perhaps something totally different.

It looks like the vehicle left the road just prior to the bridge. It then clipped a large landscaping boulder, as evidenced by the silver paint and scrapes on the rock. It seems logical that the collision with the rock would upend the vehicle causing it to come to a rest on its roof. The engaged seatbelt ensured that the driver was held securely in his seat and he quite possibly survived the initial crash. However, he must have lost consciousness and remained strapped in until he succumbed to internal injuries or just too much blood to his head. Unfortunately, I know personally that this type of accident can be fatal.

I think back to my high school days when I was a sophomore. A male friend of mine, named Mark, had gone for a late night drive, in October. I remember the timing, because I was at an Octoberfest beer tent when I heard the news of his death. I heard by word of mouth as this was well before cell phones and social media. Mark ended up in an inverted position in his car in someone's side yard, ironically in a dried-up ditch – a similar version of the scene I see here today. I remember being furious when I read an article in the newspaper a few days later that the homeowner had heard a loud bang in the middle of the night, but did not think much of it and went back to sleep. Still to this day, I wonder if my friend would have survived if the homeowner would have gone outside to check on the noise and I also wonder if the homeowner feels any guilt. I feel my blood pressure rise, just as it does every time I recall this memory. I shake my head to clear my mind just like you would with a child's Etch a Sketch toy.

My mind comes back to the matter at hand and I continue taking notes regarding the scene. I return to the vehicle with my notepad in hand. Clearly, the airbags deployed, at least on the driver's side, as the depleted airbags hang from where they were deployed. The deployments left a chalky film over much of the interior. In the vehicle cabin, I notice a nearly empty bottle of Jack Daniels lying on its side on the roof liner. The bottle is open, but some of the amber liquid remains, just even with the uncapped spout. There is a nearly full, capped water bottle also lying on its side further to the back of the vehicle. The windshield is shattered into little pieces, but held together with the film of plastic as it is designed to do. On it, I note loose change, an empty Tic Tac packet, and a Sharpie marker. I speculate that all celebrities carry a black Sharpie for signing autographs. That speculation does not go into my notes.

I go back to lean on my cruiser again and I continue taking notes. While doing so, I am sure to just state facts as we have been instructed to do throughout my schooling and career. I will leave drawing conclusions to the accident re-creation experts and the detective. I do wonder why a detective is being called in so early into this investigation, but granted, our crash victim *is* a local celebrity. The brass will want another set of eyes on the situation, just in case.

Chapter 1.3 – Detective Gaines on the Scene

The crash investigator arrives and I give a summary of my notes, to which she jots down her own notes. She thanks me and leaves to survey the scene as well.

Just then, a black unmarked Dodge Charger pulls up and out crawls a detective whom I recognize, Finn Gaines. He yells at me, "Hey Hodgy, why am I getting called to an accident scene?" I do not know why he calls me Hodgy. My friends do shorten up my name, but they call me Hodge.

I will make a point as I respond, "The driver is a VIP and we need to cover all our bases here, Finny," with some emphasis on the last syllable.

The point is made as he responds with, "Finn, just Finn, please. Okay, let us take a look, Hodge."

"Ah, you can take a hint, can't you? Who says you can't teach an old dog new tricks?"

I do feel a twinge of guilt, because I could have responded as he did. The more mature route would have been to just tell him that I prefer Hodge. Okay, it is a lesson learned.

Finn continues, "Hey Hodge, what kind of vehicle is this?"

"2019 Toyota Rav4 Limited, hybrid model. Just a couple months old according to the registration."

"Any cell phone?"

"Yes, I patted down each pocket and it looks like it is in his left front pant pocket."

Finn pulls on a pair of gloves and slides out the iPhone. He puts the phone up to the driver's left thumb and nothing happens. This is not surprising considering how swollen the hand is. I have trouble unlocking my phone when my fingers are cold, wet, or if I have a cut. Finn then tries the body's right thumb and the phone comes to life.

I bite my lip as I wonder about the legality of this action, which just draws a grin from Finn. He makes some notes and declares, "So, it does *not* appear to be a texting and driving situation here."

I say, "Considering the phone was in his pocket, I would guess not," a little sarcastically, which he ignores.

As Finn continues to look at the phone, he mumbles, "So, he texted a Jessie at 12:03 a.m. asking her to call. Jessie did call him at 12:10 a.m., but he did not answer. Before that, he got a call from a Jimmy Greyson." Finn pauses and then continues a little louder while nodding, "Ahah, so this is who this is. This is *the* Dave Stone – the new shortstop for the Tigers."

"I thought that you knew. They didn't fill you in, eh?"

"Nope, I guess information flows as needed here."

"Well, you can get all my notes, no problem."

Finn says, "I appreciate that Hodge. Please be sure to document everything here and we better get the coroner to weigh in. I am guessing that the tox screen will show some alcohol. It clearly looks like an impaired driving case at first glance."

"Will do, Finn. I do have word that Mr. Stone was also pulled over not long ago by one of our officers. He was really out of it, but the officer was starstruck and let him go."

"Seriously, in this day and age? Let me guess. Last Chance?" to which I nod. Finn continues, "I will follow up with LaChance, but why call in a Homicide Detective on top of the homicide crash investigator?"

"As I said, the brass just wants us to cover all our bases, considering who the deceased is. Personally, I do not see anything jumping out at me. Do you? Is your *spiny sense* going off?"

Finn looks at me confused and asks, "*Spiny sense*?"

"Yeah, you know how Spider-Man will say that his *spiny sense* is tingling. His spine is tingling. Chills in the spine kind of thing."

"You jackass! Spider-Man has *spidey sense*, not *spiny sense*!!"

Well, I feel foolish, but after being called a *jackass*, the guilt I felt for calling him *Finny* has dissipated. I respond, "Are you sure? I have always thought is was like spine tingling."

"Yes, I am sure, Hodge. Well, right now, I have no tingling whatsoever, but I am still gathering evidence." He hands me the phone and continues, "Can you get the phone to IT? They can clone it and get the copy to me. I know they like to do the deep dive, but I want my own copy, too. Ninety percent of the time nowadays, the cell phone holds the secret that kicks investigations into another gear."

"Sure, but hey Gaines, there is the other possibility that we cannot overlook."

"Yes, I know. No skid marks on the road, alcohol involved, and career struggles. Suicide is a possibility here."

"Those struggles on the field are minor, but who knows what other struggles or demons an individual is battling? Now, this is a new vehicle, so would it have a black box?"

Gaines replies, "Yes and no. It will have an EDR, an Event Data Recorder, but the information is fairly limited and only within less than a minute prior to the accident. We will be able to tell if the vehicle safety features operated as expected, if the driver wore their seatbelt, and if the driver was pressing on the brakes or accelerator. The scope is fairly limited."

"And clearly, the airbags deployed, he was wearing his seatbelt and we see no evidence of braking."

"The seatbelt would tend to rule out suicide, would it not, Gaines?"

"Actually, not always. Sometimes, it is a last second decision and not always well thought out."

I cannot put a finger on it, but I do have a feeling that this is not a straightforward drunk driver going off the side of the road. Spiny sense or spidey sense, something is telling me that Finn Gaines has some work to do.

I also have an overwhelming sense of sadness. I will never get accustomed to this type of tragedy.

Chapter 1.4 – Media Circus Begins

Oh boy, the circus has begun. Channel 7 Action News shows up in a panel van with a large WXYZ-TV on a diagonal across the side of the van. The driver's side sliding door opens and out slips Lucy Chan. She reaches back into the van and grabs a TV video camera and props it up onto her right shoulder. Then, an athletic looking Hispanic male gets out of the van as well and slides the door shut. He dons a TV Camera too and follows Lucy around as she approaches the accident scene.

I have seen this before where Lucy walks around with a camera on her shoulder as she talks to another camera. Most of the video is from the true cameraman's camera, but they occasionally cut to Lucy's feed. I do not understand this. What is the point of her holding a video camera too? The real cameraman can do the entire feed. Maybe, some survey says that viewers think a reporter is more credible if they are carrying a camera. I just do not get it!

As Lucy reaches the caution tape with her camera wobbling all over the place, she faces the other camera and says, "Here we are at the scene of an early morning accident. Our understanding is that this vehicle left the roadway and the lone occupant is deceased. We have unconfirmed reports that the occupant is none other than our Detroit Tigers rookie shortstop, David Stone."

I approach Lucy Chan and her cameraman to ask them to clear the area. As soon as I am within three feet of her, a microphone is jammed in front of my face. Lucy looks at my nameplate and says, "Officer Hodgson, can you share the identity of the victim or the cause of the accident?" By the way, her camera is pointing straight up into the air and the cameraman has his lens pointing directly at me.

I respond firmly, "I will have to ask you and your crew to clear the area. We have an active investigation underway and we will make a public statement if and when the Detroit Police Department deems it appropriate."

Thankfully, they oblige, but they set up a subsequent camp just a few hundred yards away. It is obvious that they are continuing to film with the scene in the distant background.

Several hours later, the investigators finish gathering evidence and we release the scene. I wonder to myself as to how long it will take for the makeshift memorial to form. I suspect we will have hundreds of flowers, baseballs, mini-bats, and candles here within a few hours. I guess this will be the first step for Detroit baseball fans, in their grieving process.

Chapter 1.5 – A Surprise Phone Call

About a week after the David Stone accident, I finally wake up from my sleep feeling rested. This is the first time since coming upon the accident scene that I actually got a solid sleep. I have to admit that the sight of Stone's distorted body impacted me significantly. The sight was truly disturbing and gave me an overwhelming sadness, that I am having difficulty shaking.

As I am getting dressed for a relaxing day off, I hear my phone do a double buzz which means I have a text message. I look and I am surprised to see that Detective Gaines wants me to give him a call. After brewing a cup of coffee, I oblige.

Once connected, I hear, "Hello, Detective Gaines, here."

"Hey Finn, it is Hodge. What can I do for you? I assume this is about the Stone investigation."

"Thanks for calling me Hodge. Yes, it is. I have two things I wanted to ask you."

"Shoot away. I am happy to help."

At first, I think he is questioning my investigative skills regarding the wallet and phone placements in David Stone's pockets, but then I realize he might be on the cusp of a breakthrough in the case.

I assure him that I put the wallet back after I confirmed the identity, exactly as I had found it. He also asks about the phone and if I moved it.

I assure him again, "No, I felt for it, but did not disturb it. I did not need it to confirm identity. It was in his left front pocket."

I get it right this time and I ask him if his spidey sense is tingling. He indicates that it is and he found another anomaly.

Finn says, "Thanks so much. I definitely need to dig deeper into this. I may be in touch again."

"Hey wait, Finn. You said that you had two things," as I figured the phone and wallet locations were just one item.

"Oh right! Um, oh, got it. I remember seeing in your notes that you noticed a puddle of water on the side of the road. I have to admit that I did not look at the puddle, nor did the accident investigator. Neither of us did. Can you fill me in as to what you saw?"

"Sure, I am not certain it is connected to the accident, but I just thought it was odd. It did not rain that night and I was working, so I would have known. The humidity was quite low and I could not picture it being from dew or any kind of condensation."

Finn asks more questions about what the puddle looked like and I wish that I had taken a picture of it. Hindsight is always 20/20. Then again, it may not even be relevant.

Finn finishes the conversation with, "Thanks so much Hodge. By the way, good for you."

"Good for me, what?"

"Well, I do not know if the puddle is significant. That said, two trained investigators did not give it a second thought, but you did. Maybe that should tell you something."

With that, I hear a click and my phone returns to the home screen. Well, I am now very curious and surprised that the almighty Detective Gaines may have given me a compliment, rather than calling me a jackass.

Chapter 1.6 – As Expected

On a day shift mid-morning, I am cruising around in my usual neighborhood. This is an industrial area and there is not normally much pedestrian traffic. However, I find myself driving eastbound on West Jefferson Avenue and I come across a homeless man near the site where David Stone lost his life. I slow my cruiser and decide to pull over when I see the homeless man pick up a hat that was part of the makeshift memorial that I had anticipated forming.

I walk up to the man who immediately puts the hat back down where he got it. I ask, "Excuse me, do you know why I stopped?"

"Yes, ma'am. I am very sorry. It's just that you know, I don't got much hair and summer is coming."

"I get that, Mister," and I pause, waiting for him to complete the sentence with his last name.

"Oh, no mister for me. My friends, they just calls me Gabby. Gabby is fine on account of I like to talk a lot. It actually annoys my friends and all."

"Alright, Mr. Gabby. You may take the hat as you could use it, but please just leave everything else."

"Okay, Officer," he pauses to look at my badge, "Officer Hodgson. I appreciate it."

"Hodge."

"Pardon?"

"My friends, they just calls me Hodge," I reply with a smile.

"Thank you, Hodge. That is very kind of you. I will be on my way. Here I go and I will leave everything else." He continues talking as he walks away towards Mexican Village, but his voice becomes inaudible. Okay, that is why they call him Gabby.

I turn back to the makeshift memorial and admire all the cards, posters, flowers, and Tigers memorabilia. Mr. Stone had a lot of potential and although he was off to a slow start, the fans did have high hopes for him and the team this season. They were calling him and

Jimmy Greyson the *dynamic duo*. I guess that dynamic duo was torn apart.

I kneel down on one knee and say to myself out loud, "No one deserves to die this young. My prayers go to you, your family, and your friends. God, please give them strength. If this was not an accident, I have confidence in our department that we will get to the bottom of this. David Stone, I pray that your soul rests in peace."

I point to my forehead, stomach, left shoulder, and right to form a cross. I conclude with, "Amen," as I stand back up and return to my cruiser.

Chapter 1.7 – Good Samaritan

Several days later, after a particularly rough shift, I am out for a run along Woodward Avenue. This is my way to release the stress of my job. As I am running, a Maroon 5 song is playing through my wireless earbuds. I really do not know which song it is, but I guess it is one of their 84 hits.

I am heading north along the famous Dream Cruise Avenue and I turn right onto East Willis Street. Up in the distance in a large parking lot, I see two men approaching each other. When they establish their positions, they are roughly six feet apart. From their stances, it is obvious that they are agitated. I debate whether I should speed up or slow down, but I maintain my pace, while keeping a watchful eye on the situation.

Damn, I see one of the males pull a knife, so I pick up my pace and yell, "Hey!" My hope of drawing the aggressor's attention has no effect. As I am yelling, "Police! Drop the weapon!" the knife is thrust into the other male's torso rapidly four times. This is not going to be good.

I break into a full sprint even though I am already five miles into my run. The aggressor sprints down the street away from me, still carrying the blood soaked knife. I do not pursue him as my first priority is this man's life. I approach the victim and tear off my shirt, leaving myself in a sports bra. I arrange my shirt to cover the puncture wounds and apply pressure with my right hand and right knee. I raise my left arm, which has my iPhone secured in an armband and I breathe deep, to steady my voice. I say, "Hey Siri, call 911." Thankfully, Siri recognizes my voice even though my pulse is racing and my breathing is labored.

The voice on the other end asks, "911, How may I direct your call?"

I focus in order to be very clear. "This is Officer Roberta Hodgson, badge 8324 off duty. Do not transfer me. I need an ambulance to just east of Woodward and Willis A-SAP. Male with multiple stab wounds. I also need police to pursue a white male, short black hair, black gym shorts, red t-shirt, black ball cap, armed with a knife, and dangerous. He headed east from this location."

"Yes ma'am. Consider both to be on their way. Please stay with the victim, unless someone else arrives with first aid knowledge."

"I am staying here. Victim has lost consciousness and I am maintaining pressure."

I hear ambulance sirens and I remember that there is a hospital less than a block away. I say to myself, "Well, if you are going to get stabbed, this is as good a spot as any."

The 911 operator responds, "The ambulance should be there within a minute. An officer is just east of you and appears to have apprehended a male who matches your description."

I look down and say, "Well sir, you are getting outstanding service today. Please hang in there."

The operator asks, "Officer, are you talking to me?"

"No sorry, talking to our victim here. The ambulance has arrived, so I am going to head east to identify the perp."

Once the EMTs take over, I jog eastward and come upon Officer Marcie Murray, whom I recognize. She has the perp's hands cuffed behind his back and he is sitting on a curb.

Officer Murray says, "Hodge, are you the good Samaritan? I just happened to see this guy running even before the call came in."

I pull up to a stop and put both hands on my knees, trying to catch my breath. "Yes, give me a minute. But yes, it was me. And yes, you definitely have the right guy. Got the knife?"

"Yeah actually, I do. He tried to throw it in this sewer, but I saw him toss it and thankfully, he wasn't a very good shot."

I say, "Awesome, well you dirtbag, you better hope that guy survives."

He responds, "Nope, Not at all. He had it coming. I should have stuck him ten times to make sure."

I turn to Officer Murray and ask, "Have you read him his rights yet?"

"Yes, I did. Not the sharpest tack in the drawer."

Right about then, Detective Gaines pulls up in a civilian vehicle and peppers us with questions. We let him know that this guy is going into custody and the other is on his way to Harper Hospital down the street.

Gaines jumps back into his vehicle and darts off.

Chapter 1.8 – Another Text

The day after the stabbing, I receive a text from Gaines asking to meet at the accident scene. Since I am working and not far from Zug Island, I let him know that I can be there as soon as he wants. Gaines says that he needs to do a few things first and will meet me there at 10:30.

I was almost done my shift, but this sounds important, so I radio in that I am extending my shift by a few hours as Detective Gaines needs my assistance. I drive around killing time, but it is actually pleasurable as there is not much going on in this neighbourhood this early in the day.

I return to the accident scene at 10:20 a.m. and I figure I will get some fresh air and sun. I am leaning on my cruiser when Gaines arrives and he tells me that he wants to run some experiments. Well, this sounds bizarre.

Chapter 1.9 – Yet Another Text

Gaines and I enjoyed running some experiments and I think that it may have been very productive. The next day, I get yet another text from the detective and I wonder if I might be in for some more fun.

Gaines: You up for another favor?

Me: Sure. What do you need?

Gaines: Wanna do some vice work for the day?

Me: Sounds intriguing….give me a ring

Within a few seconds, my phone comes to life with a picture of Inspector Gadget that I inserted for Gaines' profile picture in my contacts. I hope he does not somehow see that!

We talk for a few minutes and he details a plan for me to execute. It actually sounds like fun.

Part Two - Narrated by Jimmy Greyson

Chapter 2.1 – The Lucy Chan – Jimmy Greyson Interview

"Well, I grew up in Farmington Hills, Michigan, where I lived in a typical suburb and of course, I played baseball. As a kid, I played every position, but once in high school, my coach James Lee wanted me to play third base. He was a Sparky Anderson type of coach and I still remember him saying, 'Son, you have a rocket of an arm and I need that rocket at the spot with the longest throw.' I did not want to argue with him. You see, on third, I set up in tighter, plus the ball gets to me faster. All things considered, I have more time and a bit shorter throw than when I play shortstop. Anyway, he was right as I did have a rocket of an arm and I almost dislocated our first baseman's shoulder several times. Thankfully, by my senior year, I was moved over to my sweet spot at short."

"Thanks so much, Jimmy," Lucy Chan from WXYZ-Detroit Sports interjected, "and from there, you stayed local and went to Michigan and you were a Spartan, right?"

"Ah, no, that is like saying to a Challenger driver, 'Hey nice Charger, dude.' Lucy, you must be new to the state of Michigan. State is synonymous with Michigan State University which is in Lansing, Michigan. Home of the Spartans. Michigan is the University of Michigan in Ann Arbor, Michigan. They are the Wolverines and they have the bizarre looking helmets with the yellow stripes. I went to MSU and I bleed green as a Spartan."

"Oh sorry, Jimmy. I will try to keep that straight. And yes, I am new to Michigan, originally from Oregon. That must have been quite special for you. You got away from home, but not too far. I imagine your parents were able to come and see most of your home games."

I thought to myself that Lucy needs to do more research before she just wings an interview.

"Well, they did until they did not. You see, my dad was a huge baseball fan. He coached me up until I went into high school. Almost every night, he was coaching, umpiring, or just riding around the neighbourhood on his bike, looking for a game to watch. Then when he got home, he would camp out in his Archie Bunker chair in the basement. There, he would read the paper, while watching a game on TV. The funny thing is, it was not uncommon for him to also have an earplug in, if there was a hockey game or something on the radio, too. You know, like when seasons overlap. Unfortunately, in my freshman year, my dad found out he had cancer and he was often in and out of hospital. He had prostate cancer and it spread to his spine, liver, and pancreas aggressively."

"Oh sorry, Jimmy."

"That year, I struggled with an infection in my throwing arm too, and I missed a good chunk of the season. Just as I was returning, my dad got out of the hospital for a few days. Anyway, my dad begged my mother to take him to my game and I still remember him sitting up in the stands, far away from my mother, because she screamed too much. She was one of those fans. You could tell he was in pain, but I know he was proud to be there. Unfortunately, my coach really didn't trust my arm yet and I sat for eight and a half innings. We were down by one with two outs and our catcher, Scotty Shields got a single. Scotty was not exactly a speedster. He had these short stalky legs that yielded him the nickname, Stubby. So, I got the nod to pinch run. Well, I got the green light on a 2-0 count to our centerfielder, Dean Fransen. I got a good jump and stole second with an easy pop-up slide. There I was in scoring position to tie up the game with Dean at the plate on a 2-1 count. Dean was one of our best hitters, but he was in a bit of a slump; he was due to shed that slump at anytime. I took a big lead just thinking that I had to get on my horse if he made solid contact. Well, Dean did not get out of that slump; he popped the next pitch straight up and the catcher put us out of our misery that day. I was stranded at second. As I walked off the field, I could see pride in my dad's eyes, though. Well, that was his last game and in fact, his last time out of the hospital. We lost him about a week later and my mom didn't have much interest in ball after that. His last memory of my ball career was a stolen base at least. I guess that is why I steal second whenever I can, as I know it makes my dad proud."

I am not very religious, but I find myself looking up just a little. It has been over 20 years since we lost him, but it still hurts. I breathe deep or I know I will start to tear up on television.

Lucy was kind, "Oh Jimmy, I am so sorry to bring up your parents. I am sure both your parents were very proud of the player and the man you have become. That must have been so tough for you."

"And my family, yes. It was a very tough year. I asked my mom if I could place a baseball in the casket with my dad, so my brother and I both wrote messages on that ball. I wrote on it, *Thanks for teaching me the game.* You know for the longest time, I thought that I was thankful for him teaching me how to play ball, but as I grew older, some would say much older, I realized it was not so much his coaching. It was his time and his caring that was so important. I guess having your own kids makes you look at things from a different angle. Ironically, neither of my kids had any interest in baseball. My son plays hockey and my daughter has more fun making things out of reclaimed pallets. She will likely start renovating homes in a few years. They have their own passions and it just makes me love them more."

"So, Jimmy, you said it first. You are getting up there in years with the Tigers and as you start Spring Training under a new manager and with many new players, where do you see yourself fitting into the roster?"

"Well, we have to be on the upside. Last year was our worst record in over a decade. We are thankful to see Dave VanBuskirk take over the team, but we have to be realistic, too. In his first interview, he was clear to say that the fans need to be patient. He is not going to create a championship team in one season. He is asking for five years, but hopefully, he can create some magic a little quicker than that."

"Speaking of magic," Lucy jumps in, "there is quite the buzz around Dave Stone coming from the University of Michigan, home of the Wolverines, right? Did I get that correct?"

"Yes, you did, Lucy. Stone is a gifted shortstop, but that is my spot. Coach VanBuskirk will utilize Dave at second and hopefully we will complement each other, up the middle."

"Some are saying that you two will be the Dynamic Duo up the middle. Let us hope the descriptor is accurate. Last question for you on the lighter side," continues Lucy, "I hear that some of the guys are starting to refer to you as 'Crash' like as in Kevin Costner's character, Crash Davis, from the 1988 classic baseball movie, Bull Durham. How do you feel about that?"

"Lucy, I will let my play speak for itself. I have been a key contributor to the Tigers organization for 18 years now and I have remained healthy in that entire run. I think we know who has been the best Tigers shortstop ever and that was Alan Trammell. Tram played in 20 seasons with the Tigers, almost 2300 games, 4 golden gloves, and 6 all-star game appearances, with an on base percentage of over .350. If this season goes as planned, I should surpass all of his numbers in 19 seasons and next year will be icing on the cake! I can assure you that I still have some runway left. As for the Crash reference, well, if I can spend some time with the 1988 Susan Sarandon, I am all game!"

"Well, tough to argue with that. Thanks so much for your time, Crash. This is Lucy Chan with the future hall of famer, Jimmy Greyson."

Chapter 2.2 - The Droop

I feel good walking onto the grass at Publix Field in Lakeland, energized by that Florida sun beating down on us. This aging body is not going to fail me now; surely, it will hold up for two more seasons. The field looks perfect and I give a nod to Anthony Patrick Milton for his outstanding work. We all affectionately refer to our groundskeeper as Amp, who is such an integral part of this team, while we are here in the Sunshine State. Amp had a tough time growing up near the field, but he has certainly made a name for himself in this organization, as well as around the league. As usual, the grass here looks perfect and it is not that wide-bladed grass you normally see in all of the Florida subdivisions. This grass looks as good as Comerica Park back home in Detroit.

Amp nods in return and says, "Hey Jimmy, you up for some fixings tonight?"

I never turn down an offer of food from Amp. I absolutely love spending time with him and his five kids, not to mention his lovely wife, Amanda. I do not get to see my own kids too often since Kari and I split, but it is even worse during Spring Training. They are back in Michigan and will manage one or two long weekends here in Florida, but that is about it. I let Amp know that I would not miss it and that the field is in tip-top shape as I enter the infield, being careful not to touch any chalk. Yes, I am one of those guys. I never touch a chalk line on a diamond except in live play. I have no idea why; I just do not. I guess I am afraid to find out what would happen if I did disturb one. I wonder for a few seconds if it is superstition or just respect for the diamond itself. It is certainly one of my pet peeves when I see a batter kick the chalk lines all over the place when they address the plate. That is no way to respect the field and the work that our grounds crew puts into it.

Amp yells and knocks me out of my daydream, "See ya at six then, Crash!" He pauses slightly and then continues, "Sorry Jimmy, my kids put me up to that. They said they saw some interview with you online. I guess Susan Sarandon is a little ticked at you that you're not interested in the 2019 version of her!"

I turn around to give Amp a stare down, until we both crack a smile. I cannot get mad at Amp. Ever!

I see Dave Stone and we start to toss a ball to warm up. I have a set routine for warming up my arm: 10 throws at half throttle, 10 throws at 75%, 5 at 90%, and then I let it loose. Stone, of course, does not follow my lead. I just do not understand the rookie pushing the process. He starts throwing full speed after 3 throws. So, my routine is severely disrupted and I cannot hold back. I guess it is my ego and I speed up my progression to match his. As Stone pops my glove, I pop his as well and there you go, the testosterone is flowing.

VanBuskirk barks that he wants us to take some ground balls and one of the coaches, Wayne Bedard starts alternating grounders to Stone and myself. Stone is at second and I am at my usual home spot between second and third. I admire Stone's smooth pick-up, but you can tell that he feels a little awkward with his delivery to first. You either have to throw across your body or pivot back to make the throw. From short, you normally get a much more straightforward motion and that is how I have made a living for 18 years, now.

My arm is feeling good as I am nailing every throw to first and I am schooling the rookie. I make 5 perfect throws, but my 6th goes off the mark and the first baseman digs it out of the dirt. For the next one, I increase my setup time just slightly and I throw a strike to first. Unfortunately, as I increase my tempo, I am just not hitting my target consistently. I curse myself for not following my warmup ritual. I can only imagine what would have happened if I stepped on a chalk line.

After a long first practice, I am in the equipment room with my arm in a long bucket of ice water and VanBuskirk enters, wanting to chat.

"Hey Jimmy, so what'd you think of Stone's play at second?"

I let him know that I could see that he could field a ball beautifully, but his mechanics were off a bit while delivering the ball to first.

He acknowledges that my assessment is correct and then he says, "So, you know Jimmy, I have watched you for years now and maybe I missed it, but when did you get the droop?"

"Pardon? What droop?"

"Yeah Jimmy, you should see your trajectory from the bench. The ball flies on a laser for about 110 feet, but in the last 10 feet, it just drops like a rock. You have a droop."

I am not getting into excuses about my warmup routine, because that is what it would sound like: excuses! However, the fact that Stoner rushed my warmup was probably the cause of said droop.

"Jimmy, we have some choices to make. You can play a little tighter, but then you'll give up some range or we need to put some spinach in your diet."

I see that as one option and not really two. Clearly, I am not adopting a Popeye diet, so I ask him, "Or?"

"Well, you know Stone was the best shortstop the Wolverines have ever produced."

"That's only because I was a Sparty."

VanBuskirk ignores the retort and continues, "You clearly understand how to adjust your mechanics better than he does. I bet you can tell me every little thing that he did wrong out there today."

We continue the conversation for long enough that my arm is going numb, but I concede that he is in charge and my arm is getting old. I do have to recognize that VanBuskirk is looking at fielding a championship team five years from now and I am not likely part of that plan. I will be a team player.

Immediately after VanBuskirk leaves the room, Assistant Coach Wayne Bedard enters and throws his glove into his bag. He is clearly agitated and says to me, "Jimmy, this just ain't right. You've been with this team for how long? And then this snotty-nosed whipper snapper comes in and takes your spot. It ain't right."

I reply with, "I appreciate you looking out for me Wayne, but VanB is in charge."

My heart sinks as I realize that my dream of getting to Alan Trammel's numbers just likely vaporized.

Chapter 2.3 - Dinner at Amp's

As I kiss her on the cheek, I whisper loudly enough that my pal can hear, "Amanda, you look lovely as ever! I don't know how you do it, with five kids and a no-good husband that is never around! If you ever want to ditch that fool and start anew, you know I am your guy, right?"

Amanda rolls her eyes and does not miss a beat, "Jimmy, you know I would, but I got a threatening message from Susan Sarandon yesterday, saying that she was going to do nasty things to our pet bunny and my black ass if I didn't back away. Should I be calling you 'Crash' now, honey? What a name! All I can think of is *crash and burn.*"

Amp and I look at each other and we can each see the wheels turning and then Amp blurts out, "The country guy! Ah, um, Thomas Ray!!"

I respond, "Rhett, Thomas Rhett, but I will give you that one. I am feeling generous."

You see, we have this game between us that if someone says a song title in a conversation, it is a contest to see who can name the artist first. Sometimes, we will compete on well-known lyrics, too, but then you need to name the song title *and* the artist.

I come back to the conversation at hand, "Well, you do know that Crash Davis had an incredible season in Bull Durham, right? I could take that."

Amp chimes in, "Yeah, but it was in the Minors and it was his final season, dumbass," as he hands me a beer. "You do remember he was washed up at the end of the movie, right?"

"Geez Amp, with friends like you."

Amanda points to the cooler by the barbecue and says, "Well Crash, you do kind of look like Kevin Costner did in Bull Durham, just with darker hair. Anyway, you know where the beer is dear, so help yourself once you finish that one." She then turns to Amp, "Hey hon, can you pretend to be the chef and fire up the Q for the burgers? I hope burgers are okay guys; I promise there will be no gator in them this time!" She does an about face, to go inside through the sliding screen door, yelling, "Hey kiddos, dinner will be ready in 15 minutes. Be sure to wash up and be ready. Also, Uncle Jimmy is out back waiting for hugs from you guys!"

I think to myself, you sure know who runs this house. As Amp sparks up the barbecue, he says, "You stop looking at that fine black ass there, Crash. That would be mine and no one else's. And, you better reign in that Susan Sarandon. She better not touch our bunny or my Amanda."

Just then, the five rug rats come running out at various heights to give me hugs around the legs and waist. This family is truly blessed. Amp and Amanda live a nice, simple life. And, I do not mean that in a bad way whatsoever; in fact, just the exact opposite. A side of me would like to go back in time and keep things much simpler. Baseball has been great to me, but it has also complicated my life to no end. Well, I complicated it, but baseball enabled a weak me to do that. The fame and money went to my head. I felt indestructible and I did crash and burn in my personal life. By no means, was I a Tiger Woods, but I take all responsibility for wrecking my marriage. Kari was so supportive for the longest time, but she was right to pull the plug. I do not blame her whatsoever. If I could turn back time. Although I am not a fan of the song, I say to myself, "Cher."

Amp snaps me back to reality as he asks, "Hey Jimmy, what do you think we are in for this year? A new manager, a new rookie second baseman. Is that enough to turn the team around?"

"Oh, it's a start. I am hoping to have another year or two. I am still quite productive, but VanBuskirk is right. He has to plan for 5 years out. He's not going to create a contending team in one season. He'll have to make some bold moves."

"Yeah, I didn't mean to eavesdrop, but I heard the droop conversation. Droop, shmoop. You still have a rocket of an arm, man."

"He's right. I am losing some zip. If moving over to second base can buy me a couple more years, maybe it is the way to go."

As Amp flips the burgers, he turns to me and says, "I am shocked you are taking it this well. I thought you would be out for blood, like Bedard was. Anyway, I have to admit, I was looking forward to all the comparisons to Trammell and Whitaker. The white stud at short and the

33

black second baseman with all the sweet moves, combining for a record number of double plays."

"Well Amp, that would be nice, but times are a changing. I think when we step back and look at this rationally, I can make the transition to second base better than Stone can. He was awkward as hell out there, throwing across his body. I will concede my position. I will talk with VanBuskirk tomorrow and let him know that I will make the switch willingly. Not that I really have much choice. He will probably want me to do a press conference or something though. I hate that shit. Hey Amp, can I get that burger in the corner?"

"Of course, Princess. I know you like your burger almost bleeding. That is why it is in the corner, dumbass. Anyway, you used to love that media circus crap."

"*Used to,* is the key, Amp."

Amanda gives everyone a whistle which means the fixings are ready and she does not disappoint. We eat and drink for hours before I head home with a full belly and a bit of a glow.

Chapter 2.4 – A Big Ask

I wake up early and hit the gym that I have set up in my Florida residence. It is just a small home in a gated community, but I call it home during Spring Training. Since the split-up, this home is somewhat depressing, so I try not to stay in it very much. Amp knows that and I am sure that is why he and Amanda ask me for dinner at least once per week. They are certainly good friends.

After my workout, I shower, grab some cereal, and head to the field. Upon arrival, VanBuskirk asks me to come into the office and I cannot help but wonder what he will hit me with next.

"Jimmy, I need to ask a favor of you."

Although my mind is spinning, I give the politically correct response, "Sure boss, what can I do for you?"

"Well, Stone is staying in a hotel by himself and I don't think that is the best thing for him or for the team. We need someone to show him the ropes, keep him in line, and so on. Really, we need someone to mentor him."

"You want me to take in a puppy?"

"Yeah, kinda."

Ironically, I was thinking this morning how depressing and lonely my place is, but I was not thinking that it would be great to bring in the guy who is bumping me out of my beloved position on the field.

"Wow, this is a big ask."

"Yeah, I know Jimmy, but this kid really is just that, a kid. He needs the guidance of our most experienced veteran."

"Yeah, yeah, yeah. I get it. I do have an extra room. I will do it for the team, but he better not have a cat! A cat is a dealbreaker!"

"I am sure he is travelling pretty lightly. Thanks Jimmy. I, and the organization owe you big time. Oh, one more favor."

"Seriously?"

"Could you make this your idea? Taking him under your wing, kind of thing. He does idolize you, you know."

"Oh boy. Alright, consider it done."

I return to the dressing room and begin to get ready for practice and Stone is a couple of stalls over getting dressed, so I might as well get 'er done, as they say. "Hey Stone, you are staying in a hotel right?" I do not let him respond and I just continue, "You know, I have my own house here and it is pretty empty, except when my kids visit a couple of weekends. If you want, I would be happy to give you a room."

Stone grins and says, "VanB put you up to this, didn't he?"

I try to keep a straight face for a second or two, but then we both break the ice and laugh. "Yeah, I guess."

"Jimmy, I would love to. I cannot stay in a hotel by myself another night. I really appreciate this."

I guess it is official. I am taking in a stray puppy.

Chapter 2.5 – A Boys' Night Out

VanBuskirk is big into team building and he insists that all the players go out for dinner at a local restaurant called The Gator. It is a typical roadhouse restaurant with patio dining and VanBuskirk booked the entire patio for our team.

The staff had rearranged their tables and set up 4 long ones for us. I am sitting at one end with Dave and several outfielders: John Turner, Frank Paul, George Colman, and Ritchie Coughlin.

When we order, it is somewhat comical as Dave and two others, try to order something healthy off of the menu and meanwhile, the rest of us are looking for red meat. My idea of making my meal healthy is switching out half of the fries for Caesar salad. On the positive side, everyone orders beer.

After the team devours their meals, we all stick around for another beer. As I survey the tables, I have to admit that VanBuskirk's insistence on a team meal is a good idea. It is obvious that the team is gelling, at least socially. This will be a good first step.

I return my attention to the group at my end of the table with me. The outfield group is actually talking about fielding strategies and John says to Frank, "I could use a little help, my friend."

At that moment, I start laughing hysterically, the conversations stop abruptly, and they all turn to me with quizzical stares. Ritchie interrupts my continued laughter with, "What?"

"You guys, you guys are the Beatles! We have John, Paul, George, and Ritchie, so that makes you Ringo! That's it; you guys are now the Beatles. And you better not tell me that you don't know who the Beatles are. If you tell me that, you're all fired!"

Stone interjects with "Just humor him. They're an old English band for old white dudes. You can google it later."

John dons a fake English accent and chimes in, "Like when the tellies were black and white. Well, we have that covered!" The four laugh as three of them are black, with Ritchie being the lone Caucasian in the outfield group.

As the crowd thins out, Dave leans over to me, pulls two cylinders out of his back pocket and says, "I understand that you like these."

"Absolutely! Are those Cubans?"

"Yes, they are. I figured I needed to thank you for taking me in. I appreciate it."

"That is a good start, Junior, a good start. How about we fire up those bad boys?"

"Oh shoot, Jimmy. I didn't even think to get a lighter or matches."

"You bonehead. I will see if the waiter can help us out." I wave at him and make a flicking motion with my thumb and mouth to him, "Have you got a lighter or matches?"

Two minutes later, our waiter returns with a book of matches and we both smile.

"Hey Dave, we can go for a walk as I don't think the other patrons will appreciate these as we do. VanB will pick up the bill, so we are good."

I light my cigar as we set out on our walk, hand the pack of matches to Dave, and after a few attempts, Dave manages to get his lit, followed by a coughing fit.

Dave says, "I haven't had a cigar in a long time, or like ever, come to think of it!"

"Oh, you'll get used to it," I say as we both take another draw and I see that Dave's eyes are watering profusely. "Or maybe not,"

"I will give it a college try, but I'm not sold on them yet. We will see. As I said Jimmy, I really appreciate you taking me in. I don't think that I could handle living in a hotel much longer."

"Hah, get used to it."

"Oh, I know that we'll be in hotel rooms often, but at least we'll be in them as a team. The place I was at was just depressing. I would see all these families cycling through the hotel and there I am with no family whatsoever. Seeing the families is tough for me."

"I see."

"You know Jimmy, I saw your interview with Lucy Chan back in Detroit. I have to say that I am sorry for the whole shortstop and second base thing. I hope you know that I am fine playing wherever."

"I know Dave. It is what it is. VanB is in charge and he will make decisions on what he thinks will advance the team. I'm no prima Dona."

Dave coughs twice and says, "Thanks. I appreciate that."

"You know you don't have to finish that if it's not for you."

"My father always taught me to finish what I start. I may not take a lot of puffs, but I will finish it."

"He sounds like a wise man."

"He was. Yes, he was."

"Oh, sorry, is he no longer with us?"

"Nope, we lost him last year. You and I have that in common, losing our dads about the same age. It has been very tough and I hated leaving my mom to come down here."

"I hear ya, but I can assure you that your mother would not want you missing this opportunity to babysit her."

"You are absolutely correct, but it's hard to take over as the man of the house, when I'm not even in the house."

"Any siblings?"

"Yeah, a brother and two sisters who are still at home."

"Your mom is going to have lots of company."

"Yeah, I know. I just feel like I am abandoning ship."

"You're not abandoning anyone. You're not down here that long. And besides, they can come down here. We have room, maybe not all of them at once, but we can work something out. We will just have to coordinate with my kids' visits."

"I appreciate that too, Jimmy."

We continue chatting and walking until my cigar is down to a stub. Dave's neglect of his ensured that it lost its glow twice, but he did put a decent effort into it. We actually have a very good chat and this kid is growing on me. As we get back to the restaurant parking lot, we run into Wayne Bedard and he looks to be fuming.

I say to Wayne, "Hey Wayne, is something wrong?"

He responds with, "I don't understand you guys. You do know that this league is getting more and more competitive all the time! You need every advantage you can find. You eat like shit and then you smoke that shit. I have never seen you smoke a cigar before. Who bought those? I bet they're even Cubans! I can't believe VanBuskirk brought everyone here to this dump and then you drink and smoke like you're at a bloody bachelor party. I am done with you fools."

As Bedard finishes up his tongue lashing, he looks as if he is ready to strangle both of us. Dave looks stunned and I bet I look the same. I turn to Dave and say, "Holy helicopter parent! Well, that is a strange way to end a great night."

Chapter 2.6 – Inter-Squad Matchup

It is a beautiful day in Lakeland, Florida at 75 degrees Fahrenheit and only about 60% humidity. By Florida standards, this is paradise. It is not uncommon to be sweating profusely even in the mid-seventies when the humidity hits 90 plus percent here. You know those beer commercials, where you see the ice-cold beer with all the condensation on the glass. I swear they film all of those commercials here in Florida for maximum sweat effect.

I saw on the news in the morning that Detroit got hit with six inches of snow overnight, so I am quite happy to be here in Florida, even if it means swatting mosquitoes in the evening.

So, today is an inter-squad game, or as some call it intra-squad game. I like *inter* better for some reason, but I make note that if I ever run into one of my old high school English teachers, I will need to ask which term is more correct in the baseball context. Basically, we split up our squad into two teams. It gives a team a chance to get the rookies some field time, without taking time away from old farts like yours truly. For me, it is an opportunity to ramp up my tempo in live competition. These games also give our coaching staff a chance to experiment with different defensive formations or offensive strategies. We can see who can field a bunt when they do not expect one, for example.

Leading up to this matchup, my new roommate and I have been playing shortstop and second, respectively. I have to admit, we are looking really good. I have adjusted to second quickly and Stone is looking much more comfortable on the left side of the infield. The other players are calling us the "Dream Team" as Lucy Chan had speculated.

For whatever reason, VanBuskirk decides to give me a little time at shortstop today, although I do not get too excited, because Stone is at short as well, just on the other squad.

The first 6 innings are uneventful. Up to this point, I have not seen much action. I had two grounders for routine plays at first and I did not notice any droop whatsoever – thankfully! I attribute the lack of droop due to warming up properly. The third play for me was a fun one, as I had to chase down a blooper behind our third baseman. I made a nice feet first slide to make a basket catch and send Dave back to the dugout.

So now, here we are in the seventh inning. At the plate, I have been solid with 2 singles and one deep sacrifice fly. I am facing Greg Flajnik, who is a rookie out of Ohio State, but he is actually from Windsor, Ontario, Canada. By the way, Windsor's downtown is directly south of Detroit's Renaissance Center. Yes folks, Southwestern Ontario swings in under Michigan. Too many people just do not understand that geography.

With a runner on first and no outs, the count gets to 3-0 and the third base coach gives me the green light to take a swing at the next pitch. I have to admit, I feel like Pavlov's dog and I start to drool. For the non-baseball players, usually you take a 3-0 pitch, which means you have no intentions of swinging at the pitch regardless of where it is located. Most pitchers forget about trying to pick a corner or putting movement on the ball when they are on a 3-0 count. They just throw a fastball right down the middle and do not tend to put all of their mustard into it, either. I am not sure why the coaching staff gives me a green light, but I am guessing they just want to teach the rookie a lesson for not managing pitch placement better on a veteran. As I said, it is also part of Spring Training and in particular, inter-squad matchups: experimenting!

Sure enough, here comes a fastball right down the pipe. Well, before the ball travels the 60 feet 6 inches to the plate, my left leg is already extended and my hips are driving to give my arms a head start. Perfectly timed, my wrists snap forward and my swing feels like poetry in motion with everything firing in sequence just as it is all supposed to do. The ball launches with as much power as I can muster, but I realize that I hit the ball just a little too solid. I know that sounds counterintuitive. You see, you need to get slightly under the ball to get the lift required to clear the fence. Regardless, this is a rocket heading to right-center field. The two outfielders, John and Ringo converge quickly and both could have an outside chance of tracking this ball down. Wisely, our runner on first only goes halfway to second. If the ball is caught, he has to be able to get back to first base, to avoid a double play. If it is not caught, he will kick it into high gear and he should be able to get to third and maybe home if there is a misplay in the outfield. Our runner plays it perfectly as neither outfielder gets to the line drive in time to stop the ball from rebounding solidly off the top of the fence. The ball comes back quickly and Ringo picks the ball up off of one hop and throws a bullet into second, keeping me at first. I wince, because I know that one foot further and I would have had a dinger and more importantly, I would have taught Flajnik a lesson. Regardless, I feel it was an impressive swing. The first base coach gives me a smack on the right shoulder and says, "Man, that was a better swing than I've seen in years from you! Are you juicing or something?" I give him an *as if* grin and get ready for the next batter. I also chuckle to myself as 10 or 15 years ago, the coach would have smacked me in the ass, as he said that. Some change is good.

Now, we have first and third covered with no outs. You know what, it is inter-squad and I really do not care about the score. This is just about individual play right now and I am performing like a veteran who, like I said, has lots of runway left. After one ball, the third base coach gives us a signal for a hit and run. That means my buddy at the plate will be swinging at anything close and I am leaving with the pitch. Flajnik, or Flaj as his friends call him, tosses a light one to first to keep me honest. I get a more significant lead now and I am poised to bolt. Geez, he tosses to first a little harder and I have to dive back hard to get under the tag. No respect! As I get up and dust myself off, I try to think what Rodney Dangerfield would say right now. I bet the guys in the booth are making a respect joke on the radio broadcast, too. I also wonder if they are commenting about Flajnik's hair and how it looks like he is wearing a Howard Stern Halloween wig. Man, how does he even see the plate or the catcher's signals with that mop? As an aside, I understand that Howard Stern got his start as a DJ back home in Detroit, at the rock station, WWWW, or W4 for short. I give my head a shake to bring my mind back to the game.

Once the ball is back in Flajnik's glove, I go back to the exact same location I was last time. I even put my cleats in the footprints from the previous lead off. This little snotty nose kid better not come over here again. I get up on the balls of my feet as I see he is committing to the plate and I am off as fast as these old legs will take me. I am doing just fine. I hear the crack of the bat and I see that the ball is going right up the middle, but it is a high bounder. I should have lots of time to get there with the jump I have, but I will need to slide in order to stop at the bag. I am going headfirst just in case there is a tag and I can grab the bag with my left hand, while sliding by the right side of the base. The next thing I know, I see Stone in the air. He snags the ball on a high bounce just to the short side of second and he is coming down fast with his left cleat leading the way. I roll onto my right side, while still hanging onto the bag and that is when I feel the shearing pain in my left knee. None of Stone's cleats caught flesh, but his arch of his shoe lands squarely on the side of my left knee. I feel it bend at an angle that it should not be able to make. There is burning pain and then when Stone shifts his weight to his right leg, my knee rebounds and the burning transitions to throbbing.

I roll onto my back in pain and frustration as Stone crawls over to me, saying sorry repeatedly! Well, that pretty much cements who is the starting shortstop for the Tigers this year. That is all I can think about as I grab at my knee and grimace in pain.

Chapter 2.7 - The Medical Plan

The Tigers organization wants me back in Detroit as soon as possible, so after a quick check at a local Florida hospital, I am braced up and flown back to Michigan. Our team physician, Stephen Lemous is an orthopaedic surgeon, but he refers me to the University of Michigan in Ann Arbor. Dr. McKinlay there is supposed to be the best knee surgeon in the area.

Stephen catches me by surprise and I interject, "Hey doc, first of all, you know I am a Spartan, right? I can't go to the U of M for any reason. What about the Fowler Clinic in London, Ontario? Can't I go there? Is that not where Steve Yzerman went for his knee work? They're supposed to be the best."

Steve Yzerman was the captain of the Detroit Red Wings for years and he was in severe knee pain, but the Fowler Clinic, which is affiliated with Western University, did remarkable work with Yzerman and extended his NHL career by four years. This was even after everyone else had him written off as finished.

Doctor Lemous responds, "Your knee is not nearly as bad as what Yzerman had. His knee was completely shot, so he needed a realignment from years of abuse. He was literally bone on bone. That was a major surgery where they cut his tibia and then plated it back together to stabilize his knee and take pressure off of his meniscus, or at least what was left of it. Your injury is more run of the mill – it will be relatively routine for McKinlay. Let us get an MRI and then I want you to see him tomorrow. He will take great care of you."

Dr. McKinlay tells me that my knee is not as bad as he initially thought it would be. The MRI indicates that I have a grade two tear in my MCL or Medial Collateral Ligament. With time and physiotherapy, the ligament should be able to repair itself. He is booking me in for an arthroscopic surgery however, to fix a torn meniscus and tidy things up, as they say. He continues dryly, "You were actually very lucky with this injury. When I saw the highlight reel on ESPN, I thought things would be much worse than they are. The recovery time for this type of injury is eight to ten weeks. You are in decent shape, but with consideration for your age, you are probably going to be closer to the ten weeks than the eight. I am going to prescribe you some painkillers for tonight and for the recovery. I will need you back here at 6 a.m. for the surgery tomorrow. You will need someone to drive you in and home. Now, you will be able to walk out of the hospital with your brace and crutches doing what we call a crutch-walk." He demonstrates with imaginary crutches moving in unison with the braced knee.

He continues, "Even though you will be mobile, you will not be able to drive after the anaesthesia. Actually, for driving, you will not be able to drive for as long as you are in the brace. Yes, I know it is your left leg, but the brace will alter the way you sit in a vehicle, so no driving until we remove it."

I reply, "Thanks, Doc," but I think to myself, man, this guy needs to work on his bedside manner. There is no way that I will be down for ten weeks and yeah right, to the driving ban.

Thankfully, Kari was able to juggle things around at work and she took me home to my lonely apartment downtown after swinging by a local pharmacy. Maybe it is the swelling and/or shock of everything, but the pain is not too bad. Maybe it is because I am in *decent shape*. Decent shape, oh come on!

Once in my apartment, I open a beer and turn on the television, but I have no idea what is actually on. I stare out the window and see the good old Renaissance Center through the flurry of snow coming down to further blanket the Motor City. The Renaissance Center, or RenCen as many refer to it, is actually seven interconnected glass skyscrapers built back in the seventies. It was meant to symbolize the revitalization of the Motor City, at that time. Currently, it is actually officially called the GM Renaissance Center, as the automotive giant General Motors purchased the complex and established its world headquarters here. This is so ironic since the initial construction was spearheaded by Henry Ford II who had obvious ties to the GM rival, Ford. Currently, Marriott operates a luxury hotel in the tallest, middle cylindrical tower surrounded by the office space, shops, and restaurants. Some even refer to the complex as the *city within a city*. Unfortunately, I will be staring at the good old RenCen for many hours over the next two months. This is such a depressing thought. At least I know some trivia about the complex.

I send Stone a text: Hey Dave, take care of the house and I guess you do not have to worry about coordinating visits with my kids. Feel free to bring your fam down there anytime.

Stone thanks me and of course apologizes three more times for jumping on my knee.

I am looking at two months of almost complete isolation and I know it is going to drive me nuts to be cooped up like this. I cannot imagine what could be worse.

Chapter 2.8 – Post-Surgery

Post-surgery, Dr. McKinlay tells me that there was more work in there than he initially anticipated. He explains, "The articular cartilage was quite thin on the inside of your knee and that cartilage is there to help the bones slide over each other," as he demonstrates with two fists rubbing together. "I used a tool to poke at the top of your tibia which causes bleeding. You will not notice anything for a while, but give that a few months and your body will regenerate the area with tissue to supplement what cartilage is there. I fixed the tear as well with a few stitches. Like I said yesterday, the Medial Collateral Ligament will heal and with time and physiotherapy, you should be good as new in two or three months."

"Well, I'll be aiming for the two months, Doc, but thanks."

"So, you have some pain meds right. Take those every four hours for a couple of days. Do not wait for the pain, before you take the meds. You are best to stay out in front of the pain and take them regularly for at least the first 48 to 72 hours. Then, you can taper off and take the meds as needed. I would also lean a little towards night time to ensure that you sleep well."

"Okay, got it."

"I want you to start physiotherapy in one week. The physiotherapist will take it lightly at first, but will work you up progressively. Then, I will see you again in three weeks to see how things are progressing. Please call my administrative assistant when you get home to set up another appointment."

"Will do. Thanks Doc."

An orderly wheels me down to the lobby in a wheelchair, with me carrying my crutches across my lap. Once we are at the doors, he asks me, "So, where is your ride?"

I point to a bronze Lexus SUV and say, "I'm good from here."

He gives me a nod and says, "It has been great meeting you, Mr. Greyson. You get back out there quickly, sir. The Tigers are going to need your leadership if we are going to contend this year." To that, I smile and watch as he turns to head back inside.

I approach the Lexus and then when the coast is clear, I turn right and crutch walk my way to the parking lot. I launch myself up into my Chevy Silverado, settle in, and drive home.

Chapter 2.9 – The Recovery

Sandi, my physiotherapist, lifts my left knee and places a styrofoam cylinder underneath it. It is a short fat water noodle. She then picks up what is basically a plastic ketchup bottle you would see at a roadhouse restaurant, yet it is white. She squirts gel onto four rectangular pads with wires attached to them and then places the pads onto my left thigh in a diamond pattern. Sandi moves to a machine of some sort and presses a few buttons and says, "Let me know when you feel something, hon."

After a few beeps, my quadriceps jump to life and I say, "Oh, I feel it now."

To that, she hits the up button two more times and asks, "Is that okay?" to which I nod. "Now, every time it comes on, raise your left foot to straighten out your leg and I will come back in five minutes."

As she walks away, I admire her walk and how she can make medical scrubs look attractive. She looks like she is about 30 and in excellent shape. She has blonde hair in a ponytail with deep brown eyes and flawless skin.

I do as I was told and straighten my leg over and over. I am looking at my knee and the half inch incisions into which Dr. McKinlay had inserted arthroscopic instruments, are healing up nicely. I am sure that no one would notice in a few weeks, except for the lack of leg hair. My left leg is somewhat skinny compared to my right, but I guess that is to be expected with a brace, crutches, and not really doing any kind of exercise for my leg for almost three weeks.

Sandi returns after a couple of minutes and I see that the timer still has almost three minutes on it. "How are you making out, hon?"

"Oh, just fine. I am just looking at how skinny my left leg is."

"That is quite normal, Jimmy, but that will be my job to help you rebuild it. This is just the start. In addition to the exercises I give you here, are you doing some upper body exercises?"

"Yeah, some. There is a pretty good gym in my apartment building and I've been pumping iron."

Sandi taps my right bicep with her index finger and says, "That is good hon, but I would not recommend doing more than what you would normally do. Bulking up while on the Disabled List may mess up some of your throwing or hitting mechanics. Maintenance is the key and not increasing size anywhere, except in that left leg."

"I guess that makes sense, but can you do me a favor?"

"Sure sweetie. You name it."

"Please don't refer to it as the Disabled List? That makes it sound so permanent. I prefer to just say DL. I am on the down low for a bit."

"Sure. While you are on the DL, I am going to need you to do some cardio too. We need to think about your entire body, including your lungs and heart," to which she taps on my chest, once on the right and two times on the left. I have to admit that it makes my heart flutter a little as she continues, "Definitely use a stationary bike to start. That helps lubricate your knee to get it moving and it gets your blood flowing. But you will need more than that. In that gym of yours, do they have a pull-down bar? You can reduce the weight and increase reps. You can kind of use it like a rowing machine to start, until your legs are capable of functioning on a real rowing machine."

"The gym is really well-equipped with all kinds of stations. Maybe after your shift, you can come to check out the gym and let me know what you would recommend."

As she holds up her left hand, she says, "Nice try, Jimmy. I do not wear any jewellery here with all the gels and that, but you may see the tan line where my ring normally is. I am happily married, sweetie."

I look and sure enough, I see a faint tan line. I sheepishly reply, "You can't blame a guy for trying."

"Tell you what, you have my email address. Take some pictures of various machines and then send them to me. I can come up with several ideas to get you some cardiovascular exercises in on top of what I give you for your knee. The trick with the knee though, will be patience. I need you to take your time. That will be better in the long run."

"Yes, dear," I say sarcastically.

"Oh yeah, you have an iPhone, right. There is a great app that comes pre-loaded. It is called Health and the icon is just a picture of a heart."

I pull my phone out of my left front pocket and log in with my thumb. I search for the heart icon and open up the app.

Sandi says, "Click on Show All Health Data and you will get some great information to help you in your recovery. You really do not need a Fitbit, as your phone will keep track of your steps." She is looking at her own phone too and scrolls down. "If you scroll down, you will see Double Support Time, which measures the percentage of time when both your feet are on the ground at the same time. Yours is probably around 50% right now."

"It's 45."

"That is decent, but we will want to get that down between 20 and 40% though. There is also Step Length and Walking Speed that you may want to watch, but I want you to concentrate on Walking Asymmetry. It should eventually be 0%, but you are probably around 5 or 10 right now, because you are walking with a limp."

"Yeah, it's at 12%."

"You know they say the best way to improve anything is to start by measuring it. Just watching this number each day will help you to concentrate on improving your walking. Then we can work on the running. When you do those lunging exercises, be sure to concentrate on heel to toe and that will help eliminate stress on your knee and ultimately your limp, too."

"Okay, will do. I never knew there was this much information in my phone."

"Yep, if you overdo it and develop a limp, I can go into your phone and see when you overdid it and how long the limp lasts. All thanks to Apple! Do not be making me check into your phone there, sweetie. It might cause us to break up."

"Again, yes dear! This is certainly Big Brotherish. Anyway, I better get going. I will send you those pictures of the gym when I get home and I will see you in 3 days."

"I will be waiting, hon."

Man, she is a flirt, but she does seem good at her job and she will get me back on track.

I put my brace back on and head out without the crutches. That is a little progress. Once out in the parking lot, I get into my black 2017 Dodge Challenger SRT; she finally came out of storage now that the nice weather has arrived. I drive home and get dressed for the gym. I realize taking pictures is silly, so I take a video of all the equipment in the gym and narrate it as I go. I then dutifully email the video to Sandi for her feedback.

As I look around, I think I am not going to use a pull bar to simulate a rowing machine when there is one right there. I get onto the rowing machine and I start rowing. That being said, I take it easy on the tension setting and I concentrate on protecting the left knee.

When I return to my apartment, I grab a bag of frozen peas and a beer from the kitchen. I sit down on one of the matching recliners and look out at the Renaissance Center with the bag of peas on my knee and I pop open the beer. I reach over to the end table for my pain medication bottle and I realize that there is only one pill left, so I make a mental note to get in to see Dr. McKinlay as soon as possible. I pop that last pill into my mouth and wash it down with a cold Bud Light.

With half the beer still left, my phone pings and I see that Sandi has responded. She is good. She has given me a list of activities that will focus on cardio exercises to keep my heart and lungs in shape. She does give me heck though, because she saw my legs reflected in the gym mirror and I was not wearing my brace.

I am just about ready to call it a night and my phone rings as a FaceTime call comes in. It is Stone, so I answer it. He only apologizes twice on this call for injuring my knee, so we are making progress on that front. Dave is looking for advice more than anything. He runs several offensive and defensive play scenarios by me to determine if he made the right decisions or not. I am impressed with his desire to learn the finer points of the game; he has the skills and if he can learn the subtleties of the game, he will be outstanding.

After an hour call and two more beers, I finally call it a night.

Chapter 2.10 - Refill

With a bit of sweet talking, I manage to get his administrative assistant to move my next appointment with Dr. McKinlay up to this afternoon and I hop in the Challenger to head out to Ann Arbor for another follow-up with my orthopaedic surgeon. Upon arrival, I get the VIP treatment and they give me an MRI and x-rays, prior to seeing the surgeon. An hour after arrival, the imaging is complete and I am waiting in an examination room. I am impressed when the doctor arrives within just a matter of minutes.

Dr. McKinlay says, "Hi Jimmy, how is your knee feeling?" as he sits at a computer and pulls up my images on the screen.

"Not too bad, Doc. I feel some strength coming back, but the more I work it, the more pain I get."

"That is to be expected, Jimmy. Let us take a look at your x-rays. Really, I just had those done as a formality. The alignment of your knee looks good. Look here to see that the gap between your tibia and femur is quite uniform. This is good. If the gap starts to close on one side or the other, then that can cause issues."

"That's good to hear, Doc."

"The MRI gives us more information. Look here and I can see that the MCL is repairing itself well. And, the meniscus looks good. Can you hop up on the table and lie back for me, please?"

The surgeon grabs my leg and instructs me, "Please just relax and let me take control."

I jokingly say, "Usually, I'm the one saying that."

"Ha ha, funny Jimmy. Just relax the leg."

"It's tough to just relax it, Doc. I am getting accustomed to protecting the knee."

He responds with, "I get it, but I need to feel how sturdy it is on its own without your muscles protecting," as he starts to bend my knee from side to side. I give a grimace and he recognizes that I am in pain.

"It feels like it is gaining stability Jimmy. I take it you are religiously doing your physiotherapy."

"For sure."

"Are you doing more than you are supposed to do?"

"Well maybe a bit."

"That is why you are getting pain, Jimmy. Follow your physiotherapist's lead. They know more about rehab than you or I. You still have lots of pain meds left do you not?"

"No, I am actually out. I thought I had lots, but I took the last one last night. I could've sworn I had more. I am not sure where they all went."

Dr. McKinlay gives me a quizzical look and writes something down in his notes. He then goes to his computer and types while saying, "That is a little worrisome. I would have thought you would have had an ample supply. I really do not want to see you get into dependency issues. I will give you another prescription, but we will take it down a notch in potency. It is still a narcotic, so do be careful, but it is not as strong as the first one."

I say, "That is fine. We're on the same page," as I think that that should work just fine.

Chapter 2.11 – Karate Kid Pose

April rolls around and Sandi feels that my knee is getting close to being able to get into competitive play. She gives me approval to start light practices, but she does not want me to get into live plays at this point. Meanwhile, my teammates arrive in Detroit and the city is abuzz getting ready for our home opener. A side of me hopes that the game will get delayed due to weather, but there is not much chance that there would be enough delay to help me out. I will be up in the team box with the owners.

I am looking at myself in the mirror in the gym. Sandi has me doing this exercise where I stand on one leg and I do curls with 20-pound dumbbells. She does not want too much weight right now. She really is worried that I will bulk up too much before I come back. I get it. If you bulk up gradually while playing, that is one thing. However, if you are off for an extended period of time and you try to come back from an injury, along with new bulk, that gives you two things to work around. The twenties actually work well. As I curl on opposite sides, I can feel my whole body trying to stabilize, especially my knee. Everything around the knee is firing to keep the body in balance. I do this on my right leg for 25 alternating curls and then I repeat standing on my weak, left knee. I do not feel much difference. You may wonder why I do 25 curls. I always do an odd number of an exercise if I am alternating sides, and I start with the weaker side. That way the weaker side gets that little extra. So, it is 13 curls with the left arm versus 12 curls with the right and maybe that little extra will help out with muscle symmetry. Okay, perhaps it is right up there with not stepping on a chalk line. It is just a thing I do.

I decide to challenge myself. I flip over a Bosu ball which is one of those half inflatable exercise balls. The flat side is normally on the ground, but I want to be able to stand on the flat part and have the hemisphere on the underside. I stand on it with both feet and it is quite wobbly. It will do. I switch the 20 pound dumbbells out for 30's and I tentatively feel the surface with my right foot at the center of the flat circle. I gently lift my left leg and get into my flamingo pose. I get into a nice rhythm with the alternating curls, but I stop at 33 and I dismount. I take a deep breath and get ready to try the left knee out. Again, I reach out with my left foot and get a feel for the wobble. In a less than smooth motion, I get into my flamingo pose and things are shaking significantly more, but I am determined to do this. I do get to 33 curls, but now I am sweating and my biceps are actually burning. I jump up and backward slightly, so I dismount. It is not graceful, but it works.

Just then, I hear a voice by the door. Normally this gym is empty, so the voice startles me. It is a guy in his 20's in very good physical shape and he says, "That was impressive. I have never seen that exercise before. Strength and balance. I will have to add that to my routine."

I respond with, "Ah, thanks, my physiotherapist recommended it for my knee rehab. You can certainly feel everything in the leg working together to stabilize." I think to myself that I am glad I bumped up to the 30lb dumbbells. I would have been embarrassed if he saw me working with the 20 pounders. I continue, "It kind of makes me feel like the Karate Kid."

The gym visitor says, "Who?"

"Well, I feel old. Never mind." I thought he would have at least known the reboot with Will Smith's kid, but I am not sure they have the one-legged stance in that version.

I finish my workout and as I return to my apartment, my phone pings. It is Dave and he is reaching out to see how I am doing. I give him an update and I ask if he would be interested in getting a beer after the game. I suggest one of my favorite spots, the Old Shillelagh in downtown Detroit. It is an Irish Pub, not far from Comerica Park in Greektown. I know an Irish Pub in Greektown is a little odd, but that is where it is. Anyway, Stone hesitates and asks, "Would it not be full of Tigers fans there after the game? We would be like fresh meat in there."

The rookie has a good point and frankly, I thought of that too. I then move on to suggest, "How about the Magic Stick? We can grab a beer and play some pool."

"Sounds good. We can connect after the game and I can drive."

Chapter 2.12 – Home Opener Day

I feel acid in my stomach as I sit in the owner's box at Comerica Park. It pains me to be sidelined, but I know it is just a matter of weeks before I can return. I am doing everything the doctor and physiotherapist recommend, and then some. Sure, it causes some extra pain, but as the saying goes, no pain, no gain.

As requested by VanBuskirk, I take some notes as I see things worth mentioning. I start with the Beatles in the outfield. They have the talent, but not the finesse yet. Positioning is not just about reviewing the scouting reports. For example, I notice that our rookie centerfielder John Turner does not shift on the count or pitch call. Fielders need to anticipate the pitch and what kind of hit the batter can muster. Suppose you see that your catcher is calling for an outside pitch on a right-handed batter, the odds are the batter is going to have to go to the opposite field. Sure some batters can muscle an outside pitch to left field, but it is a matter of probability. The statisticians would say that if the batter makes contact, the ball is going to the right side of the field. Conversely, a hanging curveball will likely go to left field when a right-handed batter gets ahead of the pitch. As an outfielder, you have significant ground to cover, so you need to be smart about your positioning. Shifting even a couple of steps towards right field can make the difference between a good jump and a great jump on a play. Some naysayers will say that you do not want to signal anything to the batter inadvertently, but I would just say to move those two steps in the wind up then. No batter will be able to watch the pitcher, the ball, and the centerfielder all at the same time, at least not without whiffing on the pitch.

As I make my notes, I think about what Amp said about Crash Davis ending his playing career at the end of the movie and subsequently moving into a coaching role. Is VanBuskirk preparing me for the inevitable here?

The boys are playing well, but not great. We have had a major shakeup in players and coaching staff, so it goes to figure that it will take some time to gel as a team. We only have four veterans in the starting lineup today, so it is certainly a rebuilding year.

I make copious notes and fill four pages of foolscap as we lose a close game 9-8 to the Toronto Blue Jays. That is actually very respectable. As anticipated, the offence comes back faster than the pitching and defence, so I am not surprised at the high score.

Before going into the dressing room to join the players who were dressed for the game, VanBuskirk and I talk in the hallway. With my notes in hand, I go over a few things, but it is obvious that he wants to get inside to talk to the players before the press swarms them.

When we convene in the dressing room, VanBuskirk points out some successes on the field, but then he throws me under the bus and says, "Now, Jimmy was taking some notes up in the box about what he saw. As we know, he has more experience in the majors than anyone in this room, myself included. We need to take what he says seriously. Jimmy?"

So, I read through about a half of a page of my notes and I realize how negative it is sounding. I stop to ad lib, "That is enough of this, guys. Maybe I will talk to you as individuals about things that I noticed. No sense making a spectacle in here after a solid outing."

That son of a bitch, VanBuskirk just taught me a lesson. If I do coach, I need to make notes about the positives I see and then follow up with the players one on one, unless it is a team issue. Actually, forget about coaching, as a leader on the team, that is a valuable lesson. Man, I should have known better.

Chapter 2.13 – Magic Stick

We get to Dave's car and it is nothing like what I expected. Most rookies blow their money on a sports car, but we approach a Toyota SUV. Stone explains to me that this is a 2019 Toyota Rav4 Hybrid. This vehicle runs on gasoline, battery, or a combination of the two depending on the circumstances. As a result of having an engine and two electric motors, it has ample acceleration, but it is also very fuel efficient. His motivation for buying it was that it is more environmentally friendly than a regular combustion engine. I do not mention my gas guzzler muscle car.

As we back out of his parking space, the vehicle makes a sound like alien angels screeching. He sees my confused look and he says, "That is to alert pedestrians, because usually when you are in reverse, it runs in electric mode and it is ultra quiet."

I respond with, "I think I would rather hear the beep, beep, beep of a dump truck."

"Yeah, honestly, I would too. I have had people say that they think my power steering is shot and all kinds of things, some not so polite!"

Stoner continues on about all of the safety features, "This thing is not autonomous, but it is the next best thing. Look, I will put it on cruise while we go down Woodward Avenue. It has adaptive cruise, so it will speed up and slow down in synch with the car in front of us and it will keep us in the middle of the lane as well. It somehow senses the lines and curbs. If I am not holding the steering wheel though, it will get mad at me after a while."

"Does it sense your hands?"

"No, I don't think so. I think it just wants an adjustment periodically, because if I hold the wheel loosely and let it steer, it still gets mad at me. It is almost like it wants me to drive like they used to on TV." He demonstrates with his hands at 10 and 2 o'clock and he wiggles the steering wheel back and forth.

"I assume it has a backup camera and blindspot monitoring and all that stuff."

"Absolutely! It is one economical *and* safe vehicle! Enough about the car, what did you think about the game? I know you made tons of notes. How about my play? I want to hear from the expert."

I remember the lesson VanBuskirk taught me and I start with some positives. "Stoner, you played really well. In the field, you were flawless and at the plate, you were productive. You went 3 for 5, so no one can complain about that, but you also only faced six pitches. I don't know if you noticed, but their catcher called for a fastball on each of your first pitches. For the first three, you swung at each one and got three singles. That is an awesome start for anyone, but especially for a rookie. On the fourth *at bat* though, the catcher called for a fastball again, but the pitcher shook off the fastball call. They fed you a ball that broke out of the strike zone and you were chasing it. Were you thinking of swinging regardless?"

"Yeah, actually, I was. I was on a roll. And, you're right, I felt silly chasing that ball. The catcher pulled it out of the dirt probably a foot and a half wide of the plate."

"The scouting reports will eat you alive if you swing at the first pitch all the time. Catchers and pitchers have to mix it up, but so do quality batters. You have the skills. You just need the experience."

"What happened on my fifth at bat, Jimmy?"

"The catcher called for a low and outside fastball, because there was a man on first. Low outside fastballs almost always go on the ground to the opposite field. You gave them a grounder to second with some zip and it made for an easy double play. Either the pitcher or the catcher played you."

"How do you counter that?"

"That is where being selective can help you. If you can afford it in the count, you can lay off of that pitch and maybe it'll be a ball. Or if you know it is coming, you can try to punch it over second."

"A *Texas Leaguer*."

"Exactly. And as you gain experience, maybe you'll be able to muscle that one to left field, but it really helps if you know it's coming." I tap the side of Dave's head and continue, "So much of the game is actually up here, Stoner."

"Holy shit. You really do see everything out there. I am impressed."

"Well, I try and I have been at this game for quite some time."

There is silence for a few minutes as Stoner absorbs all of the information and then I see the bar.

"There is the Magic Stick over there on the right by the Majestic Theater and it looks like you can park out in front. By the way, I'll have to check our schedule; hopefully, we are at home and not playing on the day of the Woodward Avenue Dream Cruise. There will be classic cars cruising up and down this street all day long. It is a blast. *But*, if we come, we cannot come in this thing."

"Yeah, your SRT might be a better fit, eh?"

The kid knows about my car, so I just grin.

Once inside, I grab a pitcher of Bud Light while Stoner finds an open pool table. We throw our jackets on a shelf and I break for the first game. By the time we finish the first pitcher, we have two young girls pairing up with us to play doubles 8 ball, or as some call it, Stripes and Solids. Jenny is my partner and her friend Jessie, is Dave's.

I miss an easy shot somewhat on purpose and head to the bar to reload the pitcher. This time, I order an amber that they have on tap. I walk back with the pitcher and upon my return, I whisper to Jenny, "When I was at the bar, did I just see Stoner in my jacket over there?"

"I didn't see him over there, but maybe he was and just looking at his phone or somethin'. You don't think he took anything, do you?"

She and I walk over to the coats and I check the inside pocket of my jacket and I pull out my prescription bottle. I whisper to Jenny again, "This was pretty much full and it might have half in it now."

She inspects the bottle and says, "These are potent too, aren't they?" to which I nod.

"Don't say anything right now."

I am about to pour the beer, but the bartender shows up and says, "Oh please do not pour the amber into those glasses. I have clean ones for you, folks." He pours the four glasses of amber and hands them out.

I say, "Thank you, uh?" and I pause looking for the bartender to say his first name.

As he wipes down the stand-up bar table and picks up the used glasses, he replies, "Stefan, you can call me Stefan."

I hand Stefan a five-dollar bill and say, "Thank you for the service, Stefan."

I turn to Stoner and the girls to announce, "Here is to a great home opener and to a great night with two beautiful ladies."

Jessie looks puzzled and says to Jenny, "Home opener? What is that? You do not need an opener for a pitcher."

Stoner and I clank our glasses and laugh at the comment. Clearly, they, or at least Jessie, do not know who we are and tonight, that is a good thing. Stoner takes a long draw of the amber liquid, then scrunches his face, and says, "Ah Jimmy, can we stick to something more mainstream? This tastes like shit."

"Ah, don't be such a candy ass. Drink up. If you pony up and buy the next pitcher, you can get more of the wimpy stuff. It is nice to actually have some flavor in the beer!"

"Yeah, if you like the taste of chalk! I'll drink it, but I won't enjoy it. Candy ass, my ass Greyson!"

As we continue to play, Stoner gets more erratic with his shots and with his comments to the young girls. I pull seniority and make an executive decision to call it a night. Before leaving the bar, I exchange phone numbers with Jenny, though. You never know.

We go outside to find Stoner's car. As Stoner fumbles for his keys, I ask him if he is okay to drive, to which he responds, "We only had two pitchers and the girls drank close to half of the second one. I should be fine, but man, I'm tired. It's been a long day."

We get into the Rav4 and Stoner pulls a U-turn at his first opportunity. He starts heading south towards downtown and within a minute or two, there is a cruiser behind us with its blue lights flashing. Stoner sits upright and pulls over, a little too abruptly considering there is a cruiser behind us.

Once both vehicles are stopped, the two officers exit opposite sides of the cruiser and approach our vehicle with their right hands on their holsters. Dave turns to me and says, "Keep your hands in plain sight and don't make any sudden movements."

I look at him with a face that just tells him to relax, but he speaks firmly to me, "You are not the black guy driving a nice car. Hands in plain sight and no sudden movements."

As the officers near the vehicle, we both bring down our windows and Stoner's hands are back on the steering wheel at 10 and 2 again.

Both officers stoop down to look into the vehicle and the one at the driver's side says, "So fellas, where are you coming from?"

Stoner answers, "We were at the Magic Stick playing some pool."

"Were you fellas drinking at all tonight? We have been following you since that U-turn and the vehicle appeared to be swerving."

Stoner responds, "We had one and half pitchers between the two of us, sir." I am sure that the officers notice that he pronounces every 's' just a little too much. He continues slurring, "I do admit that I am really tired. That is why we are calling it an early night, sir. We have had a busy day and all."

The officer peers through to see me and asks, "Is this accurate, sir?" as if my answer will carry more weight. Now, I understand what Stoner meant.

I nod, lean forward, and make eye contact. I assure him, "Yes sir, we had one pitcher of Bud Light and then we split a pitcher of an amber ale with two girls while playing pool. And yes, a busy day for both of us." I then return to my normal seated position with my hands on my thighs.

At that time, I notice in my peripheral vision that the passenger side officer is pointing upward to the other officer. Both officers stand straight up and it appears they are having a conversation over top of the vehicle. They then return to our open windows and the passenger side officer says, "It is Mr. Greyson and Mr. Stonewall, right?"

I correct the officer politely, "That is Mr. Stone, sir. He is a rookie, but he will be a household name soon enough."

The driver side officer says, "Okay guys, you can head home, but Mr. Greyson, would you be able to finish the drive, please? You do not seem as *tired* as Mr. Stone."

"Well," I say, "I did not play today with the bum knee and all. All I did was take some scouting notes."

As the officers open the doors for us, we both exit the vehicle and trade places.

The roadside officer closes the door for me as I get in and he says, "Mr. Greyson, I hate to be a bother, but would you mind signing this for me?" He holds his police officer hat upside down in his left hand and a ball point pen in his right.

"Sure, not a problem, officer. We have a Sharpie here though. It will work much better." I pick out a black sharpie from the center console that Stoner has there for such an occasion and I sign the underside of the hat brim.

We thank each other and I put the SUV in gear. By the time we get a block away, Stoner's head is wobbling and before I know it, he is sound asleep in the passenger seat. It is clear that he is sleeping on my couch tonight.

I play around with the adaptive cruise control and lane departure alerts that my sleeping beauty next to me had described. This technology really is incredible.

After parking the SUV in the visitor space, I pretty much drag Stoner up the elevator and into my apartment. I deposit him onto the couch and I hear a ping on my phone.

It is a text from Jenny: Hey handsome, the waitress filled us in! Y did u not say who u are?

I reply: Aw shucks idk

Jenny: Jessie is off with some dude….want company?

Me: Sure

Jenny: Need addy…On my way!

Me: addy?

Jenny: lol…address?

Me: oops. Sorry

Well, I feel stupid as I send her my address

Chapter 2.14 – Two Show Up

I have a quick shower as I figure that Jenny will be at least 10 to 15 minutes. I pull on a pair of pants and the front door buzzes through my phone, so I let her in.

I don on a t-shirt and I go to the apartment door barefoot. I am a little surprised to see both Jenny and Jessie standing there looking around in the hallway as if they are hoping to not see anyone.

I open the door and they are still looking around, so I ask them, "Are you afraid someone will see you here?"

They both giggle and quickly squeeze by me. Jenny whispers, "No, that's not it. She just has a pretty jealous boyfriend."

"Geez, he's not in the hallway. I thought she was off with *some dude.*"

"She thought better of it. There are way too many of his friends there at the bar. It was much safer to leave with me. She is beyond tipsy right now too, so I didn't want her going too far away."

Before I know it, Jenny pushes me up against the hallway wall and she is pulling up my t-shirt. As she is kissing my chest, I look over to see that Jessie is already cuddled into Stoner and it looks like she is sound asleep. Well, they make quite the pair. At least she will be safe here.

"How about we go into the bedroom, so we don't give these two a show? If by some miracle, they wake up!"

Jenny whispers, "I'll race you," and she scampers into the room.

Well, this might be interesting.

***

At about 3 in the morning, I hear consecutive pings out in the living room, so I roll out of bed and scuffle out there to find Jessie's phone on the coffee table and it is pinging. The phone is locked, but I can see the previews of several messages:

Frankie: Jenny, who in there with u?

Frankie: u messin round again?

Frankie: Who u banging?

Frankie: Gonna slap u + kill the dude!!

Frankie: Sorry Jessie – I am not gonna slap you

Frankie: I be waiting in lobby

Frankie: Get your ass out here!

Frankie: Which guy are you with?

Frankie: I will seriously mess up the fucker!

I am reading all the texts on the locked screen, when Jenny comes out and slides an arm around my waist. She looks at the phone and exclaims, "Oh shit! Her deadbeat boyfriend must have her location on his phone. He must be downstairs."

"Well, he shouldn't be able to get in and even if he does, he wouldn't know what apartment we're in." I pause for a second, "Would he?"

"Can't see how he would. I never told him and I can't see Jessie telling him where we are."

"You didn't say that with much confidence."

"As far as I know, she has not budged since we got here."

Jenny powers off Jessie's phone and shakes Jessie to wake her up, "Hurry, Frankie is downstairs. We gotta get outta here!"

Jenny runs into the bedroom to retrieve her clothes and returns within a minute. She turns to me and says, "Hey honey, is there a way out of here besides the front door?"

"Yeah, there is a coded door to the parking garage. Just take the elevator all the way to the parking garage. Here is the code." I hand her a post-it note with the 5-digit combination printed on it. "This gets you into the parking garage and then you can walk out the back of it. There should be a guard there, but he will not bother women who are *leaving* the garage."

"Hmmm, sounds like you have been through this scenario before." She stands on her toes to kiss me on the lips and then she grabs Jessie by the arm to lead her out the door. Meanwhile, Stoner has barely moved; he is clueless to the adventure.

Alright, I am going back to bed!

Chapter 2.15 – The Morning After

I am sitting in one of my recliners, drinking a coffee and watching Good Morning America, when I hear Stoner groan. I say, "There is a pot of coffee on if you could use a cup."

Stoner just groans again and rolls over to face the back of the couch.

Ginger Zee comes on to explain that there is beautiful weather all across America today, but that will change in a matter of 48 to 50 hours as a system makes its way across the Rockies. I say, "Come on man, you are missing the best part. Ginger is on."

I look at my phone and open the Health app. As expected, my walking asymmetry is up at 15% from when I wandered around the apartment this morning. I say to Stoner, "Way to go Stoner. I pretty much had to carry you up here last night and it really messed up my knee. My phone is telling me I have more limp today than I did yesterday and my knee is giving me stabbing pains when I turn. Sandi is going to kill me."

"Ugh, do you have the license plate of the freight train that hit me?"

"You are a lightweight, dude. We didn't have that much to drink. Did you pre-drink or did you take something else last night?"

"No, I just had the few beers and nothing else. I do not take any kind of drug, not even a Tylenol. My body is my temple, man."

I notice the old English D on Stoner's inner forearm and I ask, "Hey, when did you get the tatt?"

"Last week. I wanted something that I would see every time I grab my bat or field a grounder. It reminds me that I am a Tiger, through and through."

"Well, hopefully you don't get traded."

"Ha ha, funny. In all seriousness, I am hoping that I will be a career Tiger just like you, Jimmy. Do you have any ink?"

"Nah, my body is my temple. Not messing with perfection. And no, I don't have a bumper sticker on my Challenger either!"

"Got a cane?"

"Huh?"

"Do you have a walking cane? For your bum knee. Maybe you should take some weight off of it for a while."

"Oh yeah, I do. I should probably use it for a bit. I see Sandi tomorrow, so I am interested in what she says. I really thought I would be playing soon, but it might take a little longer, now."

"You will be back before you know it. The sooner the better, too, 'cause Smitty is killing us. He is okay at second, but he can't even hit a beach ball."

"Hopefully, when I do get back, I don't have a teammate jump on my knee again!"

"Yeah, yeah, yeah. Where is that cane? I'll get it for you, then I will take you up on that cup of coffee."

"Both are in the kitchen. Cane is beside the fridge. By the way, how were things with Jessie last night? Did she pop your cherry?"

Stoner comes back into the living room, hands me the cane, and then walks to the window holding both hands around the cup. "What? Do you think we snuck off into the bar washroom for a quickie or something?"

"Ha, you don't remember the girls showing up here last night, do ya? Ya might want to check your neck in a mirror."

Rather than finding a mirror, Stoner painfully refocuses on the window in front of him and sees the reflection of a nasty hickey. "Really? The last time I had one of these was in high school."

"No need to worry. You were both so hammered, that is about all she could manage to do. By the way, if you see a guy named Frankie anywhere in the next little while, don't give him your real name!"

"Oh great. Glad we are heading to Milwaukee for a few days!"

The schedule got mucked up a bit because of a concert or something, so there is a quick turnaround and the team is on the road in short order after the Home Opener. "Yeah, maybe that's a good thing. I was thinking I was going to make the trip, but maybe not, now with the knee getting worse and all."

Dave changes the subject, "Are you sure you didn't tweak your knee while doing the samba with Jenny? By the way, you have a fantastic view here."

I love it when people admire the view here and I appreciate the opening.

"Ha ha, funny, no. Anyway, yes it is a fantastic view. To your left there, you can see Belle Isle. That is where they hold the Grand Prix races. To the right of the island is where Bob Probert had a heart attack while on his boat. His father-in-law tried to do CPR on him while they drove back to shore, but tragically, he did not make it. It was such an emotional funeral. He was way too young. Bob had some demons that haunted him and I wonder if that contributed to the heart attack. They say his brain was rattled quite a bit, too. The family gave permission for them to do testing of his brain, which has led to lots of changes in pro sports regarding concussion protocols."

"Who is Bob Probert?"

"Oh man, I am feeling old."

"You see the city on the other side of the river there? That is Windsor, Ontario, Canada. Proby grew up across the river and he was arguably the best fighter ever, in the NHL. He played for the Red Wings and then the Blackhawks."

"Are they not trying to remove fighting from the game now?"

"Yes, they are, but he played at a time when they had enforcers that would protect the goal scorers. The ironic thing was that he had hands, too. He could fight *and* he could score. Great trivia question for you. Which Red Wing held the record for the most playoff points in a single season, up until 1995 when Sergei Federov took over the lead?"

"Pavel Datsyuk?"

"Geez, he came along later, you goof! Bob Probert held that title until '95. He even had 29 goals one year. Considering how much time he spent in the penalty box, 29 goals was incredible. And, in his prime, his shot percentage rivalled Gretzky. One out of every four shots he took found the back of the net."

Dave says with a grin, "Okay, I'll trust you, but who is Gretzky?"

"Dustin Johnson's father-in-law. Man, I am wasting my time here. Anyway, that is Belle Isle. If you look at the RenCen, just to the right of it, that is where the tunnel goes over to Windsor. To your right a ways is the Ambassador Bridge. I have no idea why they painted it that godawful blueish green color. That also goes across to Canada. Eventually, we are supposed to get another bridge called the Gordie Howe Bridge, but part of the deal is that the Ambassador has to be dismantled. I am sure you have no idea who Gordie Howe is."

"Vaguely. By the way, thanks for the history and geography lesson Jimmy, but I should probably get outta here. Hey dude," he pauses for dramatic effect and then finishes, "where's my car?" He laughs and then says, "You see I know some old white dude stuff, too!"

I throw him the keys and I am shocked that he actually catches them, "It is in the visitor parking spot. Go out the front door and look right. Hopefully Frankie didn't do anything to your grocery getter."

"Do I need to worry about this guy?"

"Nah, once he finds out it was you that was with Jessie, he will probably start bragging about banging the same girl as the great David Stone."

"I didn't do anything but sleep."

"Oh I know that, but I am guessing Jessie won't let the truth get in the way of a good story."

"Yeah, yeah, as for the knee, use the cane on your good side and move it in unison with the bad knee. That will shift the weight off of the injury."

"Got it doc. Go home and rehydrate!"

Stoner heads out and within three minutes, my phone pings with a message from him. It says: Well, I guess maybe I should worry about this guy.

I am puzzled, but then a picture arrives a few seconds later. The image is of his rear window of his SUV. Etched into the glass, it says "#16 your dead."

I respond to Stoner: Hopefully he cools off….police?

I wonder if he should get the police to file a report and/or talk to Frankie.

Stoner replies: Nah…I am heading out of town anyway…I know guys like him… he will calm down. Besides, somehow it would be the black guy's fault.

That last sentence bothers me. I can only imagine what Stoner has gone through to get to this stage of his life. When people talk about White Privilege, I am starting to get it. Baseball doors have opened much easier for me than for my black friends along the way. In fact, all doors have opened easier for me than for my black friends. And, the traffic stop last night reinforced the fear that many black males face every day.

Chapter 2.16 – Disappointing Sandi

I hobble into the physiotherapist office using my cane as Stoner instructed me and Sandi's arms instantly drop to each side of her in unison with her shoulders. Clearly, body language is conveying disappointment.

"What the heck happened to you?"

"I am so sorry, Sandi. I was out last night with one of the guys and he overdid it. I had to drag his sorry ass up to my apartment to sleep on the couch. I think I twisted my knee getting him out of the car. It felt okay at first, but progressively got more and more sore since then. And, I get some sharp zings when I turn on my knee even a little."

"Okay, let me take a look at it and we will start with some ultrasound. This has put you back at least a couple of weeks I bet. Hop up here, big boy."

"What do you think about the cane?"

Sandi gels up the wand and turns on the machine. I flinch a little as the cold metal and gel make contact with my bare skin.

As she makes circles with the wand, she responds, "Well, I would rather see you walk without one, but if you caused any damage to your meniscus, keeping some weight off of that knee for a while is not a bad thing. On a scale of 1 to 10, what is the pain level?"

"About a 2 or 3, but it jumps to a 4 or 5 when I twist."

"When you get the 4 or 5, does it stick or subside?"

"It goes away pretty much right away."

"Okay, use the cane for a few days, maybe a week. It would be best if you go back to RICE: Rest, Ice and Elevate. We can probably skip the Compression, because the swelling is not too bad. I will give you some exercises to do that will not aggravate the new injury."

"Yes, ma'am."

She works on my knee for about a half hour and we agree to meet again in a week.

Chapter 2.17 – The Setback Leads to Reassignment

VanBuskirk texts me and asks me to give him a call.

"Hey boss, how can I help you?"

"I hear you had a bit of a setback."

"Yeah, word travels fast, eh. It's okay boss."

"So, what did you do to it?"

To avoid implicating Stoner, I started with, "Well, I met this girl playing pool.."

VanBuskirk cut me off with, "Enough said. I don't need to hear about the escapades. How about you stay put this week? I don't want the stresses of travelling to Milwaukee to set you back further. Can I get you to watch the games though and take some notes? You can email me or call me after the games. You be the judge which is more appropriate depending on what you see."

"Will do boss."

We disconnect and I settle into my recliner.

I send a text to our team trainer: Hey Mitch!

I see the dots appearing and I know he is online. Eventually, a message pops up: What up?

The conversation is on now.

Me: Can I share something just between you and me?

Mitch: Sure

Me: just you and me

Mitch: yes

Me: keep an eye on Stoner on the trip…I am staying back

Mitch: what do you mean?

Me: I am nervous he might be taking something … worried about an addiction

Me again: Maybe I am wrong… just watch the guy

I can see that he starts to type, stops, deletes, types, stops and then eventually a message pops in.

Mitch: I will be on the DL

Chapter 2.18 – Scouting Report

I walk into the Old Shillelagh assisted by my cane and belly up to the bar. A really cute, bubbly bartender says, "What can I get you?" with one of the worst fake Irish accents I have ever heard.

I respond with, "What have you got that is local?"

"Well, lots of guys say they like the Dirty Blonde on the tap," and she puts on a flirty smile.

I do not react, so she continues minus the flirting and the accent, "Dirty Blonde is from Atwater Brewery here in Michigan. It is very popular. If you want a red, there is the Frankenmuth Brewery Old Shillelagh Irish Red."

"I will take the red, please. Large draft. Thanks."

"On its way and here is a menu."

"No need. I will take a Shillelagh Burger, but can you change half of the fries to caesar salad?"

"So half fries and half caesar salad? I am not sure that we do that."

"Sure you do."

"Okay, I will take your word for it. Anything else?"

"Yeah, can you make sure the Tigers game gets put on up there on the bar TV in a few minutes? I am kind of working."

"You got it, sport."

I think to myself that she has no idea who I am and that is okay. Just then, I feel a vibration and pull out my phone. It is Jenny and she is wondering if she can cheer me up. Well, that message is a start.

We exchange a few messages and she is on her way here. I wave at the dirty blonde behind the bar and she comes down to me with a, "Yes, dear?"

"Can you double that order, but hold the beer for a few minutes? A friend is joining me."

"You got 'er."

Ten minutes later, Jenny comes bouncing into the bar and she makes my day. She slides her barstool closer to mine, jumps up onto it, and gives a little butt wiggle to make contact with my left hip. I smile and say, "Thanks for coming, Jenny. You are improving my day already."

The bartender appears right on cue with two plates on one arm and a beer in her opposite hand. "Perfect timing there guys. Here you go. Enjoy and let me know if you need anything else besides that other beer. I will bring that in a jiff."

I responded with, "The game?"

"Oh yeah, sorry." She grabs a remote and flips a few channels. She finds the game with our second batter in the lineup approaching the plate.

I think to myself that that is fine. I did not miss much.

We watch the game and actually have a really good time, but at appropriate times. Jenny is great at letting me pay attention and take notes when the game is active, but during commercials, she is attentive to me and me to her, as well.

The game is complete a few hours later and we both have a bit of a shine on. Jenny gives me a little head tilt towards the door and we both understand that it is time to go.

I ask the bartender for the bill, but she responds with a very cheerful, "There is none, hon. The guy at the end of the bar picked it up for you. Thank you for dining with us, Mr. Greyson!"

I look down the bar to see a guy wearing a Tigers hat, smiling at me and he raises his beer mug. I give him a wave and a smile.

I ask the bartender, "Do you have a marker or a pen?"

"Sure hon. Here is a nice black marker."

I pick up what I think is one Old Shillelagh cork coaster, but there are actually two stuck together. On one of them, I write *Thanks for dinner!* and add my autograph. I then pull out a $100 bill and say to the girl, "Please give this coaster to the guy at the end of the bar, then buy everyone at the bar a drink and the change is yours." My rough estimate is that she will be getting at least a 40 to 50 dollar tip. I add, "May I keep this other coaster as a souvenir?"

"Absolutely!" She then turns around and asks, "Would you mind?"

I grin while signing the back right shoulder of her t-shirt. I then return the marker and I slide the coaster into my jacket pocket while I turn back to Jenny.

Jenny smiles at me and we head out the door. Once outside, I ask her, "Do you mind if I make a phone call while we walk?"

"Oh sure, hon. By the way, that was very nice of you. You deserve extra special tonight!"

Jenny slides her right arm around my left elbow and she pulls in tight. As we walk towards my apartment, I call VanBuskirk. I know he will not answer and that is fine; he will be chewing out the players for a while. I leave him a lengthy message with my scouting report, but I avoid mentioning how badly Stoner played. That was obvious since he made two errors and went 0 for 4 at the plate. It would have been 0 for 5, but a player advanced on a fly out, so it was technically a sacrifice. On the positive side, I highlight that the Beatles are looking good in the outfield. I really like how they work as a unit as opposed to three individuals out there.

After I disconnect the phone, Jenny steps around in front of me and stops abruptly. We embrace. She gives me a five second hug and says, "I needed that." She backs out and we continue walking.

I am really starting to like this girl.

Chapter 2.19 – Twitter Storm

I make arrangements with Dave to get his rear window replaced when he is out of town. It is no big deal actually. I am just hanging out at his apartment for an afternoon waiting for one of the auto glass repair places that will come right to your residence.

I am lying on the couch scrolling through Twitter and I come across a hashtag #MessUpStone16. I assume this is Frankie and his buddies, but there is nothing concrete that I can see to tie it to Frankie.

There are at least 50 tweets with the hashtag and creative ways to mess up our shortstop. I text Dave encouraging him to file a police report, but he continues to resist.

I hear the buzzer and let the repair persons know that I will be right down. They literally had the window replaced within twenty minutes of their arrival. I am impressed and remind myself that if some psychopath ever wrecks my windshield, I know who to call.

Dave had prepaid for the repair and he did so out of his own pocket. If he went through insurance, they would want to have a police report, but I guess he can afford it.

Chapter **2.20** – Second Date Pizza Discovery

I text Jenny about 4 p.m. and say that I will be at her place to pick her up in about 20 minutes. To that, she responds telling me to pull up in front of her building and reminds me to bring my passport.

We decided that we wanted to get some pizza and I had suggested Buddy's pizza, which I love, but she wanted to go across the border into Canada. She says they have the best pizza she has ever had, so I figure it is worth a shot.

I pull into the crescent and she is waiting outside. She skips up the sidewalk, all smiles as I walk around to get the door for her. She says, "Nice ride. I feel like I should have my Daisy Dukes on and be sliding in the open window."

"Oh do not do that. I would be worried about scratching the paint on the door, but certainly feel free to wear the Daisy Dukes anytime you want," I give her an admiring grin and I open the door for her.

"Well, you are sweet, doll," and she plants a kiss on my cheek while on her toes.

Upon closing the door gently, I run around to the other side of the car and we are Canada bound.

Jenny smiles at me and says, "Okay, the ambiance is not much to speak of at this place. It is more of a mom and pop place or a hole in the wall, but the pizza is awesome."

We cross the border using the tunnel and I am once again amazed at how polite the Canadian border agents are compared to their American counterparts. The young lady greets us with, "Hello, bonjour." That is our cue to respond in the official Canadian language that we speak, in other words, English or French.

One time, I was crossing the border and I had just returned from a trip to Mexico. There, the tourists all try to speak a little Spanish, figuring it is polite. So, when someone says, "Ola," of course we respond with, "Ola", as opposed to, "Hello." In reality, I am guessing the resort staff just think it is hilarious that these tourists believe they are getting Mexican culture at a Dutch resort.

So, I was crossing the border and this big burly agent said, "Hello, bonjour."

Being in travel mode still, I responded with, "Bonjour," and then he started babbling a bunch of things and I had no idea what he was saying. I looked at him dumbfounded and then we both laughed. He had recognized me and was just messing with me.

Anyway, as Jenny and I are crossing the border into Windsor today, after asking for our passports, this pleasant young lady asks us where we are going. I pause and look over to Jenny. Jenny leans forward and says, "Antonino's."

The agent replies, "Oh, you will love the pizza there. It is the best in Windsor. There are a few other places like Arcata, Capri, and Naples that come close, but I think Antonino's is tops. Ask if the owner is there. His name is Joe and he's awesome. Have a great time!" She hands me the two passports and waves us through.

"Well, you're better than Yelp. Thanks so much."

As I start to pull away, she yells, "Go Tigers!"

Jenny was right. This pizzeria is really more into the take-out business, but they do have a few small tables at which we can eat. I sit down at the last empty table, while Jenny walks up to the register and says, "I ordered ahead. The name is Jenny."

The teenage boy is all smiles as he admires Jenny and responds, "What's the phone number? We have two Jenny orders tonight."

I smile and I sing softly to myself, "867, 5309, I got your number."

Jenny starts with, "313."

The boy stops her short, "Got it. The other one is a 519 number. It will be another 2 minutes. I can bring it right over to you when it's done."

"Ah, thanks hon. The lady at the border told us to ask if the owner was in. She said he's an awesome guy."

"Actually no, sorry. Oh, I mean he is an awesome guy. He just is not here right now, but he might pop in at any time. He loves to stop in and socialize with the customers. If he does show up, I will send him over. Oh yeah, do you want some pop?"

"Pop? Huh?"

"Oh sorry, you must be from somewhere other than Michigan. Do you want some *soda*?"

I chuckle and so does Jenny, "You caught me, originally from Maine and new to the area. Sorry about that. And, yes please, maybe two Cokes. Oh, actually, do you have Canada Dry? We can make it two of those. When in Rome, you know."

"Sure, just grab them out of the fridge there and I'll add it to the bill."

I see an older gentleman in the back pull a giant rectangular pizza out of the oven. I am thinking that is quite the pizza and wonder how many that would feed.

Jenny returns and says, "You probably heard. Just a couple minutes. I figured we are in Canada so why not drink Canada Dry?"

"All good. Much like Vernors, but it doesn't burn your nose so much." Vernors is a classic ginger ale made in Detroit, but not widely known in the other states.

The young boy comes over with the pizza and of course he stares at Jenny while placing it on the table. I was expecting it to come on a pedestal and he would dish out the first slice, but no, he places it on the table in a take-out box.

I open up the box and see thinly cut red meat on it along with what appears to be canned mushrooms. I give a slice to Jenny for her paper plate and I grab one as well. She just stares at me and gives me an upward nod.

"What?"

"I'm anxious to watch you try it. Go ahead."

I blow on my slice as it is still very hot and then take a bite. As I am chewing, I mumble, "Mmmm, this really is good. It's different and I can't put my finger on it."

Over my shoulder, I hear a deep voice say, "Oh, I am so glad you like it, Mr. Greyson. My name is Joe Ciaravino and I'm the owner."

"Please join us," says Jenny as she grabs an empty chair and brings it over to our table.

"I would be happy to as we do not get many celebrities in here. Sorry to hear about your knee, Mr. Greyson. I see you are still using a cane, but hopefully, not much longer."

"Yeah, the cane is for a minor, temporary setback. It's coming along though. Man, this pizza really is so good. What's your secret?" I say with admiration.

"Oh, don't let me hold you up. Eat it while it's hot," to which I take another bite as Joe continues, "My dad, Antonino, opened the first pizzeria in the area back in 1959 and today, we still follow his original recipe."

Jenny and I continue to devour the pizza and I see a sense of pride in Joe's smile.

"Dad came over from Sicily with a tiny suitcase and ten dollars in his pocket. Believe it or not, I still have that suitcase! When he kept getting laid off from his job at Canadian Bridge, he bought a little diner with the money he saved. That first diner was Capri."

Jenny chimes in, "The customs agent says they are good too, but your pizza's better."

"I think so. It's funny. When we interview pizza makers that have had experience making Windsor-style pizza, part of their interview is making a pizza for us! We have them make it using our dough, our sauce, and our toppings. Ironically, they tend to turn out looking and tasting nothing like our pizza. It really is how you stretch the dough and the ratio of sauce to cheese to toppings that makes the difference. I like to say it's the love!" He breaks out in a broad grin and lets out a deep chuckle.

I jump back in, "I love the thin, crispy crust. And, this is pepperoni right? It's not the big circles. I like this better." I mumble a little, because my mouth is still full.

Joe smiles and says, "Correct, in Windsor, we shred our pepperoni, so…"

Before he can finish, the young boy at the register completes his sentence, "So you get some in every bite!"

Joe laughs again and he asks if we need anything else. I respond, "Just one more question. I saw this giant rectangular pizza earlier. How many does that feed?"

"Well, we have a large, then queen, then king size. It is very popular, especially for those out of towners who are longing for a Windsor pizza fix. It is just over two feet by one and a half. With 32 pieces and being rectangular, only the outer pieces have crust edges. It is great for families as some like crust and some do not. It depends on your appetite, but a friend of mine always gets it for a family of 6 and it seems to be plenty. The leftovers reheat well, too."

I grab a napkin and ask Joe for a pen. "I am going to give you my number and I want to make you a deal. Joe, if you bring one of those football field pizzas over the border some time, I will get you into the VIP box at Comerica Park for a game. We just need to wait a few weeks until I am back on the field."

"Deal!," Joe says enthusiastically as he puts out his stalky hand to shake on it.

With our bellies full, Jenny and I leave the little pizzeria, my new favourite little pizzeria.

After getting into the Challenger, Jenny reaches over the console to give me a hug and a kiss on the neck. She whispers, "You really made Joe's day. Thank you for being you."

"Oh, he made my day! I loved the pizza lesson. I loved the crust. And those toppings just worked perfectly together!"

Jenny grins and says in a soft voice, "Oh honey, you take me home and I'll put some toppings on your day."

"Well, I will, but we do need to watch the game first as VanBuskirk will be expecting my scouting report."

"Then, can we watch it at your place?"

"Oh no, you know I am too weak. We would not be watching any baseball."

"Okay, okay, how about some place where we can get some whiskey?"

"I know just the right place."

"By the way, I love this car, but next date, can we take the pickup, so I can snuggle up while you're driving?"

I smile and start the car.

Chapter 2.21 - Whiskey Bar

We enter Thomas Magee's Sporting House Whiskey Bar figuring this fit the bill, as they obviously have whiskey, but they also have television screens.

As we sit down, a waiter in his thirties hands us drink menus and asks, "Would you like dinner menus as well?" He pulls out the chair for Jenny, slides it forward as she sits, and then puts his hand on Jenny's bare shoulder for several seconds, to which she hitches her shoulder backwards.

"Oh, we are full son, since we just had dinner; however we may get some appetizers later on, but that will not be any worry of yours. Could you ask Gord to come over and see me, please?"

"Can I tell him who would like to see him?"

"Sure, just tell him that Jimmy is here."

"Okay, will do."

Gord is the owner and manager of the establishment. I know him well and he runs a very respectable establishment here.

Jenny responds, "It is fine, Jimmy. Guys do that kind of thing all the time."

"And that is not fine. I will explain to Gord what the waiter did and then Gord can decide what to do with him."

Within a few minutes, Gord comes over to the table and says, "Hey Jimmy, too bad about the knee. Oh, I see you still have a cane," as he eyes my aid propped against my chair.

"Oh yeah, but it is coming along."

"My new waiter, Anthony, says that you wanted to see me."

"Well Gord, you know me. I am a straight shooter, much like you. Anthony brought us to our table and he was being very courteous. He actually pulled out Jenny's chair to help her get seated. Oh, my apologies Gord. Meet my girlfriend Jenny. Jenny, this is Gord. Gord and I go way back."

Jenny looks at me and mouths the word girlfriend and raises her eyebrows as a question, followed by a girlish smile. I return the smile to her and give a slight nod.

"Nice to meet you, Jenny. Jimmy, how do you always get the beautiful women to hang out with you?"

"Must be my charm. Anyway Gord, I thought that you would want to know that once Jenny was almost fully seated, Anthony placed his hand on Jenny's shoulder like this," and I demonstrated placing my hand on her shoulder and removing it. "Is that about right, Jenny?"

"Yes, pretty darn close, but his hand was probably on my shoulder slightly longer, before I shrugged it off."

"Oh Jimmy and Jenny, my sincere apologies. That should never occur here or anywhere else. Trust me, Anthony will not be doing that to anyone ever again, at least not in this restaurant. Jimmy, I am surprised Anthony does not have a shiner or worse."

"Well, I am still trying to make a good impression on this beauty here."

"I will take care of it, along with your bill here tonight. Enjoy yourself and do not hold back. Tonight is on me, you lovebirds."

Jenny interjects with, "Gord, you really do not need to do that."

"Oh, my pleasure."

I give Jenny a wink to let her know not to argue with Gord and then I remember my homework and say, "Oh Gord, I do need a favor. Could we ensure that one of the televisions facing this way has the Tigers game on it? I am kind of working tonight."

"Absolutely! That goes without saying!"

A newly assigned waiter named Roy comes over and asks us if we would like anything, to which Jenny responds with, "Yes, I would like to know why sometimes, whiskey is spelled with an E and sometimes it is not."

Before Roy can answer, we hear muffled yelling in the kitchen and then a slamming door. I guess Anthony is no longer an employee here.

"Good question ma'am, well you see the E is used mainly in the United States and Ireland, I understand. Meanwhile, in Scotland and Canada, they spell it without the E for some reason. To remember which is which, I think of Chris Stapleton singing Tennessee Whiskey and you can really hear the *ey sound* on the end. So, Americans spell it with an 'e'. But, really it is just a country preference. That said, there are big differences between Tennessee Whiskey and say, Rye Whisky in Canada or Scotch in Scotland."

"Oh, thank you Roy, I appreciate that. Is bourbon considered a whiskey with an E? If it is, could I get a Maker's Mark on the rocks?"

Smiling, Roy says, "It figures you would ask for that one and make a liar out of me. Maker's Mark is a bourbon and it should be spelled with an E but for some reason, it is not. Just forget all that stuff I just said. But, I most certainly will get you a Maker's Mark on the rocks."

"Make it two, please," I add.

Well, we do a tour of several countries with whiskey and whisky while watching the game. We have lots of laughs and once the pizza settles a little, we also have some jerk chicken wings which are very good,

The ball game on the other hand, is embarrassing. A few players are decent, but Stoner is worse than the night before. I need to have a heart to heart with him. In the bottom of the ninth and while Jenny is in the washroom, I text Dave. I tell him that we need to sit down and have a come to Jesus talk. I tell him that I will call him tomorrow night after he gets home and I suggest going for dinner and a beer.

Jenny comes back with a big come hither look on her face and says, "I think you need to take me home, honey."

"Absolutely, I just called one of those services that will drive us and the car home. I shouldn't be driving at this point. Let me just take care of the bill."

"Gord said he was taking care of it."

"Oh, I'll take care of Gord."

I go up to the register and Roy says, "There is no charge Mr. Greyson. Gord took care of everything."

"Nonsense, him taking care of the other business and making the offer was plenty." I put two one-hundred dollar bills on the bar and continue, "That should take care of the wings, whisky and whiskey," placing an emphasis on the *ey*, "and this is for you for being a great server and a complete gentleman." I place another hundred on the bar.

As we wait by the car, I leave my message on VanBuskirk's cell phone with Jenny wrapped around my waist. This feels nice and I smile in a state of content.

When we enter the apartment, Jenny starts discarding clothing as she slowly struts to the bedroom. I grab a bottle of scotch and two glasses, before I follow her down the hall.

Chapter 2.22 – **Xochimilco**

Jenny and I sleep until noon as we did not do much sleeping until well into the night. As she finishes up in the shower, I fix up some scrambled eggs and toast. I just finish, when she comes down the hall in one of my Spartan t-shirts and I think to myself, damn! How can anyone make a t-shirt look that awesome? She sees the admiration in my eyes. We fill up our plates and snuggle in together on the couch.

I ask her, "Are you up for a Friends marathon?"

Jenny replies, "Could I beee any more ready?"

We both laugh at her Chandler impersonation and I pull up Netflix and start it up on season 1, episode 21, which is the one with the fake Monica. I say to her, "I do not know what we will do if Netflix ever drops Friends!"

"You and me both!"

"If Friends ever leaves Netflix, the world will cease to exist as we know it. Everything would fall to pieces before our eyes."

"Hey hon, is it okay if we take tonight off? Jessie wants to hang out."

"Not a problem. Actually, I forgot to mention to you that I made plans to meet up with Stoner, too. We need to chat."

She giggles as she asks, "Do you want to double date?"

"Ah, no thanks!! Frankie is already out for blood. I will steer Dave completely clear of the Magic Stick!"

"Good call, hon."

***

I call Stoner and suggest that we meet at Xochimilco for some Mexican food and beer around 10 o'clock. Ironically, we both arrive at the same time in the parking lot I suggested. After leaving the lot, we are walking towards the restaurant and we see the Magic Stick bartender, Stefan getting out of a Toyota Corolla.

I say, "Hey Stefan, how are you doing? Shouldn't you be working at the Stick tonight?"

"Nah, I am no longer working there. We parted ways. It's fine though, as now I can get my social life back on track. I have a date with a new girl tonight."

Dave asks, "You going to Xochimilco?"

Stefan does not seem to want to engage with Dave and abruptly replies, "No, I prefer the Mexicantown restaurant."

Dave persists and asks Stefan, "Is that a new Corolla?"

That broke the ice a little and Stefan replies, "Yeah, the technology on these things is amazing. Dynamic cruise, lane tracing, pretty much drives itself."

"I know, I have a Rav4."

Stefan asks Dave, "You seeing Jessie tonight?"

"No, we are not a thing at all."

"You sure seemed like you were at the Magic Stick."

"Nah man, she is not for me."

I am sure that Dave meant nothing negative, except he just does not want to get wrapped up in the Frankie drama. However, it did sound like he was saying she was not good enough for him and Stefan took exception.

"Oh, you are some big athlete and she is just a downtown 'roit girl. Get off your high horse, dude!"

Stefan then tries to puff up his body as much as he can and begins to approach Stoner until he gets my cane smacking dead center into his chest with a thud. I interject, "Easy boy. Sit. This is not happening. You head on over to Mexicantown there Stefan. He did not mean anything bad about Jessie. It is just that there is too much drama associated with the girl right now."

Stoner and I both watch Stefan turn and walk in the direction of the other restaurant and Stoner says, "Hey Grey, I can fight my own battles, man."

"I know, I know, but your hands are gold, man. They're worth too much to the organization. And, if you call me Grey again, I will use my cane on you. I feel old enough already, buddy."

"Well, if you are threatening someone with a cane, that says something on its own."

"Hey now, how about we go get some grub?"

The restaurant is busy, but when the host sees us in line on the stairs going up to the restaurant level, he waves us up and seats us right away.

We order two Dos Equis and look at the menus.

"So, what do you recommend, Jimmy?"

I say, "You really cannot go wrong with anything in here. The tacos are fantastic, but I do like to get the enchilada or chimichanga occasionally. It is really a matter of do you want beans, chunky beef, ground beef, or chicken. If you ask the waitress, she will guide you to what works best for you."

After some dialogue with the waitress, Dave ends up ordering a chimichanga de pollo and I decide to go with ground beef burritos, which is new for me.

Dave asks, "So what is wrong with me, Jimmy? I am playing terribly out there. I am afraid I am going to be sent down any day now. And we had such a great Spring Training."

"Well, Spring Training is not Major League Baseball really, so do not judge anything by that. That said, you are better than what you have been playing, no doubt about it."

"Thanks. I appreciate that," Dave says softly and it is obvious that he is feeling deflated.

We continue into a very frank conversation. I explain to him that it appears that he is juicing. I ask him if he is sure he knows exactly what he is taking. He assures me that he is only taking protein powder that the team trainer supplies and he is not taking anything else. He makes a wisecrack that I am the one taking painkillers.

I am not too happy about that comment and I do bring up that I saw him in my jacket at the Magic Stick. To this, Stoner claims that he was only putting the jacket back up onto the shelf.

We talk about his play in more detail and I do offer some pointers until the food arrives.

As we are eating, I see a young man two tables over who is just staring at me with piercing eyes. If his eyes were lasers, I would be dead. I am thinking this is really odd and Stoner asks, "What's the matter?" and then he follows my stare. "Do you know that guy?"

"Yeah, unfortunately, I think I might have cost him his job yesterday. Well, really he cost himself his own job, but I was a part of it."

I explain the situation at the whiskey bar and how Anthony was dismissed from his employment and then we return to the food, which is amazing as usual. After we have our fill of Mexican food, the conversation does eventually turn to women.

"Hey Dave, I am not trying to set up double dates here or anything, but you know Jessie is a decent girl. She is a nice person. It's Frankie that is the lowlife and I think she is trying to find a way to get out from under that mess. She'll eventually distance herself from that fool."

"Yeah, you're probably right. Man, that Stefan sure blew a gasket when we talked about Jessie."

"Yep, I am sure he has a thing for her. I know you didn't mean anything by it, but you did sound a little dismissive when her name came up and he took exception. Kinda creepy exception. Thank goodness I smacked him with my old man cane."

"Yeah, thanks for that. I do not need to be scrapping anyone right now. Maybe I will text her later to see how she is doing."

Out of the blue, two Sol beers with double limes appear on our table. I look up to see Anthony standing next to the table, placing one beer in front of Dave and one in front of me. I flinch slightly and Anthony says, "Oh, it is okay Mr. Greyson. I am here to apologize for touching your girl like I did. I was wrong and I paid the price for it. Do not worry though. I will find another job in no time. I hope that there are no hard feelings."

Before I can say anything, he is gone and Dave says, "Well, that was kinda strange."

"Sure was, but who can turn down a free beer? I guess I read that stare wrong!"

We clank bottles and chat some more while we drink the complimentary beers.

Not too much later, we both agree that we are getting tired, but once again, Dave is really run down. This just contributes to confirming my substance abuse suspicions. That said, he did just return from Milwaukee and maybe he is just not used to the travel yet. I pay our tab right around midnight and we make our way to the stairway. As we begin to descend the stairs, some guy waiting on the stairway, yells in our direction, "Hey everyone, there are the two deadbeats that call themselves the Dynamic Duo. Which one is Batman and which one is

Robin? We should call them the Dynamic Duds. One is using a cane. The other can't catch a beach ball and throws like his arm is spaghetti."

The bouncer approaches Mr. Loudmouth and stands right in front of him, but the abuse continues, "You are useless Stoner. I hear you are a Stoner. You better watch your back dude. You are killing the team and someone oughta knock you off. I mean it dude. Watch your back you loser."

That was enough for the bouncer and the next thing you know, Mr. Loudmouth is being dragged down the stairs to the exit.

We take that as our cue to exit as well. We are most of the way out and a guy stops me and puts a Corona in my hand. The excited fan says, "Hey Mr. Greyson, sorry about that dude. Have a beer with me. I am one of your biggest fans."

Dave nods at me and says, "We can talk tomorrow. See you Jimmy. I am going to go for a bit of a drive to cool down and then maybe I will head home. Or maybe I will check in with Jessie for a booty call," followed by a mischievous grin.

I have no idea if he is serious or just pulling my leg. Regardless, I stay until the Corona bottle is empty, except for the lime and I head home.

Chapter 2.23 - Good Morning America

It is about 7:30 a.m. and the sun is just beaming into my bedroom. Once again, I forgot to close the curtains tightly and it is surprising how much sunlight can get through a two-inch gap. I rub my eyes and roll out of bed while grabbing for my cane that is propped up in the corner. I think the cane is more just a habit at this point; I should be able to discard it in a day or two.

I hobble out into the living room and power up the television to see that Good Morning America is on. I smile when I see Ginger Zee, who is attractive, but she also has a lot of spunk and she certainly knows her weather. She is about halfway through her segment when the local channel 7 WXYZ feed cuts in with breaking news. I have to admit that I am a little disappointed. A broadcaster I do not recognize, begins with, "Please pardon the interruption to Good Morning America, but we are following a breaking story on the southwest side of Detroit. We have Lucy Chan on the scene."

The feed cuts to Lucy who says, "Here we are at the scene of an early morning crash. Our understanding is that this vehicle left the roadway and the lone occupant is deceased. We have unconfirmed reports that the occupant was none other than our own Detroit Tigers shortstop, David Stone."

My chest tightens and I instantly feel acid pour into my stomach. I hear a clatter and I realize that my cane just hit the floor.

Lucy approaches an officer. The officer is an attractive female who carries herself like she knows her job well. She may have long dark hair, but it is hard to tell as it is tucked up under her hat. Lucy continues, "Officer Hodgson, can you confirm the identity of the victim or the cause of the accident?"

The officer puts up her right hand and points offscreen with the other. "I will have to ask you and your crew to clear the area. We have an active investigation underway and we will make a public statement if and when the Detroit Police Department deems it appropriate."

My left knee buckles and I fall into my recliner to stare at the screen.

Ten minutes later, I have a scotch on the rocks in my hand and GMA is interrupted again with Lucy Chan further away from the scene. "Lucy Chan here in southwest Detroit. Please roll the previous footage."

The studio crew obliges and I watch the same clip from ten minutes earlier where Lucy Chan is asked to move away from the scene.

The feed comes back to Lucy who is now further away from the scene. She stands with a TV camera on her shoulder while she talks to another camera. "That was just moments ago when I was asked by Detroit Police Officer Hodgson to leave the scene of an accident. We have obliged, but we will stay here as long as it takes to get to the facts. Preliminary, unconfirmed information leads us to believe that the deceased is a Detroit Tiger, namely rookie shortstop David Stone. We will take you back to your regular feed, but will update you when we are able."

Well, that gave us nothing new except for the name of the officer. I wonder if she was the first on the scene or if she just took charge of the scene.

Chapter 2.24 – Detective Finn Gaines

The previous day was a blur, but I was in touch with Dave's mother. I felt awful for her as she had just finished identifying Dave's body. She said that his face was unrecognizable, but she did recognize his Tigers logo tattoo. Throughout the entire phone call, she alternated between a coherent numbness and hysterical. Who could blame her?

I also talked with several senior officials with the team and they are devastated as well. I get that not only did they lose a member of the Tigers family, but they also lost a very valuable asset. Managing a Major League Baseball team is managing a business, after all.

As I sit in my recliner, I replay the blur and try to make sense of it. According to the news, they are treating the accident as just that, an accident. However, they did assign a homicide detective named Gaines, to investigate further and hopefully rule out foul play. I assume that is standard protocol, so I am not surprised to get a phone call on my cell from Detective Gaines. I was likely the last one to see Dave alive. The detective should be here any minute.

After getting through the secured door and riding the elevator, Detective Gaines knocks on my apartment door. He begins with the usual condolences and asking about my prognosis for my knee and returning to play. I have to admit that I am getting tired of being asked about my return date. I have pushed it off too many times already and I am itching to get back to playing. Now, it looks like it might be at shortstop, but that makes me feel guilty for feeling some optimism.

Seeing my limp, Gaines questions how close I am to returning, but I show him the health app that Sandi had shown me. I continue and even show him the graph. Other than the setback on Home Opener Night, I have made good progress eliminating the limp and hopefully this is just a bump in the road.

The detective is amazed at the technology in the phone and he mentions that the saying is that the majority of crimes nowadays are solved by digging into cell phones. I can see that with all the messaging, cell towers, search history and all that kind of stuff. To get away with a crime nowadays, a good criminal would have to not carry a cell phone whatsoever.

We sit in the recliners and admire the view of the RenCen while we chat and I offer him a cup of coffee. We both take it black which makes it pretty simple.

The detective surprises me at first with a request to get my fingerprints. I guess that makes complete sense since I have been in Dave's vehicle and apartment, so they probably need my prints for reference.

He does confirm that they believe this is an impaired driving case, but that does not jive with the number of beers we had. I think I had four beers, but Dave only had three. The media has hinted that other alcohol or drugs may have come into play and Gaines intimates that is possible.

I am not surprised when he wants to rewind the clock back to the Home Opener and our night at the Magic Stick. I fill him in about driving there in Dave's new SUV and its technological gadgets. I walk him through how much we had to drink, although it was not all that much, meeting the girls, and playing pool.

I did mention the fact that I thought Dave had gone into my jacket where my pain pills were and that Jenny could confirm this. This would align with the fact that Dave did get really tired, really fast, not to mention belligerent. Well, maybe not belligerent, but at least inappropriate. Not only did I suspect that Dave took pills from me that night, but I think he might have been helping himself for a week or so as I ran out of medication much faster than I thought I should. I let him know that my surgeon could confirm this as well.

Detective Gaines shows me the drug names and they match my prescriptions, so that gives credence to my theory. That said, the painkillers are unfortunately in very widespread usage in every community.

I continue with the story of the night and describe being pulled over. The cops were kind of starstruck and let us off, but I needed to drive the rest of the way home. So, I explain that I drove home and twisted my knee somewhere along the way of getting Dave out of the car, up to the apartment, and onto the couch.

I then explain how the girls showed up, but we got the text blitz from Frankie in the middle of the night. This yielded threats against Dave both by text and on his SUV to which I had a photograph. Gaines also asks me about a Sharpie and a Tic Tacs packet in Dave's vehicle and I assume that is all about fingerprinting.

The media has mentioned a bottle of Jack Daniels in the vehicle, so I felt it was safe to ask about this. Gaines indicates that yes, the rumours were true, so that gives more credibility to the impaired driving angle.

Next, we move forward from the Home Opener evening. I begin by explaining the Frankie aftermath. There were comments all over social media bashing Dave, as well as threats to his life. I thought they were idle threats, but now, we see those comments in a different light.

We switch back to Dave in general and I mention that I think he has, or had, a substance abuse issue.

I have to admit, I like this Detective Gaines. He is pretty authentic and kind of clumsy in the way he speaks. He is the type of friend that you like to have around, because he is self-deprecating when he gets twisted up. He does not know much about new technology and fumbles around with that as well. I cannot help but think man, he would be lost in the Rav4.

We come back to the threats from Frankie and I explain that I tried to encourage Dave to file a police complaint, but he refused. For the first few days, we figured he would be safe being in Milwaukee, anyways. I also fill him in that I stayed back and played scout for VanBuskirk.

As the interview is taking a while, I offer Detective Gaines a sandwich and a soda. While I am getting the grub ready, we cycle back to the health app on the phone. He has been struggling with sciatica and is wondering what his walking asymmetry would be. I return with the food and there is a noticeable change in Gaines' mannerisms. It is like he saw a ghost and just wants out of here. He takes a deep breath and we get back on track.

Now, we are talking about the night at Xochimilco. I laugh because he does not know how to spell it, but I save him, and myself actually, by handing him a coaster from my end table.

I start with the altercation that we had by the parking lot with Stefan who is, well was, the bartender at the Magic Stick. He seemed to have a thing for Jessie, who of course had a thing for Dave. I mention that I had to step in between the guys with my cane, to break things up.

I then explain that Dave and I had a very frank conversation about his playing and my suspicions of juicing and/or abusing pills and booze. The irony was blatant, as we were drinking beer while having the talk.

To that, Detective Gaines frantically jots something down.

I continue and talk about how an obnoxious guy in the stairway was yelling at Dave and me, actually made threats to Dave. The bouncer may know who the guy was.

Gaines reconfirms how much we drank and the timing. I recall seeing six beers on the bill when I cashed out. I explain that Dave had three beers and I had four, because I stayed for one more that a fan bought. I also tell him that Dave said he was either going to go for a drive or a booty call with Jessie. I mention that I was not sure if he was serious about either, but I had thought that he was okay to drive.

Gaines is about to leave, but then he stops and says, "My apologies. I thought we were done, but I have one more question, Mr. Greyson. You became friends with Mr. Stone going out for beers and all. Did you ever notice where he carried his cell phone?"

I replied, "I can't say I ever did."

Gaines concludes the interview with, "Alright, that is all for now. I really appreciate your assistance and your hospitality here today. You know most people treat me like a leopard in these types of situations."

I laugh and say, "Sorry Detective, leper. I think you meant to say people treat you like a leper."

"Oh right you are. I guess if I did that by text, you would be typing LOL or putting in a laughing emobi."

"Emoji, but ha, I see what you did there. That was funny, Detective. Good one. Best of luck with the investigation and please let me know if there is any other way I can assist."

Like I said, Gaines is somewhat socially clumsy, but I think I like the way he works.

Chapter 2.25 – The Funeral

I pull up to Jenny's building to pick her and Jessie up. As expected, Jenny does not have the bounce in her step like she did the last time I pulled up. I chose the pickup today, because I knew we had the three of us to head to the funeral. Although, the Challenger has a surprisingly roomy backseat, it is a little awkward to get in and out of the back and I figured that Jessie's attire today would not be conducive to that task.

After putting the truck in park, I climb down and give the girls a double hug with one arm around each of them. I then open both passenger side doors, but Jenny closes the rear door and grabs Jessie's hand to bring her into the front seat with her. I close the door after the girls enter and I hustle around to the driver's side. As I open the door and step on the running board with my left foot, I pause as I see Frankie standing about a hundred yards away, leaning against a fence. Even though I cannot see him clearly, I feel that his eyes are burning through me, much like Anthony's eyes did the other night when we saw him at Xochimilco. I then realize that I did not mention running into Anthony at the restaurant to Detective Gaines. For a few seconds, I debate whether or not to text the detective, but I choose not to do so right now. I will text him later when I have some time to lay out the scenario for him. Jessie snaps me out of my inner thoughts with, "Don't worry about him Jimmy. He is probably more mad at me than he is at you. Actually, he is just mad at the world."

"I do not understand why he would have an issue with me, but man, that look."

"Like I said, it is not you. It is me."

"I wish I had five bucks for every time I have heard that."

Jenny jumps in with, "Is the expression not supposed to be a nickel?"

"Yeah, it is, but there's inflation."

I thought that would lighten the mood a little, but the girls could only muster a little more than a grunt. The girls really only knew Dave for about a week, but this was still impacting them greatly. From my conversation with Detective Gaines, I imagine he suspects that Dave's death was not an accident and it feels like the girls figure that, as well. If I read them right, I believe they are thinking that we were just in a staring contest with suspect number one.

Jenny, who is sitting in the middle seat, is holding both my right hand and Jessie's left tightly, while we drive in virtual silence. I try some small talk, but then think better of it.

As I pull into the funeral home parking lot, I whisper to myself, "I am glad we came early," as I spot a nearly full parking lot. An attendant asks me if I am part of the procession and I nod, plus I add, "Also a pallbearer." He places a magnetic flag on my hood and I smile when I see that the flag is dark blue with a white old English D on it. That sparks my mind to flash back to seeing the tattoo on Dave's inner forearm.

The attendant asks me to drive around the corner and pull in behind the black hearse. I park and go around to the passenger side to help the girls down from the front seat. Jessie certainly needs assistance navigating the large step, but Jenny climbs down like an old pro. When Jenny plants both feet on the ground, she cuddles into me with a tight hug. I need that!

As we enter the funeral home, we get hit with a rush of cold air from the air conditioning. It seems odd to me to be running air conditioning this early in the year, but then I realize that they are preparing for an absolutely full house. We are just a few feet into the lobby when I hear a familiar voice behind me quietly say, "You old sack of bones, where is your cane?"

I turn to see Amp and I put out my hand which he grabs, but then he draws me in closer and gives me a firm hug. Amp whispers, "I have only known him a few months, but we really connected. This is awful Jimmy, really awful. I have to admit, I am really struggling with this." We hold the hug for a good ten seconds and then pat each other on the back.

I concur, "I am too, Amp. And you are right, this is awful. Hey friend, it is good to see you though, but I thought there was some kind of force field at the Florida state line. I didn't think that you ever left the Sunshine State."

"Wouldn't miss this, Jimmy."

"You here for a while. My place is not very big, but I would make space for you, pal. You're welcome to stay with me as long as you want."

"I booked a hotel down by the park, but..."

I cut him off and finished his sentence, "but you can cancel the reservation. I insist."

"I don't wanna cramp your style. Looks like you have two beautiful girlfriends now, Jimmy."

"Oh, I am so sorry, this is my girlfriend Jenny and her friend Jessie. Girls, this is Amp. I am proud to call Amp my friend."

"Nah, I just cut his grass down in Florida."

"Girls, Amp is just being modest. He ensures that the Tigers have the best turf in Spring Training. He is a big part of the Tigers organization down in Florida."

"I am just the groundskeeper, ladies."

"Amp, you are an important part of our family and I really do insist that you stay with me."

Amp jumps in, but more subdued than usual, "Uh, uh, Rod Stewart?"

"Nice try, but I think it was his previous band, Faces."

Amp gets back on track, with, "I only bought a one-way ticket actually, so you may not get rid of me for a while."

"Stay as long as you like, as long as you don't start singing *Take Me Home Tonight*. You treat me like family in your home, so my place is yours."

"I will check with Amanda about flights and all, but I would be happy to stay for a little while. You're the best Jimmy. My bag is in the office over there, cuz I just got here. Can I get a ride too?"

I smile and pull his shoulder in tight, "Of course you can, pal. Really glad I brought the truck today. Come and sit with us, please."

We sit near the front and then the funeral home fills up quickly. Through the windows, I can see hundreds of people who are standing outside and I speculate that the audio will be pumped outside. I note that there is certainly a mixture of attire here today. Many of the men are in suits like me, but then there are a large number with Tigers jerseys, as well as University of Michigan attire. It is obvious that this funeral is going to be a tribute to a homegrown hero who got his life cut short just when he was on the verge of making it big.

The reverend gives a touching tribute to David Stone and there are very few dry eyes in the house. Thankfully, Jenny holds my hand throughout the entire service, because it certainly helps me cope with my stirring emotions.

As a pallbearer, I help carry the casket to the hearse and then again from the hearse to the plot in the cemetery. As the casket lies on the straps next to the rectangular hole in the ground, the reverend once again says a few words. It is difficult to hear his soft voice over the sobs of Mrs. Stone and her daughters; meanwhile, Dave's brother just stares at the ground silently. The cemetery service is brief and we turn to return to our vehicles. After a few strides, I am disgusted when I see a familiar sight. About two hundred feet away, I spot Lucy Chan with a videographer along with two other crews. I think to myself, why can they not just let people grieve in peace?

The four of us get into the truck and we head in the opposite direction of the media.

Chapter 2.26 – Monkey Shoulder

I insist that Amp take the bedroom. I even promise to wash the sheets, but I lose that battle and he camps out in the living room. Unlike Dave, he pulls the sofa bed out, which is sufficiently comfortable, so Amp tells me.

We chat for a while sitting in the matching recliners and there is awkward silence. We look past the pull-out bed, out the window and see the lights from Windsor bouncing off the Detroit River. I break the silence by asking Amp if he wants a scotch and he responds after a bit of a pause with, "Is Detroit the Motor City?"

I have no idea what he is talking about and I am sure I look puzzled.

He continues, "Well, I was trying to think of a funny alternative to, 'Is the Pope Catholic?' and I was drawing a blank. That was the best I could come up with."

"Well, nice try. You probably could have gone with, 'Will the Lions miss the playoffs?'. Anyway, I will take that as an affirmative. Ice or neat?"

"Ice, please."

I go to the kitchen and come back with two glasses with three ice cubes in each, along with a bottle of Monkey Shoulder. I set everything down on an end table and pour. "I thought you might like this one. It is one of my favourites and Amanda won't get mad at you for spending too much on a bottle."

Amp looks at the bottle and declares, "Monkey Shoulder, huh, never heard of it."

"It is a unique scotch. You know how you hear about blended scotch and single malt?"

"Yeah, blended scotch is a blend of good scotch mixed with some grain whisky right?"

"Usually, correct."

"Also, when you get a single malt, it actually is not necessarily just one scotch. It is normally a mix of different barrels, but they have to all come from the same distillery to be called a single malt."

"Ah, that is news to me."

"Now, if they do come from a single barrel, they will identify it as Single Cask."

"Oh okay, I have seen those, but they are out of my league."

"I hear you. I like scotch, but I am not that much of a connoisseur. I buy by the taste and not the price tag. Anyway, Monkey Shoulder here is a blend of single malts from different distilleries and there is no grain whisky mixed in."

"Interesting, so where does the name come from?"

"Well, back in the day, the malt was pressed by hand as opposed to machinery. A man would pull down on a lever on the malt press and I guess, it would be quite common for the press guy to eventually mess up his shoulder. Probably like a rotator cuff injury. And back then, they would call that *monkey shoulder* for some reason. Hence the name."

"Good thing a baseball player didn't name it or it would be called Spaghetti Arm!"

We both chuckle and Amp asks if he can try it. I say, "Whoa, hang on. We have to make a toast first."

I raise my glass and begin with, "Well, here is to Dave Stone. We only knew you for a few short months, but we quickly became attached to you. It's such a shame to cut a life so short, any life, but you had so much talent and you really were plain and simply, a nice guy."

Amp chimes in, "And a role model to so many young boys and girls out there. You amazed me how you connected with the kids down in Florida, my kids included. We salute you, brother."

We look at each other and in unison, say, "Amen." We clink glasses and take a swig.

Amp licks his lips and says, "Damn, that is one fine Spaghetti Arm!"

Chapter 2.27 – Comerica Service

I wake up just after 8 a.m. hearing click, click, click out in the living room so I figure Amp must be up. I am guessing that he has the stupid keyboard click turned on, on his phone. I stagger out there a little slowly due to the Monkey Shoulder, aka Spaghetti Arm, that Amp and I polished off the night before.

"Hey Amp, you do know that you can turn off that keyboard clicking, right?"

He continues to type and totally ignores me.

"Yo Amp, you do know that you can turn off that keyboard clicking, eh?" I say a little louder.

"Yeah, yeah, yeah, but when you have these old fat fingers like mine, it is hard to know if you actually hit the letters. Give me a break, I am an old man."

"Okay, Amp. Why do you have the Today Show on? You know I prefer Good Morning America."

"Ginger has the day off."

"Nuf said. Do you want some breakfast?"

"Sure."

"You know where everything is," I say jokingly, as I am getting out bowls and cereal.

After dousing the cereal with milk and putting on a pot of coffee, Amp and I set up in the recliners to watch the Today Show. It catches me by surprise when they start a segment about Dave's passing. They mention that it is still considered to be an accident, but there is an investigation in an attempt to rule out foul play. However, the focus of the segment is actually on the service that will be preceding our game today against the Red Sox. They tout it as expecting the Tigers organization to pull out all of the stops.

As we are watching the segment, I get a text from VanBuskirk: Street clothes or uniform?

I assume he is wondering which I prefer to wear for the service today, so I respond: Uni

Within a few seconds, I get another message: Consider it done.

I fill Amp in on the text exchange and he laughs, so I ask him, "What's so funny?"

Amp laughs some more, but does not say anything.

We continue watching the Today Show as they honor some actor who passed away and they show several clips of old black and white movies.

In the commercial break, Amp says, "You know what I used to love watching as a kid? The old Abbott and Costello movies."

"Yeah, I have seen some of them."

"My favorite bit was the old baseball skit. You know the one?"

"Yeah, Abbott would ask, 'Who's on first?'"

"No, no, Costello was the tall, smart one. And, he did not ask. Costello would tell Abbott, 'Who's on first.'"

"Oh, okay. I always get them mixed up. And yeah, I see the difference."

"So, follow along. Who's on first. What's on second."

"Don't know."

In unison, we say, "Third base," and we both laugh.

With that, I head to shower and I don a suit. I figure if I am going to be in uniform today, I should be dressed in a suit like all of the other players when I enter the park.

***

Amp and I walk to Comerica Park. This is such a great perk of living in downtown Detroit. It is a beautiful day in southern Michigan and as we walk, Amp and I chat about nothing in particular.

We enter the dressing room and it brings back so many memories. It feels like a lifetime ago for me, meanwhile, this is Amp's first time in Comerica Park, let alone in the dressing room. He wanders around in awe.

We walk over to Dave's stall and we are both silent for about 10 seconds. Amp steps back and says, "Amen."

Amp then gives me a side hug and whispers, "Thanks for letting me come in here. You made my day. I will be behind the dugout harassing you guys, okay. Let me know if you want me to order you a beer."

"Ha ha, enjoy the VIP service there pal. You deserve it."

As Amp is leaving the room, VanBuskirk is entering, but they both stop and talk for a few minutes. Amp puts one arm around VanBuskirk and walks him out into the hallway. I think that is a bit odd, but I put on my Tigers uniform.

***

VanBuskirk suggests that I go out and warm up with the guys, which I am happy to do as I do have physio and doctor clearance to practice. Although I do not have clearance for live play, a side of me hopes that VanBuskirk will give me the nod to take short or second. Short is very, very unlikely as we do have Mark Ditmars making his debut today. The organization pulled a very quick blockbuster deal to pick up Ditmars from the Texas Rangers, although it cost us dearly in terms of draft picks and several minor league players. Hopefully, he is worth it. Ditmars has comparable talent to Dave, but he is mid-career and has significant experience in pressure cooker situations, including 3 playoff runs.

I feel good throughout warmups and I am enjoying the day. I kind of laugh to myself as I see the media taking pictures and talking amongst themselves. I bet they are figuring that I am playing. VanBuskirk has been silent in the media as he wants the focus to be on honoring Dave and not Ditmars or myself.

We regroup in the dressing room and VanBuskirk says a few words of inspiration before we head back out to the field. The plan is for us to line up in an arc between third and second. Dave's #16 jersey will be lying on the ground where he would normally set up. The Red Sox will line up in a straight line between first and second.

As we head out to the field, the crowd is silent and it feels eerie. As I near the newly chalked third base line, I alter my stride slightly, so that I straddle the line as I have done thousands of times and I head out to Dave's jersey. The family asked that I be right next to Dave's jersey, so I take my post.

Dave's uncle is at a microphone on the pitcher's mound and once everyone is in position, he breaks into a heartfelt rendition of the Star-Spangled Banner, followed by an even more emotional and passionate, Amazing Grace.

Upon completion of the songs, again, there is that eerie feeling as the entire crowd remains standing and virtually silent. To ensure that there is no cheering or applause, the Daktronics video screen displays a caricature with his hat over his heart, along with the word *Silence* displayed. The family's preacher then steps up to the microphone and promises to be brief. He starts by talking about how Dave always wanted to be a Tiger growing up.

What he says next, hits me like a punch to the stomach. The preacher continues, "Dave had a dream to not only be a Tiger, but he wanted to be a career Tiger like his hero, good friend, and mentor, Jimmy Greyson." The preacher turns and gives me a nod. Turning back to the mic, he bellows, "He achieved the dream of being a Tiger and unfortunately, he also achieved his dream of being a career Tiger. It is just such a tragedy that that career lasted less than a season. Please continue standing and say a silent prayer with me."

A side of me needs to go down on one knee as I can barely stand. I cannot help but think that I was not prepared for the preacher to speak about me being Dave's hero or mentor, but I manage to stay at attention. I feel that I did not deserve the kind comments that the preacher delivered. I adjust my hat downward, as do many of my teammates, in a vain attempt to hide the tears.

After 30 seconds of silence, three fighter jets fly over the stadium in the direction of first to third base with a large roar. As the thunderous noise dissipates, the preacher returns with, "I thank you all here today for your thoughts and prayers for David and his family. I will leave you with two things that David loved dearly." After a short pause, the preacher yells into the microphone, "Play Ball!"

I wonder briefly what the second thing is supposed to be and then, I hear the sound of successive cracking bats. The song, Centerfield blasts throughout the stadium. Even though Dave never played centerfield and the song is older than he was, he still loved the John Fogarty baseball inspired song. To that, the crowd erupts into applause and many begin singing along with the bouncing ball karaoke lyrics on the big screen. I feel a smile arrive on my face and I say to myself, "Put me in Coach, I am ready to play, today."

The Red Sox players walk to the first base side dugout and some go to the bullpen. Our players do the same, but the starting lineup takes the field. Meanwhile, I neatly fold Dave's jersey and walk towards our dugout, in front of which, Dave's mother stands. I see her as a brave, proud mother standing erect waiting for me to get to her and I tell myself to hold it together.

As I near the third base chalk line, I look down and whisper to myself, "Piss on it," and I step directly on the chalk while en route to Mrs. Stone. I position myself in front of her as John Fogarty continues to sing and I present Dave's jersey to her as if I were in the military and I was presenting a folded flag to a grieving family member.

Mrs. Stone holds the jersey with one hand and leans in to hug me with the other arm. All she can manage is a whisper, "Thank you Mr. Greyson. We were blessed for the short time we had him. And thank you for welcoming him into your home and to the team. He really did look up to you with the utmost respect. He literally wanted to be you."

I wipe the tears from my cheeks and I am speechless. I give Mrs. Stone a grin and I walk her arm and arm to her seat in the VIP section, right next to Amp.

As I help Mrs. Stone get settled into her seat, I muster the nerve to speak, "Mrs. Stone, you should be so proud of what your son did accomplish so quickly. He had potential to be much better than me at baseball and life in general. It is me who should have looked up to him. I hope you enjoy the game. Amp here will take care of anything that you may need or want."

Amp smiles at Mrs. Stone and I know that he will take good care of her.

I return to the dugout and VanBuskirk is waiting for me. He gives me a hug and when we separate, he says, "Thanks for doing that. I am sure the family really appreciated it."

The top of the first does not take long and we retire the Red Sox's first three batters in order.

As our fielders are trotting into the dugout, VanBuskirk approaches me and says flatly, "Who's on first," pauses and follows with, "What's on second."

I just laugh and he continues to just stand there. After a few seconds, he says,"Well? What do you say?"

Oh geez, Amp put him up to this. "Okay, I'll bite. Don't know."

All the players join VanBuskirk in yelling at me, "Third Base!"

After the laughter fades, VanBuskirk continues, "Well, you are in uni. Get out there and coach the offence as you see fit. And, don't be lookin' over here for any signals. I have complete faith in your ability to call the game. Hell, you can probably do it better than I can!"

So, I make my coaching debut at third base. I am sure that the media is having a field day, speculating that my playing career is over. It just so happens my coaching debut is a success. I do fumble some of the signals, but we manage to pull out a 4-2 victory over Boston, thanks in large part to a clutch bunt and subsequent hit and run, both of which were plays that I called late in the game.

I find comfort in the fact that my knowledge of the game can help our team succeed; however, I still itch to play.

Chapter 2.28 – Green Light

I really appreciate having Amp stay with me, although just as during the first night, we repeatedly drink far too much while chatting late into the night, almost every night. I show him around Detroit: Greektown, Fox Theater, Renaissance Center, and of course the Old Shillelagh, Xochimilco, Buddy's Pizza, and of course my new favorite pizzeria across the river. Amp actually leans towards liking Buddy's better, but I will not hold that against him.

Each morning, I hit the gym for two hours, while Amp walks all over downtown Detroit. I go extra hard at the rehab, both to benefit my knee and also to address my waistline, which has expanded somewhat from all of the beer and scotch that Amp has made me drink. I am seeing tremendous progress and the cane is a distant memory, and none too soon. In fact, I probably kept using it a little longer than I really needed.

Eight days after the funeral, I meet with Sandi and she is amazed at the progress I have made. I pass every test that she throws at me and she assures me that she will communicate with the team doctor and management to move me beyond just practicing.

I am pumped when I get back to the apartment, but my excitement comes crashing down when I open the apartment door and see Amp's suitcase in the kitchen. I call for him but he cannot be too far if he is still in the apartment. He is actually just out of view in the Dining Room and he yells, "What? I am right here. I am just admiring your view one last time before I head back to the swampland, we call Florida. We don't get to see rivers and lakes that you can actually swim in."

I chime in with, "Well, without dodging gators I guess, yes."

"I talked with Amanda this morning and the kids are anxious to get me home. She also found a nice direct flight home on Spirit. Checking my bag will probably cost me more than the actual flight."

"Yeah, and it is a good thing you are only 5'9", otherwise you would be chewing on your knees the entire flight."

"It's a short flight, so I'll be fine. I can't thank you enough for everything, but can I ask you for one more favor?"

"Sure, anything for you, Amp."

"Can you drive me out to the airport?"

We both laugh as I say, "Of course. Want the Challenger or the pickup?"

"I drive a pickup all the time, so let me drive the Chally."

"I need to grab a shower first and we can leave whenever you'd like. And yes, you can drive. Just do not leave any rubber on the road. You would not believe how much those tires cost!"

"Who drives a muscle car and doesn't want to lay rubber?"

"Yeah, yeah, give me five minutes."

***

As we leave my underground parking space, Amp gives the car a little too much gas and of course, lets out a chirp that echoes throughout the garage, so much so, the security guard asks Amp to roll down the window as we approach the exit. He says, "None of that please, sir."

Amp turns to me and says, "A white kid calling an old black guy, 'sir'? We are making some progress in Detroit after all."

"Yes, we are, but there is still a long way to go, Amp. Long way to go!"

Amp barely gives the car any gas as he rolls out of the garage, but then as soon as he is on the road, he gives it a steady push on the pedal which results in some rubber transferring from the rear tires to the asphalt. Thankfully, he does not give it full throttle or he would have the ass end kick out on him, before the traction control actually activates.

I warn Amp, "If you're going to give it pedal to the metal, please give me a heads up so I can grab the *oh shit handle.*"

"The what?"

I raise my right hand above my head and grab the handle above the window and then grab my right wrist with my left hand and yell, "Oh shit, oh shit," while lifting my knees and wobbling around in my seat. "This is the *oh shit handle!*"

Amp looks at me while smiling and then he nods while pressing down the gas pedal a little harder. As he accelerates through the on-ramp onto I-96, his smile increases in direct correlation to his speed. He is certainly enjoying himself.

112

Amp stops smiling for a minute to say, "So, I am guessing your love life is going to make an improvement with me headin' back home."

"You got that right. I love you man, but no offence, Jenny is much better in bed."

"You just don't know how to meet my needs, Jimmy," Amp adds with a completely straight face.

I shake my head. "That may be true, but I am honestly afraid of Amanda."

A few minutes later, Amp is cruising along I-94 towards Romulus and the Detroit Metropolitan Wayne County Airport, or DTW for short. I fill him in on the good news that I am reactivated, but it is still up to VanBuskirk who really has the final say regarding live play. My mind wanders back to my college days and I silently hope that I get more than just a pinch run in my return game.

Amp says, "Whatever will be, will be."

I jump in with, "Eddie Money. Uh, uh, Baby, Hold On."

"Yeah, yeah, you got me. Anyhow, you have been around a long time and you still have lots of time left. Do not rush it. Be patient and you will have a better chance of returning strong."

"Yeah, I will survive."

In unison, we both say, "Gloria Gaynor." That one was a little contrived.

I know Amp is right, but I am anxious. I need to have a good season to ensure that I am playing in 2020 and not being a part of some coaching staff in the minor leagues somewhere!

Chapter 2.29 – The Return

The day after Amp leaves, I wake up to the sunlight streaming into my room once again. I have this alarm clock on the bedside table that I really like, as it projects the time onto the ceiling with a fine, red light emitting from the top of the clock. I open my eyes and tilt my head back just slightly to read the time off of the ceiling. It is 7:16.

Even though I barely move, somehow, I disturb Jenny and she rolls over and turns away from me. I stare for a moment and admire her bare back and shoulder length, wavy blonde hair. I cannot help but think that I am one lucky guy.

I reach over to the bedside table and pick up my phone. I decide that I am going to text Detective Gaines about the former Whiskey Bar waiter, named Anthony. I type a text that describes him getting fired and also that we ran into him that fateful night at Xochimilco. I realize he was mad at me and not Dave, but you never know, it may be relevant. Also, he bought us each a beer to apologize, so Dave and I had four beers each at dinner and not three like I initially reported.

So, it is three and a half weeks into the season and I have the green light from everyone from Sandi up to Tigers Management to make my season debut. However, I dread going to the park and talking with VanBuskirk. I have this nagging feeling that I may not play at all today. Most importantly, I better not be coaching on third.

I finish the text and put my phone back just in time for Jenny to turn over again and snuggle into my chest. We sleep for another half hour before we get moving for the day. It is a big day!

***

I walk into the dressing room to cheers and things being thrown at me to welcome me back to the active roster. Towels and socks are flying about and I am not too impressed when a jockstrap hits me right in the face. I am thankful when I realize there is no cup in it and that it smells like fresh laundry detergent. I thank the guys for the warm welcome and then proceed directly to VanBuskirk's office. I might as well get this over with right away.

I rap my knuckle on the door frame and ask through the open door, "May I come in?"

"Absolutely. I am happy to see you back, Jimmy. Close the door."

"So, I am just wondering what you are thinking today. It does kind of dictate how I warm up and all."

I brace myself for what I might hear.

"Jimmy, we really don't want to push it too fast. We need to ease you back into things. It's a long season, you know."

"Yes, I understand." I am starting to steam as I just want him to get to the point.

"Jimmy, I have you in as DH this afternoon. You will be batting ninth in the lineup."

"Alright, thank you, sir. I will do my best. Do you want the door open or closed?"

"Closed please."

As I leave the office, I cannot help but think, well, that is better than a late game pinch run. When I think about my situation, from his perspective, it makes sense. As the Designated Hitter, I get to hit, granted, in all likelihood, one less time than the first part of the order. However, hitting and running should be straightforward and safe for my knee, unless I get into a rundown or some fool jumps on my knee again! My movements can be less predictable in the field, as I adjust to bouncing balls or running players. It makes sense. I will bat for the pitcher for today or maybe a game or two, but then, the big question will be, where do I get to play after that? He has been practicing me at short, as well as at second and I can see the logic for either, but I am not likely to dislodge Ditmars. He is a younger version of me. Well, that is for another day.

Chapter 2.30 – Pitching Duel

Flajnik is pitching today and he has had a solid start to his career. His lanky frame generates great velocity and he can peak at 99 miles per hour, a few innings into the game. On top of that, he has a wicked curveball and a decent changeup, but that is about it. Teams will get to know him and eventually start to light him up if he does not add another couple of pitches to his arsenal. However, so far, so good this season.

Today, he is off to a great start as well, putting down their first nine batters in the first three innings, much to the pleasure of Flaj's new fans in Detroit. There are 20 adoring fans in centerfield who are all wearing Flaj's #8 jersey with matching black, curly-haired wigs. They are jockeying over each other to get the best camera angle for the group photo on the large screen above the crowd. I wonder if an entrepreneur will begin selling a Tigers hat with the wig built right into it. Anyway, as well as Flaj is pitching, unfortunately, the Red Sox pitcher, Frank Donner is matching him in this contest, virtually batter for batter. By the time I get to the plate, there are two outs in the bottom of the third and the game has no score and no hits.

As I walk up to the batter's box, my nerves are as shaky as during my first professional *at bat* years ago. I enter the box being sure not to touch any chalk with my cleats and I dig my right foot into the dirt with my right hand up in the air, signalling to the umpire to give me a few seconds. Once I feel secure in my right foot placement, my left foot finds its location and my two hands are now on my bat. I calmly say, "Game on!" However, there is so much crowd noise, I doubt even the Red Sox catcher heard me.

As I give my bat one last loop back to my ready position, I try to put myself in Donner's mindset. If I was a pitcher and I am facing a guy who has not had a major league plate appearance in months, what would my first pitch be? Clearly, he would be thinking that I am taking the first pitch in order to gauge delivery and velocity. That would lead to the logical conclusion of delivering nothing too fancy: something with heat near the center of the strike zone. The second pitch would likely be a big breaking ball trying to mess with my confidence. I know I gave Dave a lecture about being selective, but what do I have to lose? There are two outs and both pitchers are on fire. What is the best way to rattle a pitcher? Well, there are two ways: one is to fire a rocket right back at him and the other is to break up a no hitter. Here goes nothing as I decide to go for the *two for one.*

My mind is made up that I am taking a rip at the first pitch. I am not going to be greedy, so I am aiming for a liner right back at Donner. Donner is right-handed and the shortstop has pulled to the left slightly. If I aim at Donner's delivery hand, I should be good. That is where I envision the ball going.

Sure enough, Donner puts one right down the middle, probably about 98 miles per hour and I launch a rocket right back at him. Rather than to his right or my left, it goes directly at his torso and thankfully he decides to extend his follow through and dives to the ground before the ball would have impacted his right kidney. It was close to where I was aiming, but not quite. That said, I know I rattled Donner.

I know I am not getting to second on this hit, because the ball got to the centerfielder in record time, so I run at about three-quarter speed to first. As I am standing on the bag, our first base coach slaps me on the ribs and says, "Well, you rattled Donner! Welcome back, Jimmy."

I respond with, "Mission accomplished. That was the plan and it is good to be back."

Well, I got stranded at first, as the next batter lined out to third, also on the first pitch. I was hoping for a chance to steal second, but that did not happen. I am okay with it though, because I cracked the egg. I got a hit in my first at bat in my season debut and more importantly, Donner is going to be off of his game, now.

Donner exits the game after giving up four hits in the fourth inning, but Flaj continues his roll. He accumulates nine strikeouts after eight innings, but there is action in the bullpen when we return to the dugout in the middle of the eighth. I ask Flaj how his arm is feeling and he responds, "Like a wet noodle – I'm done," and we both laugh. I congratulate him on a great outing as he puts a bag of ice on his shoulder and another one on his elbow. As I walk away, I laugh to myself again thinking about my Spaghetti Arm night with Amp. Well, Flaj won that pitching duel, but we need to close things out for him.

In the bottom of the eighth inning, our second baseman, Smitty, despite Stoner saying that he could not hit a beach ball, does get a hit. Unfortunately for him though, he appears to pull his hamstring on the way to first. VanBuskirk puts Ritchie Coughlin in to pinch run for him and I cannot help but once again think that I am happy that was not me repeating my college return. Ritchie aka Ringo is normally an outfielder, so I silently get a positive thought.

VanBuskirk walks through the players standing in the dugout and sits next to me. "You want Ritchie to take second or," and he leaves his words hanging.

"I got it, sir," I respond quickly and I go to get my glove as I see the inning wrap up.

As if on cue, and maybe it was, I step onto the turf and I hear John Fogarty sing, "Put me in coach," as the song, Centerfield floods the park once again. I smile, and I pick up my pace to head to my spot at second. As I take a warmup bounder and throw it to first, I realize that I did not even look for the chalk line. I have no idea if I stepped on the baseline or not.

So, we enter the top of the ninth with a 3-1 lead. The Red Sox lead off with a single, strikeout, and a single, so they have one out with a man on first and second. The next batter extends the count to full, three balls and two strikes. I see our catcher call for an outside, low fastball on the right-handed batter, so I am thinking that this is perfect. If the batter makes contact, it should come my way and hopefully on the ground. It should have some zip to it, so I need to be ready. I shift a little to my left with the pitch, expecting the ball to be hit between myself and our first baseman.

The ball is hit and I anticipated correctly, but it is moving fast. My first step is a side step and then I dig in to run hard to my left. After two full strides, I dive and get the ball on a short hop. I quickly rotate a 180 degrees counter clockwise and try to get my legs under my upper body. As my eyes find Ditmars approaching second base, the ball is cocked in my right arm, but I am on my right knee with my left foot planted in front of me. My throw is all arm and it sends a burning sensation through my ribs on my right side as the ball leaves my hand. My throw reaches the bag just as Mark crosses it and he throws a strike to first for a double play. My right side burns, but I will survive. That is why we have ice and anti-inflammatories.

As they say, the fans go wild! We win by a score of 3 to 1, with no need to hit in the bottom of the ninth. The game is in the books with a solid team effort and several bright spots for the team.

Chapter 2.31 – New Dynamic Duo?

Lucy Chan and her videographer enter our dressing room after the game and come directly to me. Thankfully, she does not have a video camera on her shoulder too; I really do not understand the two video camera thing. Lucy asks, "Jimmy, can we chat for a minute?"

"Sure, Lucy." I learned a long time ago that that is always the correct answer, even when you have a bad game and do not want to talk with anyone.

The cameraman points to Lucy and me, then Lucy jumps in to set the stage, "We are here in the Tigers dressing room after a 3-1 win over the visiting Red Sox. But more importantly, we are here with none other than Jimmy Greyson, who just returned from injury and completed an outstanding comeback. How does it feel, Jimmy?"

"Oh, it feels good, but it is far from a comeback. I played one game and only played the field for one inning. There is a long way to go."

"You are being modest, Jimmy. You went two for three at the plate and made a game saving play to close out the game. Can you tell us what it felt like at the plate for your first *at bat*?"

"Well, actually, I was quite nervous. It took me back to my first major league *at bat* kind of nervous. Anyway, I figured the first pitch would be a fastball, so I was swinging for sure and I saw a spot where I wanted to put it. I got solid contact and missed my location a little, but I am just glad that Donner got out of the way of it."

"Yes, I think we all are. That ball was moving. So, you saved the game in the top of the ninth. Please tell the viewers about coming up with that play."

"Well, even a blind squirrel will find a nut once in a while."

"Oh Jimmy, you are being far too modest. There was no luck involved there. Can you tell us about that play and how your were feeling?"

"Well, it was not just me and I wouldn't say that play saved the game. We had a two run lead and still had our bats to play out if necessary. However, the play did close out the game which felt good. I saw the pitch call and that allowed me to get a good jump on the ball. I was happy with my catch and getting the ball to second on target for Ditmars to do his thing. He turned the double play very smoothly. I was impressed with his timing and throw."

"Yes, Ditmars looked good out there and especially on that play. The management certainly made a good trade with the Rangers to bring in another middle infielder. So, is it safe to say that we have a new Dynamic Duo out there on the field?"

I am in shock that she asked this question and I just stand there. I gulp and lower my head to count to three.

After a few seconds, Lucy realizes her insensitivity and continues, "I am so sorry Jimmy, that wasn't an appropriate question," and motions to the cameraman to cut.

I reply dryly, "I expect that question will be edited out before airing."

"Absolutely, Jimmy. And again, I am sorry. Thank you so much for your time and keep up the great work. You looked awesome out there."

"Tell you what. Go ahead and turn the camera back on and ask me about the Ditmars trade."

Lucy points to the camera and the red light comes on. "Jimmy, I would like to ask one more question if you do not mind. What do you think of the Ditmars trade?"

"Well, the organization is still mourning the loss of David Stone, may he Rest In Peace. We lost a good friend and valuable team and family member, but I know that he would not want the Tigers to shut things down for the season. He would want us to become contenders for the playoffs. A side of me had hoped to move back to shortstop, but bringing in Mark is what is best for the team in the long run. We can rebuild the infield around Mark, and me at second is part of that plan. I fully expect that we will be in the mix to make the playoffs here in 2019. I know VanBuskirk talks about a 5-year plan for our rebuild, but I think good things will come much faster than that. The Tigers will be contending in 2020 for sure, thanks to VanBuskirk's strategic moves he has made for this team. I am really looking forward to seeing his work come to fruition."

I know I sound somewhat robotic, but oh well.

Chapter 2.32 – Clarification

I am lying in bed, just staring at the ceiling, watching my alarm clock projection and trying not to stir and subsequently wake Jenny. I am reviewing my return game play by play. This is what I do. My memory may not be too good for some things, but for baseball plays, I have a photographic memory. I am in the middle of the fifth inning in my mind when I hear my cell phone do a double buzz.

I retrieve my phone with an outstretched arm and look at the preview. It is a text from Gaines: Can we talk?

I reply using just my thumb: Sure. Will call in 15

I slide my arm out gently and whisper to Jenny, "Shh, stay sleeping, hon. Gotta take a call."

A few minutes later, I am brewing a pot of coffee and calling Detective Gaines.

"Good morning Detective. You are up early."

"I am so sorry. Did I wake you?"

"No, I am good. I was just lying in bed replaying yesterday's game on the ceiling. Have you heard of the novel about the girl chess protégé? I kinda do the same thing as her, but with baseball plays. By the way, I can't play chess for the life of me!"

"No, I have not heard of it. What is it called?"

"Queen's Gambit, I believe; it's getting made into a mini-series."

"I will wait for the series then and binge watch it if I ever get the time. Anyway, great game yesterday, Mr. Greyson. You seem to be fully recovered."

"I am feeling ready. Thank you, sir. I do not imagine you want to talk about baseball, though."

"Correct, I hate to bother you, but do you mind if we review the events at the Magic Stick on Home Opener Night in more detail?"

"Sure, Detective. I don't mind at all. Do you have some leads?"

"Actually, I think it is better that I not divulge too much. I do not want to skew your recollection."

We continue to talk for about a half hour going over all of the details that I can remember. By the time we are done talking, I have a pretty good idea that the good detective is thinking that the night at the Magic Stick is pivotal to the investigation. In fact, I believe I know who he is thinking might be responsible for Dave's death.

Once I end the call, I send a text to a new friend: Does today work?

I shuffle back down the hallway towards the bedroom and before I get into the room, I see a return text: Sure does. I will bring 6 and I have a plan!

I smile and slide into bed and cuddle into Jenny's back. She reaches behind her and pulls me closer.

Chapter 2.33 – Person of Interest

I am in my bedroom packing a bag for our road trip to Cleveland. We will leave a couple hours after our afternoon game today. My phone buzzes twice, along with a ping. I check the text message icon and it is Amp: Turn on CNN – breaking news.

I hustle to the living room as I do not believe in having a television in the bedroom, but that is another story.

I get to the living room just as they cut to a CNN correspondent who is standing in front of the entrance to Comerica Park. I miss the name of the reporter, but I listen attentively to everything she has to say.

"We are here in front of the Detroit Tigers Comerica Park with breaking news regarding the sudden death of David Stone early in the morning on April 14th. It was reported as a single car crash and confidential sources initially indicated that it was an unfortunate fatality due to impaired driving. It now appears to be otherwise. A confidential source close to the investigation has informed us that the Detroit Police Department has identified a person of interest in a newly opened homicide investigation."

Next to the correspondent appears a still picture of the front of the Magic Stick, as she continues, "Although we are not at liberty to identify the person of interest, we have unverified reports that the person has connections to the Magic Stick bar and pool hall here in Detroit. We do not know at this point if the person is male or female, or if they are an employee or customer."

I say out loud to the television, "Not at liberty, my ass. If you knew the identity, then you would know that if the person of interest was a customer or employee. Why are you acting like you know, but cannot reveal?"

I realize my phone is still in my hand as I feel it vibrate. Amp's next message: Well, who do you think?

I reply: Well, I am hoping it is not Jenny! Lol

Amp: You better hope not! Or you will be sleeping with one eye open.

I bring the exchange to a close: It ain't her. Gotta run pal. Gotta pack for Cleveland before I head to the park for today's game. You gonna watch?

Amp: Of course! Good luck brother! Hopefully you get to play a full game today!

My final text: Hopefully is right! And, hopefully the Detective arrests the person I am thinking he is going to arrest.

Chapter 2.34 – Game Two

We are finishing our home stand with the Boston Red Sox this afternoon and I really am hopeful that I will be starting at second. I cannot believe that is where I am at, but I know that in the long run, this has potential to be a good thing.

Jenny and I walk to the park and we look rather sharp together. I am wearing a new charcoal grey double-breasted suit that Jenny picked out for me, along with a narrow collar white dress shirt. Jenny insisted I not wear a tie, so this is my look for today, totally designed by my girl. And damn, Jenny looks awesome in her heels and short tight black skirt, along with a white Tigers jersey. On the back, she has of course, my number 13 and above that in big block letters from armpit to armpit, it says JIMMY'S GIRL! And yes, including the exclamation mark.

As we approach the front gate, I ask Jenny once again, "You are okay waiting for him here, right?"

"Absolutely, Jimmy. My pleasure." She then reaches up to kiss me, although with those heels, she does not have to reach as much as usual. "Best of luck, big boy! Break a leg!"

"Oh, you should never say that to a guy with a bum knee, but thanks hon. I will see you in the party room after the game."

"Yep, wouldn't miss it! I will be there with bells on!"

When I get into the dressing room, VanBuskirk yells out through his open door, "Hey princess, before you start giving me the whole *I need to know how to warm up* crap, you are playing second."

To that, there are a bunch of hoots and hollers and I just smile, followed by a big sigh of relief. I cannot help but wonder if it is because VanB thinks I am ready or if it is because Smitty has a blown hamstring. Either way, I will take it.

Well, to make a long story short, I play really well. Nothing dramatic in the field, but I fielded everything cleanly and every throw was bang on, and with significant zip. At the plate, I was three for five in the number three batting slot. Unfortunately, the rest of the team was somewhat flat, nothing terrible, but nothing with spark either. We fell to the Red Sox by a score of 4-1.

After the game, VanBuskirk reminds us that we are to get changed back into our dress clothes and then we are hitting the road in two hours. I remind the players that we are heading down the hall to the party room, until it is time to board the bus.

I am walking down the hall with Ditmars on my left side when we see Jenny. Ditmars says in a low voice, "Well, hello there." It sounds like this is his version of Joey Tribbiani's, "How you doin'?"

I punch him in the shoulder and let him know, "Easy boy, she is with me."

"You stud you. Good job, old man."

I stop and put my right hand on his chest to stop him as well. "Excuse me?"

"I did not mean anything by that, Jimmy. You are an all-star in my books. I idolize you, dude! Nothing but respect! Sorry, man."

"Okay, we can move on."

"But seriously, dude. You are the stud. She is smokin'."

"I know, how about we move on, Dit?"

"Yeah, yeah, what smells so good?"

"Oh, you just wait. You will find out soon enough."

We meet up with Jenny and she is all smiles. I quickly introduce Jenny to Mark and then we go into the party room arm and arm. There is our new buddy Joe, in jeans and a Tigers jersey, pulling pizza out of a portable pizza oven.

I ask, "Joe, where did you get the oven?"

"I have some paisanos on this side of the border."

We can all see the pride in Joe's face as he pulls another reheated football field pizza out of the borrowed oven and he slides it back into its Antonino's box. He says, "I have one more and that is it. You guys can start on that one down there. They are all the same, pepperoni and mushrooms. That is our best!"

The guys start streaming in and begin digging into the king size pizzas. VanBuskirk enters and asks, "What is going on here? Pizza and beer when we have a game tomorrow?" He tries to act all serious, but cracks a smile before he finishes the sentence. He then cracks open a can of Bud Light and grabs two square pieces from the middle of one of the pizzas. He bellows throughout the party room, "Enjoy this guys. Maybe this will put a spark in your asses for tomorrow! Cause there was no spark today!"

All the players just moan, but I know in my heart, I was not to be included in that comment, unless VanBuskirk expects me to supply the spark for them. Then again, maybe he does.

Once Joe has the sixth pizza set up, I give him a big hug and thank him for coming across the border with the pizza. I ask him if he had any trouble at the border.

He replies, "Well, you do know that we are not allowed to bring meat or vegetables across the border, right? I told the customs agent that I had six cheese pizzas."

"Did he buy that?"

"No, but I dropped your name. I actually showed him your text and he let me through! So, I hope you guys enjoy the contraband pizza!"

I hand Joe a can of beer and we tap aluminum!

The pizza is awesome and I learn another new tip from Joe. He tells me that they do offer fresh mushrooms, but he prefers using canned mushrooms. The reason being, fresh mushrooms tend to give off a lot of moisture, so they have to cut back from their usual generous amount of sauce. Less sauce means less flavor. I tell him, "Well, I am converted. This is the best damn pizza I have ever had! Thanks so much and I hope you enjoyed the game."

"I really did. You know I played a little bit of baseball when I was young, but I was not all that great. I had fun, but hey, look at this body. I am not exactly built for speed! But you know what, I made a lot of good friends. We may have moved all over the place, but some of those guys are still friends in my heart."

We laugh together and enjoy each other's company for the short time we have before departure.

VanBuskirk pops back into the room to give us a 5-minute warning, so I give Joe another big bear hug and thank him profusely for coming to the game.

Joe says, "No, grazie a te amico! No, thank you, friend!"

To myself, I smile and I think about the, "Hello, bonjour," greeting at the border.

Chapter 2.35 – Road Trip

The trip to Cleveland was a quick one, but with a double header. I feel like I am back to about 95% physically and the team is beginning to gel. We win both games handily and it is obvious that VanBuskirk is feeling good about our prospects for the remainder of the 2019 season. Ditmars and I are working well together and he is on fire at the plate. The dressing room has come alive with an overwhelming sense of optimism, even though we all hope for some closure with regards to Dave's passing.

After a tiring trip home, I enter my apartment and my spirits are lifted immediately when I realize that Jenny has used the key that I gave her. She is lying on the couch, sipping white wine and watching a Friends episode – the one where Ross whitens his teeth excessively. When Jenny realizes I am there, she runs at me and pretty much slams into me for a long hug.

When we separate, I feel a buzz in my pocket, so I pull out my phone to see a text from Amp: There has been another murder!

I am amazed that I get my news tips all the way from Florida.

Part Three – Narrated by Detective Finn Gaines

Chapter 3.1 – Early Morning Drive

7 a.m. comes too dang fast nowadays. Maybe I am just getting old and rickety, but retirement is coming too darn slowly. I start off with a coffee and check my iPhone every morning, but go figure, the phone did an automatic update overnight and it wants me to see what is new with whatever new operating system it has just downloaded. Version 13.5.2.3a or something or other. I just want to see if I have any email or text messages, but I am in this stupid tour of new features. I had put off the operating system upgrade for days trying to avoid exactly this, but it just did it on its own while it was plugged in for charging.

I am old, but I am actually pretty good with the technology. You know, I like the Google and the Facebook. I just do not like them changing everything once I get used to where things are located. I will take a tour of the new stuff when I have more time. I just skip through everything and sure enough, I have six new text messages and I need to be at Zug Island ASAP.

Living in Harper Woods, I floor it down I-94 as fast as I can safely travel. As usual, I grin as I drive by 8 Mile Road. I think of how popular Eminem got, but meanwhile, I do not think I would recognize a single song of his. I just know that one of his songs was called *8 Mile*.

There are so many songs that refer to Detroit, but there is one that makes me laugh. Journey's *Don't Stop Believin'* has been popular for decades and it gets played in timeouts at just about every sporting event in North America. It is even played here in Detroit at Little Caesar's Arena, Ford Field, and Comerica Park. You all know how it goes, "Just a small town girl, livin' in a lonely world, she took the midnight train goin' anywhere." Clearly Steve Perry has trouble saying "ing," but regardless, it goes on with, "Just a city boy, born and raised in South Detroit, he took the midnight train goin' anywhere."

Well, the Renaissance Centre is right downtown Detroit. Granted, core Detroit has shifted a bit as Joe Louis Arena and Tiger Stadium were replaced with Little Caeser's Arena and Comerica Park. Ford Field has also been an added bonus to the core, as the Detroit Lions and Pistons moved downtown from Pontiac and Ann Arbor, respectively. Downtown Detroit has gone through some ups and downs, as well as a shift, but it is currently thriving, just a little more east than previously.

Now, the funny part, downtown Detroit is right on the Detroit River. There is a west side and an east side, along with a north. There is actually even a southwest area where the Detroit River turns southward, but there is no gosh darn South Detroit. It just does not exist. South of downtown is water and I am sure that boy on the train did not grow up there.

Anyway, I am on my way to the southwest section, which is an industrial area, so I exit onto I-96 to head towards the river and then get onto I-75 to go west, skirting Mexican Town or Mexican Village. No one really knows what to call it. Regardless, it was hit hard by the downtown shift. I pull into the accident scene on West Jefferson Avenue, just east of Zug Island. What a name for a place! It sure is not Tahiti, by any means. Zug Island was an uninhabited Native American burial ground for hundreds, or maybe even thousands of years, and it was actually a peninsula. In the late 1880's, a canal was cut around the property and it became an island, a very industrialized island eventually.

As I exit my Detroit Police Department issued Dodge Charger, I see a silver SUV on its roof beside the roadway. Had it travelled another 20 feet or so, it would have ended up in the Rouge River, which feeds into the Detroit River. I cannot help but wonder if we would even know about this accident had the vehicle made it a little further and into the water. I approach the scene and encounter Officer Hodgson, whom I have known for most of her 10-year career.

"Hey Hodgy, why am I getting called to an accident scene?"

Officer Hodgson approaches me and says, "The driver is a VIP and we need to cover all our bases here, Finny." I am taken aback by her calling me Finny. What is up with that?

"Finn, please. Okay, let's take a look, Hodge."

"Ah, you can catch a hint can't you?"

I guess she is trying to make a point. I honestly thought she liked being called Hodgy, but apparently not. I will make a mental note of that preference. That said, many believe my mental notes are literally just random post-it notes scattered about my brain. It is somewhat true, as my thought processes are not exactly linear; my mind does jump around more than most.

Chapter 3.2 - The Scene

This is a horrific scene. It appears the vehicle left the road at full speed, with no evidence of any braking, before or after leaving the roadway. I see silver paint and scrapes on a large boulder which obviously upended the sport utility vehicle.

"Hey Hodge, what kind of vehicle is this?"

"2019 Toyota Rav4 Limited, hybrid model."

I look inside and it appears that the multiple airbags attempted to preserve the driver's life. Several deflated bags hang from different parts of the driver's side of the cabin. The airbags look like they actually accomplished their goal of protecting the driver from hard objects, just as the seatbelt did its job of keeping the driver in the vehicle. However, it appears as if gravity might have been the killer in this instance. The driver hangs upside down in the vehicle and blood has pooled into his head, as well as his one hand and arm. One arm is hung up in the steering wheel while the other is extended like he is haling a taxi, but because of the vehicle inversion, that arm became the lowest part of his body.

I take notes and pictures: I document a nearly full water bottle, a partial uncapped bottle of Jack Daniels, an empty Tic Tac container, loose change, and a Sharpie. Often in these types of accidents, we spot a cell phone smashed somewhere in the vehicle as they often leave the driver's hand at impact, or just before.

"Hodge, any cell phone?"

"Yep, I patted down each pocket and it looks like it is in his left front pants pocket."

Okay, so this was *not* a case of texting and driving gone bad.

I pull on a pair of gloves and slide out the iPhone that looks just like mine. I put the phone up to the driver's left thumb and nothing happens. I try the body's right thumb and there you go, the phone comes to life. Hodge gives me an inquisitive look like she is not sure I should be doing this and I just return a lopsided grin. I see that the driver asked a Jessie to call him just after midnight the night before, and she did call, however, he did not answer. Prior to that, there was a call at 8:32 p.m. and it was from a Jimmy Greyson. I begin connecting the dots and realize who my VIP is.

I continue to look at the phone and say, "He got a call from a Jimmy Greyson. Ahah, so that is who this is. This is *the* Dave Stone, is it not?"

"I thought that you knew. They didn't fill you in, eh?"

"Nope, I guess information flows as needed here."

"Well, you can get all my notes, no problem."

"Okay Hodge, please be sure to document everything here and we better get the coroner to weigh in. I am guessing that the tox screen will show some alcohol. It apparently looks like an impaired driving mishap here."

"Will do, Finn. I do have word that Mr. Stone was pulled over not long ago by one of our officers. He was really out of it, but the officer was starstruck and let him go. Had the passenger take over behind the wheel and sent him on their way."

"Seriously, in this day and age? Let me guess. Last Chance?" which gets me a nod. "I will follow up with LaChance, but why call in Homicide on top of the homicide crash investigator?"

"Like I said, the brass just wants us to cover all our bases, considering who the deceased is. Personally, I do not see anything jumping out at me. Do you? Is your *spiny sense* going off?"

I give Hodge a confused look and respond, "*Spiny sense?*"

"Yeah, you know how Spider-Man will say that his *spiny sense* is tingling. His spine is tingling. Chills in the spine kind of thing."

"You jackass! Spider-Man has *spidey sense*, not *spiny sense*!!"

"Are you sure? I have always thought is was like spine tingling."

"Yes, I am sure Hodge. Well, right now, I have no tingling going on, but I am still gathering evidence." I hand her the phone and continue, "Can you get the phone to IT? They can clone it and get a copy to me. I know they like to do the deep dive, but I want my own copy, too. Ninety percent of the time nowadays, the cell phone holds the secret that kicks investigations into another gear." I actually have no idea what percentage of investigations are aided by cell phones, but it sounds good.

Hodge does bring up two very important considerations. First, this could also be a suicide. If it was, Stone wearing a seatbelt would indicate that it would have been a last minute decision. It does happen and alcohol was involved, so judgement can be impaired. The second is that the little black box or EDR will give us some information in the half minute or so, just prior to the crash. We should be able to answer questions like: Was the driver accelerating or braking? Did the airbags deploy at the correct time? How fast was the vehicle travelling? Was there a malfunction? I imagine there are other pieces of data that I would not anticipate as well, since this is a fast evolving technology.

Chapter 3.3 - The Autopsy

As I enter the Coroner's Office, I swear my internal temperature drops five degrees. This place just gives me the chills. I call out for Dr. Walker, "Hey Walk, are you here?"

Dr. Walker, in a crisp, open white overcoat, comes walking out of his private washroom, tucking his shirt into his pants. "Hold your horses. Who is here any…" He stops short when he sees that it is me. "Oh hey Finn, what gives me the pleasure? Just seeing you, handsome, gives me pleasure. I did not think that I had any homicide victims in here today."

So, I have known James Walker for years and he looks like he could play college football, because he did. He played for Bowling Green, where he was an outstanding offensive lineman. He had no aspirations of playing professional football, but he used football to fund his ambitions of becoming a doctor. He eventually found his niche in the role of coroner.

As they would say on the Canadian sitcom Schitt'$ Creek, James drinks both red wine and white wine, if you know what I mean. He thinks that the flirtatious talk makes me feel uncomfortable, but it does not. I just laugh along.

Anyway, I respond to Dr. James Walker, "Well, there was a traffic accident that had a fatality, so it is considered a homicide accident until we can prove it otherwise."

"Yes, I know that, hon. I am no rookie here, but that is usually determined by the scene investigator. They don't normally bring in the big guns unless there is proof of intentional death."

"I hear ya, but our vic is a VIP. Where is our David Stone?"

Dr. Walker says, "Oh, right over here. We can take a look now," as he goes through an open door to the examination area. "Mr. Stone is one fine specimen of a human being. He was in excellent physical shape. I had already done a fair amount of work, when I had to take a break."

Dr. Walker snaps on some surgical gloves and approaches the body. "Blood screening has indicated alcohol in his system to the tune of 0.04 and also two different painkillers. Potent ones, too. They are in my notes over there. Oh, and there were traces of both of those painkillers in the Tic Tac container retrieved from the vehicle. The 0.04 will get you a suspension in some regions, but it is not legally impaired in Michigan. That combined with the level of painkillers, however, would knock out you or me."

I remember Hodge's comment about another possible impaired driving episode, so I ask, "Any evidence of Mr. Stone being a heavy drinker or drug user?"

"No, on the contrary. His liver was in tip top shape. Like I said, everything about him is in incredible shape. Other than that Tigers logo tattoo on his arm, this gentleman is in perfect condition."

"If he was actually breathing, I assume you mean. So, what can you tell me about his demise?"

"Oh, yes, yes. That is what I mean. Any-who, in layman's terms, hanging upside down for hours is what killed him."

"I figured that much."

"Well, there are a few factors. His heart was unable to pump blood throughout his body against its normal direction of flow and the blood would pool in the lower extremities of his inverted body. His brain would get overwhelmed with blood and cause hemorrhaging."

"Makes sense."

"Also, the lungs are light and airy compared to the other organs in the torso. That is why they are up on top. When inverted, the heavy organs will compress the lungs over time. Breathing will get harder and harder as time passes, so the body will eventually get starved of oxygen."

"So, it is like having someone sitting on your chest, I guess?"

"Yes, and not in a good way, hon." He does not miss a beat and continues, "Finally, because of the inversion, blood will get to the heart very efficiently, but the heart will have a hard time moving it out. The heart will get overwhelmed and this would cause heart failure. So, my initial guess is that Mr. Stone's hemorrhaging and lack of oxygen probably caused him to be brain dead before he eventually succumbed to heart failure. I can firm that up with a bit more work."

"So, what about the alcohol and drugs?"

"They were likely a contributing factor, as he would have passed out before or after the collision. There was no internal organ damage, so if he was sober, he likely would have been able to undo his seatbelt and exit the vehicle unscathed, really. The airbags did their job of cushioning all the impacts and unfortunately, the seat belt did its job too well."

"Is there any reason for you to believe that this could be a homicide?"

"Well, that is your job to determine, hon. From my perspective, if Mr. Stone consumed the alcohol and/or painkillers willingly, then this is an unfortunate accident and thankfully, no one else was injured. If Mr. Stone did not willingly consume the alcohol and/or drugs, then it could be homicide. Does that make sense?"

"Yes, it does Walk. Thanks for your help. I guess I cannot close the book on this one just yet."

As I was about to leave, I pause as I remember something that I should ask, "Were prints run on the car and the items from the car?"

"Yes, they were. I will send you the report. Although it should have been sent to you already."

"I do not check my email continuously. Can you give me a summary?"

"Sure, the bottle of Jack had Mr. Stone's prints on it and a few others as well. Probably the cashier and stock person in the store. The Sharpie had two sets of prints. The water bottle and the Tic Tac case just had Mr. Stone's prints on them. Oh yeah, the steering wheel and gear shifter had two sets of prints and happened to be the same two sets as the Sharpie: Mr. Stone and someone else not in the system."

I think to myself, well, that raises some questions. First of all, I need to figure out who also drove the vehicle. The Tic Tac case also piques my interest.

Chapter 3.4 – Officer LaChance

I am in the office and reading over the fingerprint report, when Officer LaChance walks into my workspace.

"Hey there Detective Gaines, I understand you wanna see me about Dave Stone." He then sits down across from me and puts his DPD issued hat on the table between us.

"Yes, thanks so much for meeting with me. I understand you pulled Stone over not too long ago. Can you fill me in? It might be pertinent to my investigation into his fatality."

"Sure, no biggie!" LaChance then switched into testimony mode, "It was the evening after the Tigers home opener. They had a matinee game of course and I was patrolling near the Magic Stick on Woodward Avenue several hours later. I observed Mr. Stone's vehicle make a U-turn to begin proceeding southbound. We followed for a few hundred yards and then Officer Jenkins and I both observed that the vehicle was weaving within its lane."

"Okay. Good."

"We engaged our lights and the vehicle pulled over right away, a little too abruptly actually. We both exited the cruiser and approached the vehicle. I asked them if they had been drinking."

"They?"

"Oh yes, there were two occupants in the vehicle. David Stone was driving and Jimmy Greyson was in the passenger seat. So, they responded that they had been drinking beer, but it did not seem excessive."

"How did you know that?"

"They indicated that they shared one pitcher of beer and then shared a second pitcher four ways. I determined they could handle that much. Mr. Stone looked exhausted more than drunk. Mr. Greyson seemed fine."

"So, you sent them on their way?"

"Well, yes and no."

"You either did or did not."

"Should I have my union rep here?"

"No Officer LaChance, I am not Internal Affairs. I am just trying to determine if there was an unfortunate accident or a homicide."

LaChance's guard seems to come down, "Okay, well, like I said, Jimmy seemed fine, so we, I guess I, had them switch seats and Jimmy drove home."

"Jimmy? You seem pretty chummy with Mr. Greyson."

The officer lifts his hat and turns it over as he says with a smile, "He was a swell guy. He even signed my hat."

I think to myself. Okay, mystery solved on the double set of prints on the steering wheel and likely the Sharpie.

"So, how did he sign your brim?"

"Uh, what do you mean?"

"What did he sign it with?"

"Oh, I was going to give him my pen, but they had a black Sharpie in the car's console, so Jimmy used that."

"Okay, did you see anything in the vehicle worth noting?"

"No, it was pretty tidy. Nothing out of the ordinary that I saw anyway."

"No bottles, nothing?

"Other than the Sharpie, nah, nothing. Hey Detective, do you think I did anything wrong here?"

"Well, only time will tell on this one, but suppose that Mr. Stone had an addiction problem. Did your *catch and release* help him? Or enable him?"

"Uh, oh."

"But hey, you got a cool autograph while defacing city property."

Officer LaChance excused himself and I went back to my fingerprint report. Okay, so I need to get Greyson's prints to verify that he was the other recent driver of the vehicle and the Sharpie. Can you drive a Sharpie?

Chapter 3.5 – Mr. Stone Residence

"Thank you, Mr. Sylvester, for letting me in. I can lock the door on my way out."

The building superintendent responds, "Great, but please still stop by my office on the way out, cuz I will want to come back up and engage the deadbolt."

"Will do."

"This is such a shame, Detective Gaines. Mr. Stone seemed like such a nice young man. I can't believe he is gone."

"That is what I am hearing. Thanks again, Mr. Sylvester. I really appreciate you accommodating me here, today. Like I said on the phone, if you can think of anything unusual with regards to Mr. Stone or his apartment, please call my office line. Here is my business card."

He replies, "Didn't think anyone still used these," while quizzically analyzing the small piece of card stock.

"You may be right. I guess I am a dying breed. Thanks again."

Mr. Sylvester had told me earlier that he never saw anyone come or go to Mr. Stone's apartment. He had only seen Mr. Stone enter the apartment, but he certainly does not see everyone who enters the building.

I pull on a pair of latex gloves and begin wandering around in the apartment. It is obvious that the occupant had not been living here very long. It was, as they say, minimalist.

I open the fridge and it contains mostly restaurant leftover packaging, but there are a few light beers on the door and in the crisper, there are all kinds of fruits and vegetables. On the counter, I note that there is a Ninja blender with a large container of protein powder beside it, so I surmise that our rookie shortstop's food preparation routine consisted of making smoothies.

I open the pantry door and I see an open case of water bottles. The plastic wrap is peeled back slightly and four bottles are missing. I note that the brand is the same as what was found in the vehicle.

I see a basket on the counter near the apartment door. It looks like this is where Mr. Stone would empty his pockets upon entering the apartment. There was a partial pack of cinnamon Dentyne gum, some loose change, a cherry chapstick, and some receipts.

I look through the receipts and I come across one for a Speedway gas station. On the receipt, I see $15 worth of gasoline, a pack of Dentyne gum, and a package of Tic Tac mints.

I think to myself that $15 of gasoline is not exactly a tremendous amount and I rationalize that since he drove a hybrid, he probably did not use much gas. He does care about his breath, however. Then it hits me and and I say out loud, "Well, I will be damned."

I continue the search of the apartment and touch base with Mr. Sylvester before leaving the building.

Chapter 3.6 – Black Box

I return to the office to gear up for a meeting with Sergeant Brown and I check my email. As I do so, I receive a pop-up box telling me that I have a message from someone in IT. I open the attachment with anticipation as the subject line is Event Data Recorder.

It takes a few seconds to load and I realize that I am hopeful for some relevant data, but also not overly optimistic that anything earth-shattering will come from this report. The report is in PDF format so it opens in Adobe Acrobat. I do prefer paper, but at least in this program, I can still highlight in yellow and type some comments. I will print it later to add to my pile.

I skim most of the report, but hone in on the technician's summary section which highlights key items:

* Initial crash impact speed was 56mph
* Cruise Control was engaged
* Neither the brake pedal or accelerator depressed in the data window
* Driver's seatbelt was engaged throughout the entire data window
* Airbags deployed appropriately for a driver only impact

I process this information in my mind. Stone was speeding, but not excessively. Although lack of braking can indicate suicide, seatbelt use, cruise control and lack of acceleration would likely rule that out. Finally, the airbags deployed as if there was no passenger, which was evident from my visual inspection.

As suspected, there is nothing too revealing; however, the report does help me to rule out suicide.

Chapter 3.7 – Better to Ask for Forgiveness

"Sergeant Brown, I think that I need to keep investigating this David Stone case as a homicide."

"It's not an impaired driving case?"

"I do not think so."

"Any indication of suicide?"

"No, the black box has pretty much ruled that out."

"How so?"

"Stone was wearing a seatbelt and had the cruise control engaged. Although he did not brake before impact, he also did not accelerate."

"I see, but what makes you think homicide?"

"I came across something."

"Do tell."

I ask myself who says that phrase anymore. "It was the victim's apartment search. I came across a case of water bottles and a receipt."

"Okey doke Gaines, but you will have to elaborate on that."

"Yes, of course, well you see the fingerprint report indicated that the water bottle in the vehicle had only Stone's prints on it. This makes sense, because he bought a full case of water bottles. You know the type in a shrink wrap. He would have taken the water bottle out of the case himself, so it makes sense that there are only his prints on the water bottle."

"Okay, where is the homicide part?"

"Well, I found a receipt where he bought a single packet of Tic Tacs. You know the kind. They are clear plastic with a colored lid. This one had a white lid and part of the top flips open. Well, there was an empty Tic Tac box in the vehicle and it had only Stone's prints on it."

"Yeah, so?"

"Have you ever seen Tic Tacs in a gas station? They are almost always right by the cash register, so that customers pick them up at the last minute while checking out. It is a *suggestive selling* tactic. Often they are in a plastic contraption that kind of looks like a tree. I went by this gas station and that is how they are displayed there. I talked with the attendant and they load this little tree by hand, one packet at a time."

"Okay?"

"Well, one of the attendant's fingerprints should have been on the Tic Tac packet then. Someone must have wiped the container clean at some point and then Stone handled it."

"You are declaring this is homicide based on a Tic Tac box?"

"No, no, no sir, but it is an anomaly and I think I need to make sense of it."

"Okay, we need to do our due diligence here. It is high profile and many people are watching. The Tigers organization, the mayor, the press. So, what's next?"

"Well, I need to talk with Jimmy Greyson as he has spent some time with Stone. I also want to get to know this vehicle some more, so I want to rent one for a few days."

"What? You better not be expensing that. Google the thing."

"But sir, it is a hybrid and it has…"

"No, I will repeat once and not again. You better not be expensing that. If you want to take a car for a joyride, do it on your own dime."

"Okay, Sarge. I will keep you in the loop."

As I leave the Sergeant's office, I realize I learned a lesson. On occasion, it is better to ask for forgiveness than permission. And, this was one of those occasions.

Chapter 3.8 – Car Rental

After five calls to different car rental companies, I finally find one with a 2019 Toyota RAV4 Limited Hybrid, albeit in black as opposed to silver. It will do. I ask the agent at the desk if they can give me a quick lesson on the features of the Rav4, but the agent is really just a recent Business graduate and does not know much about the vehicles. I leave the lot looking around the interior, but I am severely overwhelmed.

As I am driving towards downtown Detroit, I notice several car dealerships in a row. I guess they like to stick close to their competitors, just like Lowes and Home Depot. How does the saying go? Keep your friends close, but keep your enemies closer. Sure enough, I pass a Nissan dealership, then a Kia, followed by Toyota. I do a quick right and drive by several Highlanders, Rav4s, and Corollas in the Toyota lot.

I park and meet Hugh, a Sales Associate in a sports jacket with patches on the elbows, a dress shirt, jeans, and penny loafers with no socks. I show him my badge and explain that I am working a case that involves a hybrid Rav4 and I need to get to know the car better. He says, "I would take you out for a test drive, but we cannot keep the hybrid models on the lot; they are selling like hot cakes."

"Hot cakes must sell well. I never understood that expression."

"Come to think of it, I have no idea what that is supposed to mean. Anyway, I don't have a hybrid Rav on the lot."

"That is okay. I have one here. Would you mind going for a drive with me?"

"Sure, not a problem as long as you promise that if you are in the market for a new vehicle, you will give me an opportunity to at least show you a few cars."

"Deal!"

Hugh enters the passenger seat with a grunt and says, "I could lose a few pounds, so the wife says."

"I really appreciate this, Hugh."

"It is a slow day and I figure it can't hurt to have a friend in the police force. So, what would you like to know?"

"Maybe just go through the routine as if I was taking it out for a test drive. Or if I was picking up a brand new purchase. Whichever is more detail."

"Okay. Things are pretty simple. Let us start over on the left. Down below, you have automatic bright light adjustment if you hit that button, but you still have to have your headlights on which is on the signal stick. Being in Michigan, the next button turns on the heated windshield. This model has wires in the windshield just like a typical rear defrost. So on a cold morning, you press that button a minute or so before you turn on your wipers. The wipers will be all warmed up and ready to go!"

"That is a neat feature."

"In the middle console, there is your traction control. You can turn it off by pressing this button, not that I recommend doing that. Here and here are your heated seat controls, or as I like to call them, your bun warmers. Again, handy in Michigan. In the hole there, you have a wireless charger for your phone, as well as a USB and aux jack to tap into the audio and navigation system."

"Being a cop, I am not crazy about the phone charging in such an accessible location."

"Good point. Now, if we move up to the steering wheel, the radio functions are pretty simple. There are your cruise control buttons right there on the right side of the steering wheel. This button turns the cruise on and off, whereas this button cancels temporarily. The set and resume also double for down one mile per hour and up one mile per hour. To the left, you can see the picture of what looks like a wifi signal coming out of the front of a car; that one adjusts the distance between you and the next vehicle in front of you, while you are on cruise. This vehicle has adaptive or dynamic cruise control. And that button there turns on or off the lane tracing. Oh and of course, it has a Blind Spot Monitoring System. These features all combined make up what Toyota calls Safety Sense and it is standard on all Rav4's. Basically, Toyota believes in safety first."

"Wow, information overload."

"You will catch on. How about we go for a drive?"

As I back out of the parking spot, I hear screaming angels and I am sure that I look confused.

Hugh sees my look and says, "That is a safety feature. You know how your golf cart will either go beep, beep, beep or play a buzzer when it is in reverse, it is to give pedestrians a warning. That is especially important in an electric or hybrid vehicle that is normally ultra quiet at low speeds."

When I put it into drive, Hugh continues, "As I said, it will be very quiet when it is running in electric mode. This vehicle has a gasoline engine up front and two electric motors, one on each axel. The vehicle knows what to use when and will engage or cut each of them as needed. An added bonus is that you get all-wheel drive because of the electric motor on the back axle. As the battery drains or if it needs more power, the gasoline engine will kick in. You can see what is running at any time up here on the console display. By the way, when you see the green arrows pointing at the battery, that means it is recharging. Every time you coast or brake, you will see that the battery is gaining juice."

"Whoa, what happened there?"

"What do you mean, detective?"

"The car just seemed to turn a little on me."

"Yeah, if you get too close to one of the lane markers, it will give you a little nudge. It will do even more so, when you are on cruise control. Give it a try."

I tap the cruise button, press the set button, and then I lift my foot off of the accelerator. Sure enough, the vehicle stabilizes at 32 mph. A few seconds later, a pickup truck pulls in front of me and the Rav4 slows up slightly. I ask, "That is the adaptive cruise, right?"

"Yes, exactly. If you want more or less cushion with the vehicle in front of you, press that wifi looking button. Take your hands off the wheel for a bit and see what happens. Now, you are not supposed to do this as it is not an automatic pilot car, but it is darn close."

I put my hands to the side and the car continues driving perfectly. The speed goes up and down with traffic, no problem. As we come to a slight curve in the road, I go to reach for the wheel, but the vehicle navigates the curvature on its own. I am truly amazed. Out of the blue though, the Rav4 centre display shows an orange picture of a steering wheel. Hugh says, "That is the computer telling you to get your hands back onto the steering wheel. If you do not, it will shut off the cruise control on you."

I grab the steering wheel again and steer for myself. I do notice that when I veer away from the center of the lane, it nudges me back in and gives me a beep from the console. When I change lanes without signalling, it beeps at me, too.

Hugh says, "It encourages you to stay in the middle of the lane and also to use your signals. If you do not signal while changing lanes, it will give you a nudge back in. It will eventually let you change lanes, but it does take some extra effort on the wheel."

"You can tell that Toyotas come from Japan. Detroiters do not use signals to change lanes."

"Well, if you drive one of these, you will learn to use your signals properly and very quickly. By the way, these babies are assembled in Kentucky and Ontario."

We continue the drive and we chat. I am truly amazed at the technology compared to my 2008 Dodge Journey. After about 20 minutes, Hugh and I exchange business cards and we part ways. I realize that Hugh and I are newly found friends. By the way, even though Hugh had a business card, he was surprised that I had one as well.

Chapter 3.9 - Jimmy Greyson Interview

"I am so sorry to hear about your colleague, Mr. Greyson. And thank you for taking the time to speak with me. I am Detective Gaines, but you can call me Finn, if you would like."

"Thank you for the condolences, sir. At the beginning of the season, Dave and I were rivals and in fact, he was the one who caused my injury, but really, we became close friends."

"Yeah, I noticed your limp there when you answered the door, but I thought you were close to returning."

"Yeah, I was close to returning to the lineup, but I did tweak my knee. I suspect it has knocked me back somewhat, but it is improving again."

"Really, it still looks fairly bad."

"Oh, it is improving. Here look, I have to show you something that Sandi, my physiotherapist showed me." Greyson pulls out his iPhone, opens an app, and shows me his walking asymmetry. I did not know there was such a thing. He continues, "You can see a graph of how my walking was gradually improving and then bang, my limp came back when I twisted my knee."

"These phones are amazing and I need to learn more about them. Some are saying that phones hold the keys to solving most crimes nowadays."

"Here, we can sit in the recliners and admire the RenCen and the view of Windsor, while we chat."

"That sounds good. This really is a beautiful view."

"Thanks, can I get you a coffee or anything? I have a pot starting to brew."

"Yes please, a coffee would be awesome. Just black is great."

"Remind me to get it in a few minutes. So where do you want to start?"

"Oh, before we get going too far, I am hoping you will cooperate with regards to fingerprints. We dusted Mr. Stone's vehicle and its contents for prints and I understand that you have been in his vehicle, so we need your prints to understand the entire picture fully. I have also recently secured Mr. Stone's apartment, so again, we need your prints for reference there, too."

"Detective Gaines, does it look like we are talking homicide now? Do I need a lawyer?"

"Possibly and no, sir. I have discovered a piece of evidence that has me confused, so I am open to the possibility that this was not just an impaired driving fatality. And, I need your prints because we know you have touched things in Mr. Stone's vehicle and I assume his apartment."

"Okay, sure. I have nothing to hide. By the way, I think I hear the pot finishing up." Greyson gets up and returns quickly with two cups of coffee, both black.

"Good and thank you sir, for both the prints and the coffee. It should hit the spot." I take a sip and continue, "Dang, this is good. It ain't Nescafé."

"No, it's not. It's a blend I like to use."

"So, I understand you were in the stands for the Home Opener and then you and Mr. Stone went out for drinks afterwards. Can you give me a summary of the night?"

"Sure. Is it okay if we refer to him as Dave instead of Mr. Stone?" to which I nod. Greyson continues, "So, we left from the park and Dave had volunteered to drive."

"He drove a Toyota Rav4, correct?"

"Yes, correct Detective. A hybrid and it was pretty cool. He was bragging about its fuel efficiency and all of its safety features. Well, we drove out to the Magic Stick on Woodward Avenue. It is a great place to have beer and play some pool."

"Mind me asking how much you had to drink? And can anyone corroborate that?"

"Sure Detective, I bought two pitchers of beer and the bar probably has the receipts and I assume my credit card records would match. Dave and I split the first pitcher and then we got friendly with two girls: Jenny and Jessie. Jenny and I have become a bit of an item. I have Jenny's phone number in my phone, so I can give you that. As for Jessie, I think her last name is Williams. Anyway, that second pitcher was split four ways."

"Did Mr., uh, Dave have anything else that night?"

"Well, I can't say for sure, but when I went to get the second picture of beer, I thought I saw Dave go into my jacket pocket. And, some of my pain pills were missing. Jenny can confirm that."

"She saw Dave take the pills?"

"I am not sure, but she and I talked about it looking suspicious and quite a few pills were missing. In fact, I have had two prescriptions and I have gone through them a lot faster than I think I should have. The doctor gave me some hassle about renewing, so he knocked me down a level on the pain meds. In hindsight, I think Dave was skimming from me."

"What were you taking?"

"Here are the two different bottles." Greyson pulled them out of the end table drawer and said, "Here, take a picture of them if you want. One is empty and that is the stronger one. The partial bottle is the weaker one."

"Okay, thanks. Continue. Do you think he would have blown over the legal limit if he took a breathalyzer?"

"Don't think so. We had the same amount to drink and I felt fine. That being said, he was really groggy. He had a busy day with his first major league home game and all."

"Alright, keep going."

"We started to drive home and Dave was behind the wheel. Within a couple minutes, we got pulled over. The officers were a little starstruck, so they gave Dave a break and just had me drive the rest of the way home. I dragged his sorry ass up to my apartment and messed up my knee doing it, too."

"Oh no, that is how you tweaked it?"

"Yeah, so I put him on my couch and I went to go to bed."

"So, you called it a night?"

"Well, not really. I got a text from Jenny and she said she was coming over. When she got here, Jessie was with her. She was hammered and cuddled up next to Dave for a sleep. They were quite the pair. Snooze fest!"

"So, I assume you and Jenny had some fun in the bedroom."

"Yes, correct and then about 3 in the morning, Jessie's phone blew up. Her boyfriend Frankie was going crazy train on her phone. He must have a tracking app on her and he was outside the building. He was threatening her and Dave in a series of text messages."

"Oh, I will have to track down this Jessie and Frankie."

"Jenny will be able to help you. Anyway, Jenny shut off Jessie's phone and then the girls snuck out through the parking garage."

"Oh, okay."

Greyson says, "Well, that is not all. Frankie or maybe one of his tag alongs did this to Dave's SUV," as he pulls out his phone and displays a picture of Stone's vehicle. "#16 You're dead was etched into the back window."

"16 is his player number?"

"That is why they call you Sherlock eh?"

"Ha yep, did he report this to insurance or police?"

"Sorry about that wisecrack, Detective. Ah no, unfortunately, he did not report it even though I encouraged him to do so."

"No problem. Can you send that picture to me please?" to which, Greyson nods. I continue, "Oh yes, Mr. Greyson, another question. Did you touch anything in Dave's vehicle besides the steering wheel and gear shift?"

"Well, probably the signal thingy, although I feel like I am the only one in Detroit who uses signals."

"I hear ya. I know exactly what you mean!"

"Oh yeah, I did use Dave's Sharpie to sign an autograph for the one officer who stopped us."

"Do you know his name?"

"No sorry, I might have seen his nameplate, but I am terrible with names."

"Sir, did you happen to touch a water bottle or a pack of Tic Tacs?"

"Hmmm, I do not recall seeing a bottle of anything in the vehicle. I do remember picking up the Tic Tac package out of the console though and asking if I could have one. Dave was very abrupt and told me, 'No, I need to have fresh breath – leave them alone dude,' so I just put them back. I thought that was a little strange."

"And that was the Home Opener evening?"

"Actually, come to think of it, I am not sure when that was. I do remember I was a passenger though and I have been in his car at least a couple times now. It was not when I was driving though – he was pretty much passed out at that time."

The timing is opportune as I turn to a new page in my notepad, "Okay, we can move forward now from the Home Opener Day. Anything of interest after that?"

Greyson interjects with, "Would you like another cup of joe before we move on?"

"Oh, absolutely! That would be great. Thanks."

Chapter 3.10 - Jimmy Greyson Hospitality

"Okay Jimmy, fill me in as to what has occurred since the Home Opener and the aftermath of it."

"Sure, well, I was hopeful that Frankie might be content knowing that he had sloppy seconds from a Major League Baseball player, but he wasn't. I'm not on Facebook, but I guess there was all kinds of trash talking on there bashing Stoner. I mean, Dave. I'm sorry. Stoner is just a common nickname for guys with the last name Stone. I am not implying anything. Like I said, I suspect he might have had a substance issue, but me calling him Stoner has nothing to do with that."

"Understood. I called someone who I figured was a friend, *Hodgy* and she got all mad at me."

"Oh, you mean the very attractive traffic cop that secured the scene?"

"As a matter of fact, yes."

"Yeah, ah no. She does not look to me like the type you should be calling *Hodgy*. No dude. I mean, sorry detective."

I am sure I look a little embarrassed and say, "Okay, go on."

"Well, Frankie lit up Facebook I guess and there were threats against Dave from Frankie and several of his friends. I am on Twitter and I saw some stuff there. They had a hashtag #MessUpStone16 running with all kinds of comments. There were some nasty threats. There was even a picture of Dave's vehicle with a comment something like, 'I will pay someone to cut his brake line,' but I have no idea if that was Frankie. It may have been him or a friend of his. The picture looks like it was taken here on that night, so the picture was likely taken by Frankie or one of his thugs if he had company with him."

"Okay, we definitely will have someone follow up on the social media stuff. That is beside my wheelhouse."

"Not in."

"Pardon?"

"The expression is *not in my wheelhouse*, not *beside my wheelhouse*, sir."

"Oh, okay. I actually appreciate that. I do not like to sound stupid. Trust me, I am not."

"Anyway, on the positive side, the team was on the road to Milwaukee, so I figured Dave was safe. I stayed back with my knee tweak and all. VanBuskirk wanted me to just rest the knee and he asked me to do some scouting reports on the boys while watching them on TV."

"Did you?"

"Did I what? Oh, scout, yes. I watched both Milwaukee games and I touched base with VanB after each game."

"How?"

"By phone. I would call when I knew he would not answer and just leave a message."

"How did Mr. Stone play?"

"Not very well, which led me to believe he really had been hitting something stronger than beer. He seemed to have lost a step or two from his normal speed."

"Oh, that would not have been good."

"Hey Detective, we have been at it for a while. Would you like me to fix up a couple sandwiches and some soda? I really don't mind and it will only take a minute."

"That would be great. Actually, before you do that, can you show me where you get the walking asymmetry thing on your phone? That sounds interesting. I have been struggling with a bad case of sciatica for months now and I feel it has something to do with my gait. Maybe I am imagining it, but when it is bad, I limp a bit. But then again, what is the cause? And, what is the effect?"

"True. Here. It is this app here." He touches the app on my phone to open it and he continues, "Then you tap on Show All Data and it is down a bit on that screen."

While Greyson is in the kitchen, I play around with the phone and look at my walking asymmetry. It tracks it over days and provides graphs. I touch on one of the entries and wow, it gives me even more information.

I pull Stone's cloned phone from my right breast pocket of my sports coat. I pull up the health app and check the asymmetry data. Well, I will be damned! This is a bigger anomaly than the Tic Tac case.

At this point, I just want to get out of here and follow up on the lead I just discovered, but I better not. I have Greyson here and he is being quite helpful. I need to call Hodgy. I mean Hodge!

Greyson returns with sandwiches and I thank him for his cooperation and his hospitality. In between bites, I continue, "Okay, so can you tell me about the night of the accident?"

"There is not much to tell. I called Stoner when I knew he would be back in town and we met at Xochimilco for some Mexican food and beer."

Okay, I will bite, "How do I spell this Soshi Milko you say?"

Greyson laughs. "Here is how to spell it," and he tosses me a cork coaster that was on the end table. "I like to collect coasters from my favorite places, as you can see. There are a few strewn about, here. Anyway, it is a fabulous Mexican restaurant on the west side. It has taken a huge financial hit though since Tiger Stadium was abandoned and dismantled, but it has incredible, authentic Mexican food. It also took a hit when Ontario extended their last call from one to two in the morning. Back in the day, I understand that a swarm of Canadians would cross the border at 1 a.m. to get tacos and a couple more beers. That is the story anyway. It was before my time and probably before 911 increasing security at the border."

"Okay, so how did that evening go?"

"Well, this might be relevant. We both drove there and arrived at the same time in the parking lot, so we walked a short distance together to the restaurant. We ran into a guy named Stefan. He was the bartender at the Magic Stick the night we were there. He and Dave ended up having words. It appeared that Stefan had a thing for Jessie and I had to get in between the two of them at one point. It was actually an advantage having the cane that night. This Stefan character sure acts like a big man, but Dave would have torn him apart. I stepped in, because I was more worried that Dave would injure something if an altercation broke out." Greyson chuckles after that.

"What is the joke?"

"Well, the guy pretends to be a big man. Meanwhile, he drives a Corolla. It just seems funny. He was bragging about his new car. Yeah, I know I am the stereotypical jock driving a pickup and a sports car. I guess I should not be so judgemental, but the Corolla just seems like a grandma car to me."

I think to myself that it is interesting that Stefan has a new Toyota as well. I imagine it probably has similar technology to the Rav4. I make a mental note to check to see if the Corolla has the Safety Sense features as well.

"Okay, thanks, I will follow up with this Stefan. So, how did it go after that?"

"Not badly. We chatted and Dave kept asking me what he was doing wrong. He felt like his play was sliding and it had been. I asked him again about drugs and he denied taking anything. He wondered about what his trainer might be giving him. Maybe something laced into his supplements. He asked me if steroids could be messing him up. Making him lethargic maybe. I have no idea; I have never juiced, not even in college."

Ding, ding, ding. Another light went off for me.

"And who would be the trainer working with Dave?"

"His name is Mitch, but believe it or not, I just don't know his last name. He is Mitch the Trainer to all of us."

"Okay thanks", I write down the name and continue, "so when were you at the restaurant and how much did you drink?"

"I think I called him around 8 or so. We got there about 10 p.m. and I paid the bill about midnight. I seem to remember having 3 beers each on the bill. Bottles. Oh sorry, I had 4. Just as we were about to leave, a Tiger fan put a beer in my hand and insisted that I tell him a few game stories. So, I left slightly after Dave."

"Okay, with guys your size, I am not thinking that would get him to the 0.04 that Mr. Stone was at, but maybe."

"Yeah, but the media said there was a bottle in his SUV too. Is that true?"

"I am not at liberty to say, Jimmy," but I am nodding my head slightly as I say this. I continue, "Did he seem capable of driving?"

"I thought so. He was tired looking, but that was about it. Oh yeah, we had another altercation that night. Some dude waiting to get into the restaurant started yipping at Dave, calling him a loser and a stoner. Really ripping into him and even telling him to watch his back. The bouncer stepped in and dragged the guy out."

I make note of another follow up item.

"Okay, I think I am done now Mr. Greyson. I will head out now, but if I think of anything else, can I call you?"

"Absolutely. And, I will call or text you, if anything else comes to mind."

As a kid, I fondly remember watching the series Columbo which ran in the 70's. Columbo was a homicide detective who was somewhat unkempt, wore a stereotypical trench coat and smoked a cigar often. He tended to act like a bumbling detective throughout most of the show, but he was actually quite brilliant. While interviewing suspects and witnesses alike, he had this habit of throwing out these seemingly random questions while rubbing his forehead. The point was to gather information, but also to see if the question made the person sweat. Greyson is clearly just a witness at this point, but you never know. I will see if he sweats.

As I am about to leave the apartment, I pause at the doorway and rub my temple. I try to do my best Columbo impersonation. After a couple of ums and ahs, I continue, "My apologies when we thought we were done. I have one more question, Mr. Greyson. You became friends with Mr. Stone going out for beers and all. Did you ever notice where he carried his cell phone?"

Greyson indicates that he was unaware, but more notably, the question did not phase him one iota. This is good.

"Alright, that is all for now. Thank you."

By the way, if Columbo asked two or three of these seemingly random questions, you knew that he was onto something!

As I am riding down in the elevator, I text Officer Hodgson asking her to call me as soon as possible. I get into my rental vehicle, anxious to get my cell connected to the Bluetooth of this Rav4.

Chapter 3.11 – Anomalies

As I am driving down Woodward Avenue, the phone that is sitting in the console getting charged rings throughout the vehicle speakers.

"Hello, Detective Gaines, here."

"Hey Finn, it is Hodge. What can I do for you? I assume this is about the Stone investigation."

"Thanks for calling me, Hodge. I have two things I wanted to ask you."

"Ask away. I am happy to help."

"First, I know you took out Stone's wallet to verify his identity, right?"

"Yes, and I put it back exactly as I found it – same pocket and same orientation."

"That is what I figured. You knew where his phone was. Did you take it out to check it?"

"No, I felt for it, but did not disturb it. I did not need it to confirm his identity. It was in his left front pocket."

"Perfect. Thanks Hodge."

"Is your spidey sense tingling, Finn?"

It certainly is. When I looked at Stone's iPhone clone, I discovered something. If you dig deeper in the Walking Asymmetry data, it gives you data for multiple time segments when the phone holder is walking or running. In each time segment, you can dig deeper. In each and every entry down at the bottom of the data for David Stone, the phone said Device Placement: Right Side of the Body. The phone told me that David Stone religiously carried his iPhone in his right pocket and not the left! Someone else must have inadvertently put the phone into his left front pocket before the crash.

I respond, "Oh yes. The phone is telling me that the deceased always carried his phone in his right pocket, not his left. Thanks so much. I definitely need to dig deeper into this. I may be in touch again."

"Hey, wait Finn. You said that you had two things."

Oh yes, the Tic Tac packet and the phone location discrepancies got me looking for more anomalies. In between the text to Officer Hodgson and when she called, my mind wandered to the puddle referenced in her notes.

"Oh right! Sorry about that. I remember seeing in your notes that you noticed a puddle on the side of the road. I have to admit that I did not look at the puddle, nor did the accident investigator. Neither of us did. Can you fill me in as to what you saw?"

"Sure, I am not certain it is connected to the accident, but I thought it was odd. It did not rain that night. I was working and I would know. The humidity was really low, so I could not picture it being from dew or any kind of condensation. Also, the water was not clear. It was dark in color."

"Black?"

"Well, not quite. Yeah, I guess it was like really dark grey. I didn't think it looked like oil or anything like that. It was separated a bit, if you know what I mean. It was like there was almost black at the bottom and clear water on top. Does that make sense?"

"Not sure if it makes sense or not, but it gets me wondering. Thanks so much, Hodge. By the way, good for you."

"Good for me, what?"

"Well, I do not know if the puddle is significant; two trained investigators did not give it a second thought, but you did. Maybe that should tell you something."

I think she took that as a compliment. I hope so, as she is one smart cop.

At this point, I now have three items that make me wonder. None of the three are screaming at me that this was a homicide; however, my spidey sense is tingling louder and I need to stay on this case. It is not getting closed out in the short run, that is for sure.

Chapter 3.12 – It is Official

"Good morning Sarge," I say as I enter Sergeant Brown's office.

"Top of the morning to you, Gaines. What can I do you for?" he responds.

I hate it when he talks like this, but what can I say? "Well, I have an update on the David Stone case for you."

"Okey doke. Lay it on me."

Again, what adult talks like this in 2019? However, I jump right in.

"Okay, I have come across three pieces of information. None on their own raise much suspicion, but combined, I am thinking that there has been foul play."

"So, one is the Tic Tac container, right?"

"Yes, the Tic Tac container had only Stone's fingerprints on it, which is unusual. One of the gas station attendants should have handled it before Stone bought it. Also, Jimmy Greyson said that he did handle a Tic Tac container in Stone's vehicle, but Stone seemed protective of the container. Now, we did find traces of two different painkillers in that container, which happen to be the same painkillers that Greyson had been prescribed."

"Really, do tell." Again, an annoying saying!

"Well, Greyson believes that Stone was skimming painkillers from him. I need to go track down a young girl that can possibly confirm this. That is my next stop today. So, if Stone was stealing some of the pills for himself and storing them in the Tic Tac container, that would make sense that he did not want his colleague finding them there. But, and it is a big but, why would the container get wiped down?"

"Okay, continue. This is sounding a little more promising."

"The second is Stone's cell phone. At the accident scene, I retrieved the cell phone from Stone's left front pocket. That in itself is not unusual. However, did you know that there is a software app on all iPhones that tracks your steps much like a FitBit?"

"No sir-E."

"Yes, it tracks your number of steps, flights of stairs, and the interesting thing is that it tracks your walking asymmetry."

"What in blazes is walking asymmetry?"

"Here I will show you on Stone's clone phone here." I pull up the app and continue, "Here. Basically, if it reads zero, you have a normal walk, but if you have a limp, it will read some kind of percentage. Greyson showed it to me. It was something his physiotherapist put him onto, to monitor his knee rehab progress."

"Interesting, but what is the relevance here, Gaines?"

"If you dig deeper into the data, you can see where the user carries their phone. In every piece of data in here, it says that Stone carried his phone on the right side of his body."

"Well, knock me over with a feather. And, you said that you found his phone in his left front pocket, correct?"

Seriously, can this guy just not talk normally for a few minutes? I pause for a few seconds and continue, "Yes, sir. A second anomaly."

"And the third?"

"Well, for this one, I am puzzled. Officer Hodgson noticed a puddle on the shoulder, where Stone's vehicle left the road. Meanwhile, there was no rain and literally no dew that night. It is a mystery how this puddle would have formed. I do not know if it is relevant, but it has me scratching my head. And by the way, that Hodgson has a nose for sifting through a crime scene. She has potential, sir."

"Duly noted about Hodgson. As for the puddle, yeah, that is weak, but the first two have me curious too. Not so curious that I am going to pay for a rental vehicle for you though, Gaines."

"Yes boss, I hear you. Stone's apartment has been secured and I will get a team in there to do a thorough search of it – fingerprints and everything. And, I definitely want his protein powder tested as Greyson wondered if Stone was juicing, perhaps unknowingly. Mitch the Trainer would have supplied Stone with his supplements. I will have to follow up with IT, as well. They have a clone of Stone's phone too and they have completed a deep dive. I just do not understand all the techno lingo in their report. I will need a translator when I talk with them."

"Well, the ships pulled anchor and we are moving on this one, I guess. I will talk with the communications folks. Not sure how we should play out our hand in the media here."

"That is why they pay you the big bucks, sir. I will let you figure that out. I will just keep working the evidence and the case."

"Right-E-O on that Gaines."

Oh my, I wish he would just speak English!

Chapter 3.13 – Magic Stick

I talk with the IT technician as I drive to the Magic Stick and once again, I am amazed at the safety technology on this Rav4. Clearly, it is not an autonomous vehicle, but for the price, it is incredible. Anyway, the technician is telling me that they are striking out with the phone.

I ask about any suspicious images and apparently, Stone never took any pictures with his phone. I ask if we can track where he went on the night in question. The technician informs me that his cell phone did ping off towers in West Detroit, but as we talk through this, it appears the phone followed the exact route that we would have anticipated based on the information we received from Greyson.

I mention what I found in the Health App and the technician complimented me, saying that he had never ventured into that data. "That must be a relatively new app. I guess I better take the new features tour that my phone keeps telling me to do," he says.

I thank him and he responds, "Sorry sir, but we have really struck out with the phone on this one. Meanwhile, usually the phone is a treasure trove in any investigation nowadays."

"Well, I think what I found is a pretty good nugget, though."

"True enough detective, true enough. I think you have made more progress than we have! Well done and if you're ever looking for a reassignment, you know where to find us!"

We disconnect our call just as I pull into a parking spot in front of the Magic Stick. It is three o'clock in the afternoon on a Tuesday, so it is not exactly hopping. However, I made some calls ahead of time, so Jenny and Jessie told me they would be here. Jessie did tell me that Stefan was no longer working at the bar, but she gave me a phone number for him. I decide to call Stefan before entering the bar.

Stefan answers on the third ring and he tells me that he is very happy to help with my investigation, although he is confused as are many others, considering the crash is being reported in the media as an unfortunate drunk driving accident. Stefan is able to verify that Greyson bought two pitchers of beer and that the girls had participated in the second pitcher.

Apparently, he has a thing for Jessie and watches her often. I ask him, "Can you fill me in on what went on with Jessie that night?"

"Well, the girls were playing pool with Greyson and Stone. I watch the Tigers all the time up on the television screens in the bar, so I know the boys. I used to play ball myself you know."

"Okay, but how about we stick with the night at hand?"

"Okay, they were playing and flirting. Jenny was touchy with Greyson and Jessie just kept eyeing Stone. You could tell she wanted him and I hate it when she gets that look in her eyes. But, it was strange 'cause all of a sudden, the guys just decided to scoot."

"So, what happened after the guys left?"

"Well, I think the Stone fella had Jessie all revved up, 'cause she started coming onto me. We have had a couple of flings over the last year, but I try to steer clear now, because her guy Frankie is a whack job, if you know what I mean."

"So, did you leave with Jessie?"

"Well, ah…"

"What? Just tell me."

"Well, ah, we met up in the storage room back in behind the washrooms and had a little bit of fun. It didn't take long, so I don't think Jenny even noticed."

"I see. Did you see Frankie at all that night?"

"Yeah, not long after Jessie and me had our storage room fun, Frankie showed up. I think he could sense that Jessie got it on or something, because he was wound up jealous. She kept telling him that she did not leave the bar," Stefan smiled and continued, "which is true."

"So, did they argue? Did it get physical?"

"Yeah, they argued and yes, it got physical. Frankie shook her a bit, but he did not hit her or nothin' like that. I woulda been right in there had he. Frankie left in a huff and then the girls left together a bit later. Frankie was pissed and I wouldn't be surprised if he hurt Jessie later. And, I am sure if he would have seen Mr. Stone, it woulda been ugly."

I thank Stefan for his cooperation and disconnect the phone as I exit the vehicle and then I head into the bar.

Jenny and Jessie are both waiting for me at the bar, but I ask Jenny to go play some pool while I talk with Jessie. I like to keep witnesses separate during interviews to ensure that they do not inadvertently influence each other's recollections.

Jessie's account of the evening matches perfectly with Stefan's version while she is at the bar, except she leaves out the storage room rendezvous. Her story of course continues further into the evening, but then it aligns with Greyson's account. In other words, she ends up on Greyson's couch cuddled up with Stone, her phone has a text explosion, and then the two girls make a hasty exit via the parking garage.

Before closing out the interview, I ask Jessie about the bartender, "Do you know Stefan well?"

She replies, "Yeah, I have known him for a while. He kinda has a thing for me, you know, but no, I would never. I mean he is not my type. He is way too clingy. If we ever did get it on, I would never be able to shake him. Besides, I only need to date one psychopath at a time. No, I do not mean Frankie is a psychopath. Oh man, that came out wrong. Are we done, sir?"

Well, that part of the conversation certainly put Jessie into a tailspin.

Talking to Jenny on the other hand is actually quite pleasurable. She is obviously very attractive, but she is also intelligent and likeable. She explains how the evening went. In particular, I ask her, "Did you see the guys partake in anything other than the two pitchers of beer?"

Jenny replies, "Well, actually yes. When Jimmy went up to the bar to buy a pitcher, I saw Dave go over to where the guys had their jackets over there on that ledge." She points to a ledge that is behind the pool tables. "Dave took some pills out of Jimmy's jacket."

"You actually saw him take the pills out of the jacket?"

"Well, I think so. Actually, I am not sure. I think I did."

"We can put it this way. Which hand did he stick into the jacket? Left hand or right hand?"

"Actually, I do not know. You know, as you say that, I do remember seeing him lift up Jimmy's jacket by the collar with his right hand and place it further up on the shelf. It must have been hanging down a bit, maybe close to falling. I do not actually recall seeing him reach into it. How did you do that?"

"Simply. Your memory is usually more accurate when you focus on details as oppose to general perceptions."

"Oh okay, that makes sense. Now, when Jimmy came back, he said that he saw Dave with the jackets and then when we checked his pill bottle, there were pills missing. Maybe my memory just filled in the blanks. I am sorry if I misled you."

"Oh, do not be sorry. Mr. Stone may very well have taken the pills, but I need to know exactly what you saw and could testify to, while under oath."

"Am I going to court? Did someone murder Dave?"

"No, I just mean that in general terms. Whenever I interview a witness, I can only count on things they saw first-hand."

"Oh, like on TV when they say, 'Objection, that is here say.'"

"Yes, exactly."

I thank both ladies, but I also get contact information for Frankie. I do not want to interview him here. That interview will need to be at the station.

Chapter 3.14 - Experimentation

As I leave the Magic Stick, I call Frankie's cell number and I leave a message, "Hello, Frankie, it is Detective Finn Gaines with the Detroit Police Department. I am wondering if you would come into the station to talk about your interactions with a Mr. David Stone. Please give me a call at this number." I continue by repeating my phone number twice to ensure that he gets it accurately.

I drive south towards the Detroit River and make my way westward towards Mexican Town in Southwest Detroit. I walk around a little and check out the restaurants and bakeries on Bagley Street. Xochmilco Restaurant is at Bagley and 23rd and the dining area is actually up on the second floor. I survey the area and get back into my rental vehicle.

I press the map button on the large touch screen that sits in the middle of the dashboard and I look at the map to determine what would be the most logical route to get to the crash site. I head west and then south on Clark which eventually makes a sharp right turn to become West Jefferson Avenue. At this point, I pull to a stop and look around. I am now facing a little south of west and the Detroit River is on my left. I accelerate up to 30mph and engage the cruise control and take my hands off of the steering wheel. The vehicle continues at 30mph plus or minus a mile per hour and on its own, it navigates the minor turns in the road flawlessly. I do notice that the vehicle likes to drive closer to the center line than I normally would. I guess it centers itself between the lines, but I probably hug the shoulder a little to keep clear of oncoming traffic. I note that as interesting.

Eventually, a message appears saying that I need to be holding the steering wheel, so I give the steering wheel a little nudge and again, let the technology take over. The vehicle drives on its own, but I keep my hands and right foot at the ready, because I do not fully trust the car on its own. Several miles later, I am approaching the crash site and the Rav4 continues past the location where Stone's SUV left the asphalt.

So many questions are in my mind. Was Stone alone in his SUV? Was Stone the actual driver? If he was, was he impaired? Was he even awake? Was the vehicle basically driving itself? Yes, I know it is not autonomous, but it is pretty darn close. Theoretically, Stone could be passed out and his car would continue on its own. But then again, not for too long. The vehicle literally gets mad at you if you do not wiggle the steering wheel periodically. Okay, I know that it is not literally getting mad at the driver. I wonder out loud if I could tie a belt to the steering wheel like in the movies, but then a murderer would have to retrieve the belt after the crash. There are so many questions going through my mind, that my head is ready to explode!

I look around to ensure there are no other cars and I start driving again, I engage the cruise control and let go of the steering wheel. Once the warning comes on commanding me to hold the steering wheel, I ignore it, but I keep my hands nearby. The steering control shuts off and the vehicle slowly loses its track, but the cruise control remains engaged. I would have thought the vehicle should have disengaged the cruise control too in case someone fell asleep at the wheel. I guess it is more just to ensure that drivers do not treat it as an autonomous vehicle.

My mind is spinning and I continue talking to myself. "Suppose someone wanted to kill Stone using this vehicle. Suppose he was incapacitated. The killer could put him in the vehicle and engage the cruise control. The vehicle would drive itself, but not very far before the lane tracking assist or LTA for short, would shut off. But, if you were trying to kill him, would you not choose a spot for him that would cause the most damage. The site where he went off the road was dangerous. Maybe the killer was aiming for the Rouge River and missed, but still got lucky with the vehicle turning over. Perhaps the intent was to only harm Stone, not kill him, and the death was actually an accident. But then, he was left for dead. Regardless, how could a murderer get the vehicle in motion? It is not like the movies where someone will jump out of a moving vehicle, drop and roll, and then get up like nothing happened."

Oh, my imagination is getting away from me. I do not have any evidence indicating murder really. What about motive? And means?

Okay, suppose it was murder; anyone with Google could find the means potentially. I silently wonder what I would get for results if I typed, "2019 Toyota Rav4 Murder Weapon," into a Google search.

How about motive? Well, I have the sex lives of Stefan, Frankie, and Jessie, where David Stone might have been perceived as changing the love triangle into a rectangle.

Now, I think of what Dr. Walker and I have both said. Maybe the key is in the cell phones.

Chapter 3.15 – Cell Tower Pings

I park on the shoulder and pull the IT report up on my phone and I look up the section about cell phone tower pings. According to the report, Stone's phone was in Xochimilco for the time frame Greyson had indicated. There are small gaps, although that is normal, because phones do not ping off the towers constantly. Then, it appears that Stone's phone was near where Clark turns into West Jefferson. From there, there are regular pings that coincide with Stone driving down West Jefferson. The phone becomes stationary at or around 12:19 a.m., which I already knew from seeing the report before. That may have been the time of crash plus or minus a few minutes, but the autopsy indicated that the time of death was more likely between 1:00 and 2:00 in the morning. What a way to go. The poor guy.

The IT Department had also pulled up Greyson's phone records to verify locations and timelines. The information aligns perfectly with Greyson's recollection of the evening's events.

I drive back to where Clark turns into West Jefferson and pull up the crash site on Google Maps. I begin talking to myself once again, "I am several miles away and Stone's vehicle drove there at a speed of roughly 50 to 60 miles per hour according to the pings and the black box report on the collision speed. If, and that is a big if, he drove himself, he would have had to drive most of the way, because the lane tracing would not stay active that long without him making periodic adjustments. Then, potentially, he could have passed out as he approached the crash site. That is only if it was truly an impaired driving accident. If somehow Stone ingested drugs unknowingly, then it could be murder, but it appears there is evidence he had a substance abuse issue. Stolen pills and the Tic Tac container, albeit there is a question mark around that Tic Tac container with the fingerprints."

I continue rambling, "Suppose someone got Stone incapacitated and put him in his own vehicle. Then, somehow, they got the vehicle moving at say 50 miles per hour and found a way to not let the car shut off the lane tracing. That would still be leaving a lot up to chance. The vehicle could potentially just roll out into a vacant lot. How could the killer aim for a river miles down a somewhat curvy road?"

I look out the window and I see a homeless man wearing a Detroit Tigers hat walking very slowly, pushing a grocery cart full of his personal belongings. I wonder how long he has been staring at me talking to myself. I hold the button to lower my driver's side window, raise my phone, and I point to it as if I have been on a phone call. I then retrieve a five dollar bill from my wallet and hold it out, "This is for you, sir."

He responds, "Gabby, my friends just calls me Gabby. I cannot remember the last time someone called me *sir*. I do not deserve that kind of respect."

"Well, sir, everyone needs and deserves respect. Have a nice day."

"Well, thank you, sir," he says with a kind emphasis on the word sir.

"You can just call me Gaines or Finn, whatever you prefer."

"Thank you, Gaines! It has been mighty fine meeting you."

As Gabby walks away, I continue to hear him, but I have no idea what he is saying.

My mind goes back to my wondering, but I clearly need to sleep on this.

Chapter 3.16 - Juice

I stop into my office, which is a place I do not like to spend too much time; however, there is a report sitting on my desk that I would like to review. I know I have an emailed version of it, but I seem to have better luck scouring over printouts. The technicians obliged my request for paper and they sent me a hard copy in addition to the electronic version.

I begin scanning the documents and I make mental and physical notes of a few items. Jimmy Greyson did supply his fingerprints and there are some of his prints in Stone's apartment, but nothing out of the ordinary. They were on the television remote control and the hallway door. Pretty routine for someone who has been in the apartment.

The water bottle case literally has no fingerprints on it, except for Stone's on the underside of the shrink wrap. Logically, this is from him carrying the case into the apartment. As suspected, there is some evidence of PEDs (Performance Enhancing Drugs) in Stone's protein powder and I wonder if the PEDs were there with his knowledge or without. I cannot think of a logical reason why someone who is intentionally taking a drug would hide it in their protein powder, but you never know.

The search team found two zip lock bags with painkillers in them, in the bedside table drawer. The painkillers match what was found in the Tic Tac container, as well as Greyson's prescriptions. Again, this seems logical, considering Greyson suspected that Stone had been skimming some of his medication.

In the report, it is described that a crumpled note was found in the kitchen garbage can. I am looking at a picture of the flattened note. Printed in blue pen and block letters is, "YOU FUCKIN SCUMBAG PRICK – I KNOW WERE YOU LIVE AND WHAT YOU DRIVE! YOUR DEAD IF U GO NEAR MY GIRL AGAIN!" There is also a comment that the piece of paper is being sent away for further analysis.

Well, I think I have a lead to pursue.

Chapter 3.17 – Frankie

"Thanks for coming here willingly, Frankie. There is a bottle of water for you, if you would like. I just wanted to let you know that while we are chatting here, I do have a team executing a warrant on your apartment."

Frankie replies sarcastically, "Oh really?"

"Yes, now is there anything that they will discover that might incriminate you?"

"Damned if I know. I have a gun, but it's registered and it is properly stored. I don't do drugs, so no worries there. They might find some sex toys, but there's no law against that, is there?"

"No, everyone to each their own, I guess. By the way, please state your name and birthday for the record."

I am surprised when he tells me that his name is actually Frances Ticklewood and with no middle name. Thankfully, I did not laugh.

I thank him for the initial information and continue, "Anyway, Frankie, can you tell me anything about this?" I hold the picture of the note that was found in Stone's garbage and then I slide it across the table facing Frankie.

"That ain't mine. Never seen it before!" Frankie exclaims.

Right on cue, I feel a double buzz in my pocket. I pull out my phone and I have a text message from one of the technicians. I pull up a picture of a post-it note, on which is a shopping list. On the list, in printed block letters, I see:

OJ
TP
BREAD
PREP H
JAM
CONDOM
PIZZA

I put my phone face up on the table and slide it over next to the note. "Frankie, it looks like you have some haemorrhoids that are bugging you. Does that steel bench bother you? And your printing looks very similar to this note. The shopping list is a little neater, but then again, you were likely much calmer when you printed your shopping list compared to when you wrote that threat." I chuckle a little and continue, "You only need one condom? What is up with that?"

Frankie stirs on the bench as if his haemorrhoids are acting up and says calmly, "Do I need a lawyer?"

"Well, if you have not done anything wrong, no. Let me know if you do want a lawyer."

The room falls silent and I take a deep breath, hoping he does not *lawyer up*. I silently give him a count to five and nothing, so I continue, "Where were you on the night that David Stone was killed in the car accident?"

"What's it matter? Like you said, it was a car accident."

"There are some inconsistencies in the evidence and we suspect that there could have been foul play. We do know that you did threaten Mr. Stone by text. And again on his vehicle. Tell me about those threats."

"Yeah, yeah, I am sure you have the text messages. Just talkin' smack, that all."

"And etching the rear window of his SUV?"

"Well, I was mad. I pay for Jessie's phone so I have her on Find My iPhone. I knew she was in that dude's apartment. That ain't right. It was just a threat. I didn't mean anything by it."

"Well, a threat usually means you want the other person to believe that you will follow through with said threat, there Frankie. So, you admit to threatening David Stone by text and then scratching into his car window?"

"Yeah, but I would not hurt the dude. I just wanted to scare him."

"I have to step out for a few minutes. You want some more water or anything?"

"Yeah, a coffee would be nice, with a shot of Bailey's Irish Cream in it, if you're being really sweet."

***

I step out into the hall and watch Frankie through the one-way window. I like to let suspects stir awhile. It does not hurt to let them think for 10 to 15 minutes. I also like to fill them up with liquids, because they will get uncomfortable after a couple of hours of questioning.

After five minutes, I am still looking through the window and Frankie winks, then sticks out his tongue. Whatever, I go to the washroom, because I do have the luxury of being able to relieve myself and I grab a water bottle from the staff room. There are some in the fridge, but I grab a warm one out of the case.

At roughly thirteen minutes from the time I left the room, I re-enter and roll the water bottle across the table to Frankie. "The coffee pot was empty and of course, we are not allowed Bailey's Irish Cream in here."

Frankie opens the water bottle and takes a long draw. Then he says, "You know, you should be lookin' at that bartender Stefan. He is one strung out dude and he has a thing for Jessie and you know, he is really jealous of me with her. He would have been really wound up if he saw this Stone guy getting friendly with Jess."

"What do you mean by, 'strung out dude,' Frankie?"

"Just that. He has been popping oxies and percs for months now. I think he might actually be dealing prescription drugs. And, there have been rumours that he will put roofies in girls' drinks to loosen them up. I heard that he takes girls back to the storage room on breaks and after closing. Does his thing and throws them in a cab."

"That is quite the accusation, Frankie. Do you have anything to back it up?"

"Well no, but the Magic Stick does have a camera on the bar area to watch the tenders. You know, so they are not drinking or giving out free stuff. I bet you could find something there."

I pause and I am thinking about this. I do know that Stefan has allegedly used the storage room and reportedly with Jessie, unless he fabricated the rendezvous. Jenny seemed to think that Jessie was a willing participant, at least initially, but then Jessie did crash hard on Home Opener Night. I think I need to get a warrant and check that video footage at the Magic Stick.

I respond, "I will do that, Frankie. I believe you son, but I do have to do my due diligence to rule people out. But this note here really does look like your printing."

"It ain't, I swear."

"Well, we will get experts analyzing it, so I guess that is irrelevant right now. Okay, we can move on."

"Where were you the night that Stone was killed?"

"Man, I have no idea. I remember hearing about it on Twitter in the morning, but I don't know what I was doing the night before. I was probably at the Stick until closing. Yeah, I think I was. If you get that *warren* thing, you can probably see that I was there. I know I bought a couple pitchers at the bar. I will be on the video then."

So, we dance around for about three hours and I eventually let him go to the washroom. After he takes an extraordinarily long pee, I walk Frankie out of the precinct.

Chapter 3.18 – Magic Stick Video

I drive over to the Magic Stick, even though I do not have a warrant yet. I may have to bluff my way through this one.

I ask for the owner or manager and I get one person who is both, Cindy Mason. I explain to Cindy that I am working on a case that might involve a patron named Frances Ticklewood and perhaps one of her bartenders, Stefan Johnson.

Cindy laughs, "I guess now I know why Frankie has never shared his last name. I assume that's Jessie's on again, off again no good boyfriend. And Stefan, he's a dirtbag, too. I let him go a week or so ago. How can I help you?"

"Well first, I need to be able to verify that Ticklewood was here until closing on April 13th. He claims he went up to the bar to buy pitchers of beer. Would he be on camera?"

"Oh, that shouldn't be too hard. Do you want to wait while I look up the bar videos?" "Sure, do you mind if I join you?"

"Absolutely, uh, oh, no, I mean yes. Sorry." Cindy pauses and formulates her response, "No, I do not mind if you join me. Please do."

I make a mental note to not ask a question like that. Something like, "May I join you?" would be much more straightforward.

Anyway, Cindy leads me to the storage room and she sits in front of a small desk with a laptop. After a few seconds, she has a screen full of 8 different camera angles. She quickly pulls up the camera behind the bar. "You said the 13th right?"

I nod and say, "Yes."

She scrolls to that night and says, "It will just take a minute. Oh, yep, here. I have him getting beer at 11:19 p.m.," she pauses while searching and continues, "again at 12:52 a.m., and here we go, hang on, again at 1:30. So, yeah, he was here all night and we close at 2 o'clock. Hope that helps."

I think to myself that it does help, but there is still a window of time that he could have left the bar. It is not that far to Xochimilco.

She closes the bar feed and the screen returns to the eight realtime live feeds and I see the back of my head in one little square. I point to it and turn around to say, "Oh, you have a camera in here?"

"Yeah, but that's new. It used to be by the kitchen, but I had it moved into here, when I got rumors that Stefan was using this room for extracurricular activities. First night the camera was in here, I caught him and canned his filthy ass."

"Oh, I see. Can you go back to the Tigers Home Opener Night?"

"Yep, April 4th, right?"

"Yes, you got it. I would like to see when Jimmy Greyson buys a pitcher of beer. Actually, the second pitcher."

"Oh, that will be easy enough."

We watch Jimmy get the first pitcher and Jimmy carries two glasses with one hand and the pitcher in the other. Later, he returns for another pitcher. This time, Stefan puts 4 glasses on the bar. Clearly, Jimmy cannot carry four glasses and a pitcher, so Jimmy leaves with the pitcher. After Jimmy leaves, we see Stefan put something into two of the glasses.

I say, "Well, I will be damned,"

Almost at the same time, Cindy says, "Well, that little pecker!"

I look to Cindy and say, "Cindy, you have been so helpful, but I think at this point, I should get a warrant so that I can get a copy of all of this. Trust me, you made the right move firing this guy. You probably saved a number of women from horrifying experiences by letting him go."

"I feel bad that I didn't let him go earlier or call the police earlier. Well, call them at all. I am so stupid. How many girls did he do this to?"

"You did not know. It will take some digging, but we will find out. I work homicide, but I will hand this off to another detective. Stefan may be involved in more than one crime here."

As I am exiting the Magic Stick, my phone rings and it is Sergeant Brown, who opens with, "Well, hang onto your hat Gaines, if you have one!"

Chapter 3.19 – Dumb Luck

Brown says, "This will knock your boots off. The report has come back on that crumpled-up note that was sent out for analysis. We have good news and bad news. I will start with the bad. The handwriting analysis does not provide a match for Frances Ticklewood. What kind of name is that? And no wonder he just likes to be called Frankie."

"Okay, thanks Sarge, I thought the printing looked close, but I was far from convinced. So, what is the good news?"

"Well, the paper must have come from a pad as it had a bit of residual plastic on the top edge."

"Okay?"

"You know when you write on a pad, it kind of embosses the paper below it."

"Yeah. I would shade with a pencil when we were kids to try and decipher things. It rarely worked unless you pressed really hard when writing."

"Well, the lab has better technology than a kid with a pencil. Anyway, they found an imprint of a note and it said, 'Be back in 5' and then, get this, it said, 'Stefan' down a little lower. It looks like this Stefan is your guy."

"Sarge, I need you to help push through a warrant for the surveillance recordings at the Magic Stick. It looks like this Stefan Johnson has been drugging girls and taking advantage of them. I think he drugged Stone as well. Things are piling up here."

"Yep. Consider it done. I will be on it like a wet blanket."

"Oh, and we need a warrant for Johnson's residence, vehicle, and phone records."

"Gaines, I thought you were coo coo for Cocoa Puffs earlier, but maybe you are onto something here. It looks like we have ourselves a *person of interest*."

Chapter 3.20 – Person of Interest

As I drive to the Magic Stick once again, I have the Home of Rock and Roll, WRIF on the stereo. The news breaks in and I just about crap my pants when I hear the announcer, "We have unconfirmed reports that the police have a suspect in the death of the Detroit Tigers shortstop, David Stone. We do not have an actual name, but our understanding is that the *person of interest* was a former bartender at the Magic Stick on Woodward Avenue. Sources close to the investigation, but not authorized to speak on behalf of the DPD, have also indicated that the *person of interest* is also under investigation for a number sexual assaults."

That did not take long. Nothing like taking the element of surprise out of interviewing the guy. Clearly, someone leaked this to the media and I am ticked. I do not think Brown would unless he is thinking that this is good press for the Detroit Police Department. However, he would know that this would hinder my investigation. The owner of the Magic Stick would know that we were looking at Johnson. That said, of all people, Cindy would know that making this public knowledge would not be good for business. Hey, come have a beer and shoot some pool here where we hire killer rapists as bartenders. That would be a sweet advertising slogan. Maybe the leak was Frances Ticklewood? He is the one who pointed us in Johnson's direction in the first place. Regardless, I am not too happy about the leak.

I pull up to the Magic Stick and Cindy Mason is waiting for me at the front door. She says, "Well, thank you for wrecking my business. Who is going to want to come to a bar that hires rapists and murderers?" Then, she jams a memory stick into my chest. Obviously the leak did not come from her!

"I promise you, Cindy, I did not leak that information. I cannot believe anyone at the DPD would either."

She mumbles, "Whatever," and turns to go back into the bar.

I think to myself, well, I better not come here for a beer or I will be getting a spitter for sure!

Chapter 3.21 – Stefan Johnson Interview

Well, the forensic guys have gone over the apartment, vehicle, phone records, and the Magic Stick video, so now I have significant material to review with Mr. Johnson. I map out a plan that meanders somewhat and I hope that I can get to the good stuff before Johnson bolts and demands a lawyer. Part of my plan is to avoid the sexual assault of Jessie as another officer will be following up on that and I do not want to taint their investigation. Also, if I go there, he will clam up.

"Thank you, Mr. Johnson for coming here today under your own volition. You are not under arrest and you may leave at any time."

"Stefan is good. Yeah, I hear I'm a *person of interest*. Although I have no idea why."

"Okay, so as you know, we searched your apartment and your vehicle, so I will start with your car."

Before Johnson answers, I see him take a glance at his phone which he had set on the table when he sat down. I imagine he knows we have his phone records, too. You can see him thinking and I wonder if it hurts.

Johnson then responds, "Okay, go ahead. It's a Corolla. Big whoop."

"It is brand new, right? 2019?"

"Yeah, so?"

"Well, that is a pretty expensive vehicle for a bartender. Well, unemployed bartender. How can you afford it?"

"Tips are actually really good in bartending and have you ever heard of financing? The interest rates are rock bottom right now. It makes sense to buy something that's quality and good on gas."

"So, it is a hybrid, right? And comes with all kinds of technological and safety features."

Like Greyson had mentioned, Johnson demonstrates a sense of pride and says, "Yeah, it's a hybrid. Jumps back and forth between electric and gas. And yeah, it has what's called *Safety Sense*. The cruise will adjust to the vehicle in front of you and it pretty much drives itself when you put it on cruise."

"Did you know that David Stone also had a hybrid Toyota? A Rav4 and that is the vehicle he died in?"

"Yeah, I did. I ran into him and Greyson in Mexican Village. Stone saw my car and mentioned he had a Toyota as well."

"So, tell me about that run-in."

"Not much to tell and I wouldn't call it a run-in. I saw Stone and Greyson coming out of a parking lot. They asked me why I was not tending on a Saturday night and I told them I was no longer working at the Stick. That's about it."

"It was all cordial?"

He knew I knew more, so he continued, "Mah, Stone made a negative comment about Jessie, so I told him that he shouldn't put Jessie down. She is a classy girl and all. He got all upset because I was telling him to chill. The old guy Greyson then smacked me in the chest with his cane. Is that assault? Can I sue him with assault?"

"My understanding is he just stopped you two from fighting, so probably not. I do not imagine a tough guy like you was hurt by an old guy with a cane." There is no sense in explaining the difference between charges and civil suits. "Stefan, what were you doing in Mexican Village?"

"I had a date. That ain't a crime as far as I know." To that, I am thinking that I am amazed he would have a date with someone who is fully conscious. Cindy is right in that he is a dirtbag.

"And with whom was the date?"

"A girl."

"Come on, Stefan. I have enough already to arrest you. We can go that route. But, you say you are innocent. Help me, and yourself, if you truly are innocent."

I can almost see the gerbil running on the wheel inside his head as he then says, "Her name was Starr with two R's. I met her at the Magic Stick a week or so earlier and she gave me her number. Oh yeah, it was April 1st, 'cause one of the customers joked that her giving me her number was probably a prank. We texted back and forth for a bit and then we set up a date to go to the Mexicantown restaurant."

"What is Starr's last name?"

"To tell the truth, I never got it."

187

"You know how to spell Starr, but you never got a last name? Anyway, tell me about your date."

"You a perv or what?"

"Stefan," and I give him a stern look implying once again that we can go the arrest route.

"Okay, I met Starr there at the restaurant at 10. As I said, it was after I ran into Greyson and Stone, I went into the restaurant and she already had a table. She even had two margaritas waiting for us. Nice, attentive girl!"

"Continue."

"We had food and drinks and she was all over me," to which he looks very proud.

"So, what time did the date end? Did you take her home?"

"We drank until midnight and then I thought for sure that I was taking her home. We went outside and after a couple minutes, we got into my car. I thought she was giving me directions to her place, but instead, she was trying to find an isolated spot for, you know."

"No, I do not know, Stefan."

"Well, she ah, you know." He points between his legs. "Then, when she was done, I drove her back to the restaurant, so she could get her car."

"So, you are alluding to that she gave you oral sex?"
Johnson nods.

"What time did you drop her back off at the restaurant?"

"No idea, man."

"What kind of car did she get into?"

"No idea. I dropped her off at the front door."

I think, what a gentleman. "You dropped a woman off after midnight and did not ensure that she got into her vehicle?"

"Guess not."

"Have you been in touch with her since?"

"No, she ghosted me."

"Ghosted you?"

"Yeah, she stopped responding and in fact, text messages started bouncing like she cancelled her phone."

Well, I am not surprised. What a clown. I jot down a reminder to myself to dig into the cell phone records and find this Starr Whomever.

"Let us switch over to the Magic Stick. So, why did they let you go from the bar?"

"Well, it's funny. Some girls flirt with me at the bar. It is kind of a cycle thing. They flirt with me hoping I will give them a heavier pour of liquor in their drinks. Then, when I give them a little extra, they flirt with me more. It's a win-win and nobody gets hurt."

"Okay, so they fired you for giving away alcohol. I wonder if they could lose their license for that? Is that it?"

"Well, I didn't pour that much more. They watch you like a hawk there. They even have cameras on us behind the bar."

"So, what was it?"

"Well, like I said, some of the girls get quite flirtatious. That's the word right? Some want to get it on like right away. And, I am just a guy. I can't say no and all. So, they put a camera in the storage room and caught me in there with a girl. I swear it was the first time, too."

"So, you are telling me that on the first night they put a camera in the storage room, it happened to be the first time that you had sex with a girl in there? Seriously?"

Johnson shrugs one shoulder and then the next and sits up straight. With a grin and demonstrating pride, "Well, maybe it was the third or fourth time."

"Ever go in there with Jessie?"

Johnson's eyes dart to the door and back to me, "Well, ah, yeah, ah, maybe once I think."

"Was she drunk? Impaired?" I immediately regret asking this question. I really wanted to avoid this topic, so I need to redirect as soon as possible.

Johnson replies, "She may have had a glow on, but she knew what she was doing."

I am shocked Johnson did not bolt already, so I say, "Okay, that makes sense." I need to keep him on the hook for a little while longer as I have the zinger coming up from what I found in the apartment. "Oh, I need a coffee. Do you want a water or something? Bag of chips?"

"Yeah, Yeah, a bag of chips and a water would be great."

"I will see what I can do. I will be right back."

Chapter 3.22 – The Zinger

Eight minutes after leaving for snacks, I return with a bag of barbecue chips and two bottles of water. Johnson rips open the bag and unfolds the foil so that he has easy access to the chips. The first water bottle is open after two chips and is pretty much gone in one chug.

I take a sip of coffee and continue, "So, you know that this Frankie character is not a fan of Stone. He has made multiple threats against Stone: bodily harm and death threats."

"Yeah, heard dat."

"Did you ever threaten David Stone?"

"Course not. We exchanged words, but Greyson can vouch for me that I didn't threaten Stone. Or touch him, actually!"

I pull out a piece of paper from my file folder and slide the photocopy of the threatening note onto the table in front of Johnson. "Does this look familiar?"

Johnson shakes his head, purses his lips, and folds his arms.

I laugh slightly as I think I would enjoy playing poker with this guy. I repeat, "Stefan, does this look familiar?"

"Well, Frankie is the guys whose been threatening Stone. Does it look like his printing?"

"Stefan, we need you to tell the truth here, okay?"

"What? I am telling the truth."

I pull out another piece of paper. This is a copy of the imprinted note that the lab managed to pull from the indentations in the paper. Before I place this onto the table, I say, "So Stefan, you know when you print on a notepad, it leaves an imprint on the paper below it." Then, I slide the paper onto the desk. "This must have been printed on the piece of paper directly above the threatening note that you say Frankie wrote."

Johnson squints, looks at the paper, and shakes his head. "Okay, I wrote that note, but I did not mean anything by it. I am not going to kill the guy. And how could I have anyway? It was a car accident."

I need to pull back a bit or he is going to bolt and I need to get to my best piece of evidence. I take a sip of coffee and that reminds Johnson that he is thirsty. He opens the second water bottle. He must be ready to pee his pants by now. I decide it is time for the zinger.

I take two steps to the door and open it with my right hand. I pause when the door is fully open. Then, I count to three and I say, "Oh, I almost forgot." I let go of the doorknob to slap my hand onto my forehead. I walk back to the table and pull out another piece of paper from my file folder that is under my left arm and I place the paper on the table. Johnson squints his eyes again and moves his head closer to the table to see a picture of a Tic Tac packet. I am watching his reaction carefully as I ask, "Do those look like Tic Tacs in that picture to you?"

This guy is not as dumb as he looks. He immediately stands up and says, "I am free to go, correct?"

"Yes, you are. And thank you for confirming what I thought." I open the door for him.

Johnson asks, "Where is the nearest washroom?"

"Oh sorry, it is out of order. You will have to hold it until you get home, Mr. Johnson."

I go back into the room and see the two bottles, one of which is empty and the other just has a couple inches of water consumed. What a waste!

Chapter 3.23 – Follow Up

Well, the Stefan Johnson interview is causing me some homework. I make a list of follow-up items that I need to address.

First, as much as I hate to waste anything, I am not going to drink out of a water bottle after this lowlife has already drank from it. However, the thought of that sparked a couple of thoughts. No matter how careful anyone is while drinking out of a bottle, there is almost always some backwash. I send an email to the lab to do a DNA and drug test on both the water and the Jack Daniels that remained in the bottles in Stone's vehicle. That one is easy.

Second, while I am at it, I might as well have the lab run Johnson's DNA. The two water bottles will go to the lab, as well.

Third, I need to comb through Johnson's cell phone records to see if they are consistent with his story. This will mean reviewing text messages and cell tower pings, which will take some time and I will need some assistance. Of course, a high priority is to get in touch with Starr. I find her phone number in the documents and I call it. Not surprisingly, I receive a message stating that the number is not assigned. I try texting it and I get a red message saying that my text was unsent. This is what Johnson meant when he said that she ghosted him. Alright, what is my plan B to find Starr.

Okay, item three-B: I email the IT department. I ask them to check the Magic Stick bar video for April 1st, to see if they can get me a picture of Stefan Johnson getting a phone number from this mystery woman.

Fourth, I text Jessie to let her know that I need to speak with her again based on newly discovered information. I assure her that she is not in trouble and I need her to confirm some items. I am sure she has heard about the person of interest, so she is anxious to make arrangements for another interview.

I hear a bell sound on my laptop and I check my email. Well, that was quick. I pull up a picture of an attractive girl with long dark hair and olive skin. In the picture, she is handing her cell phone to Stefan Johnson while leaning onto the bar at the Magic Stick. Clearly, Stefan is looking at her extensive cleavage. I have to admit that I am staring a little as well and then I am startled by a noise behind me.

I hear a loud, slow clap and I turn to see fellow detective Paul Antaya who then segues into a DJ sounding voice. He bellows, "Put your hands together for," followed by a pause and then finishes with a drawn-out, "Destiny!"

I look at him puzzled and ask, "What? Do you know her?"

"Well, I might. It looks a lot like a girl named Destiny at the Riv. It is a strip joint out in Dearborn. The Riviera."

"I will not ask how you know this, but are you sure?"

"Yep, quite sure and get your mind out of the gutter. It was from an investigation."

"Well, that was some dumb luck. Thanks so much, Paul. If this pans out, I owe you a couple of beers." I realize what I said and continue, "And, not at the Riv!"

I cannot believe this, but I think I am going to a peeler bar.

Chapter 3.24 – Anthony

It is somewhat of a drive to Dearborn, therefore I figure I should try to do some work while in the car. I remember that I got a text from Greyson this morning about a waiter named Anthony. I doubt there is any relevance here, but I might as well follow up on it, while on the road.

Greyson suggested that I contact Gord at Thomas Magee's Whiskey Bar, which leads me to ask Siri to call Thomas Magee's Whiskey Bar. Unfortunately, Siri tells me that there is no Thomas Magee in my contact list. Well, I know that!

On the second attempt, Siri asks me if I want to call St. John's Church in the Wilderness. That is a miss and I am getting frustrated, so on the third attempt, I yell, "Hey Siri, call the feckin' Thomas Magee Whiskey Bar." Go figure, it works this time.

After three rings, the call is answered by a cheery female voice. I identify myself and ask for Gord, who answers the phone within seconds and informs me that he was actually expecting me to contact him. I guess Greyson must have given him a heads up.

"Thank you for taking my call, Gord. It may be nothing, but I figure I should follow up on this as you never know what pieces are relevant until they are. Relevant, that is."

"Understood," says Gord, "I am glad you called. I can fill you in on how things rolled out here that night. Jimmy and his girl Jenny came in together and Anthony seated them. Before they ordered, Anthony informed me that Jimmy wanted to see me. I did not think much of it at first. In fact, I thought the request was more a social request. However, when I got to their table, I could see that Jimmy was agitated. Jimmy explained what happened, actually surprisingly calmly too. I have a feeling that this Jenny is helping mellow Jimmy's temperament."

After a few seconds of silence, I reply, "I do not have many details, so you better fill me in."

"Oh, okay, I guess when Anthony seated the two of them, he put his hand on Jenny's bare shoulder and held it there for a while. I am shocked that Jimmy did not smack him with his cane. Maybe his bum knee kept him from going after Anthony."

"Maybe, or as you said, he was being a gentleman in front of Jenny."

"So anyway, I terminated Anthony's employment immediately. He was not too happy and he actually broke my back door on his way out. I had to call in a repairman to fix the door that night and the whole event was quite costly."

"What is Anthony's full name?"

"Actually, it is Norbert Andrew Wohlers. Anthony is not even his middle name. Not sure why he goes by Anthony."

"Well, I have a guess Gord. Do you do reference checks when you hire?"

"Not really. I just interview them. I either get a good feeling or a bad feeling, you know."

"I would suggest you beef up your process, Gord."

"Maybe I should."

"Thank you so much, sir. This might be helpful. If you think of anything else, please call me or text me at this number. Take care."

"Will do. Actually, I can text you his Social Security Number, address and phone number."

"Oh yes, please do. That could prove to be very helpful."

Within a minute of disconnecting, Wohler's information is displayed on my phone. I then call the station to request a records check.

I feel like this is a waste of time, but I am just driving anyway.

Two minutes later, Sergeant Brown calls me. "Excuse me Detective Gaines, but why are you looking into Mr. Wohlers?"

"He popped up in the Stone investigation. I guess Greyson got him fired and then he showed up at Xochimilco the evening before Stone died."

"Okay, there is a warrant out for his arrest, out of Toledo. He has an extensive record: Assault, Trafficking, Insurance Fraud, and he is the prime suspect in his ex-wife's murder. The FBI is actually involved for some reason. Your records request fired off several red flags in multiple agencies."

"No way."

"And get this. With the insurance fraud, he somehow overrode the computer of his neighbour's vehicle and managed to get him to hit his wife's car. There was a major civil suit and the insurance company paid out half a mill in damages. The insurer however, hired a private investigator who blew the scam wide open. They got the majority of their money back, but Wohlers went into the wind, just as his ex was found dead in a ditch."

"Thanks Sarge, I will forward you a cell phone number and last known address. Can you send someone to pick him up? I am on my way to a strip joint in Dearborn. I will fill you in later."

After disconnecting the call, I think to myself that other than me saying that I am going to a peeler bar, this was the most normal conversation I ever had with Brown. There were no stupid sayings. Hey, this is progress, but I wrap my knuckles on the side of my head and say, "Knock on wood."

Chapter 3.25 – The Riv

I flash my badge at the front door and I ask the bouncer to point me towards Destiny. The large man just stands there with his arms crossed and grunts. Had I not called before I left the station, I would be a little nervous that Destiny is not working today.

I ask again, "I am Detective Gaines with the Detroit Police Department. Could you point me to Destiny?"

Again just a grunt, but then I see Mr. Bouncer looking at his left elbow. Behind his elbow, I notice that he is rubbing his middle finger and thumb together. I retrieve a twenty-dollar bill from my wallet and direct the bill at his still moving fingers. Somehow his hand gobbles up the twenty with the efficiency of an ATM.

Mr. Bouncer then tilts his head towards the bar and he mumbles, "Leopard skin dress and black booties at the bar."

I squeeze between his huge frame and the door jam to make my way to the bar. As I approach the bar, I note that it is good that Mr. Bouncer mentioned the black booties, because there are two girls at the bar in leopard skin dresses. The other one is wearing furry slippers though. Go figure. I approach Destiny and she says, "I heard you were coming out here, Detective." She grabs my hand and leads me to a dark corner of the room. "It's a slow day. I will only charge you ten bucks per song."

"I do not want any dancing. I just want to talk, Destiny."

"If I had a Ben Franklin for every time I heard that!"

"There are like three guys here in the whole place right now and they are all busy. How about we say twenty bucks until I have all the answers I need?"

"Make it forty and we have a deal," to which I nod. She continues, "What can I do for you, Detective?"

"Well, I guess you met a Stefan Johnson at the Magic Stick. Can you tell me how that came about?"

"Well, a couple weeks ago, my girl and I went out to get a few drinks downtown and when I went up to the bar, I sees this guy and he was kinda cute."

"Do you remember when that was?"

"Yeah, it was April 1st, because I remember everyone was doing stupid April Fools jokes."

"Oh, okay, good."

"He kept staring down my top, so I knew he was interested. Anyway, he asked for my number, so I handed him my phone and he put his number into it. I texted him later that evening and suggested that we go out, but he wasn't available. He kept saying he had to work, but I think he eventually quit that job 'cause it was a damper on his social life. Any who, we decided to go for a late dinner the other day."

"So, where did you go?"

"I love Mexican, so I suggested Mexicantown restaurant."

"What time did you get there?"

"About 10 I think."

"I have always wanted to go there. What did you have? Was it good?"

"Can't really remember. Ended with changa or something or other. The margaritas were good and more memorable."

"So, how long did you stay there?"

"I am pretty sure we left by midnight."

"Did you leave together?"

"Hey, I may dance, but I ain't easy. I don't sleep with a guy on the first date. We went outside and he tried to make out with me right there on the street. I pretty much had to fight him off. He pouted and got into his mommy car. Didn't even make sure that I got to my car okay. What a jerk! So, I ghosted him."

"So, this was at midnight?"

"Let me check. I called my sister right after he left and we talked for about half an hour. She's having marriage troubles you know. I sat in the parking lot for the call." She pulls up her history and shows it to me, "See, I called her at 12:02 a.m. and we talked until 12:34."

"So, you talked in the parking lot? You were not driving home during the call?"

"No, my old jalopy don't got Bluetooth. It isn't safe to call while driving, officer."

"Okay, makes sense. And, call me old, but how did you ghost him?"

"Oh, you are not old sugar. You are actually pretty cute." She pauses, giggles, and then continues, "Sorry, that is just kinda habit, now. Well, I use an app on my phone that gives me a second phone number. I can text and call through the app, just like a normal phone. So, if I meet a new guy, I use that number. Then, if it doesn't work out, I just burn the number and get a new one. It's actually pretty slick."

I am amazed that now you can just burn a phone number instead of buying a new burner phone. Wow. Everything matches Johnson's story except the way the date ended. Johnson claims that Starr/Destiny did him a favour on a dark street. She claims they parted ways. I better just double check.

"Just to clarify, did you get into Stefan's car at any point?"

"No, not at all. Never. Did he say I did?" which got no response from me. "No, I just walked to my car and went home."

"Straight home?"

"Yeah, actually I did after chatting with my sister. I had a long day. Worked an afternoon shift here."

"Well, that pretty much answers all my questions. Thank you, ma'am."

"Oh, you are welcome, hon. By the way, you still have half a song left."

"I am good, but thanks though."

I start to leave, but then I turn back to her and squeeze my temples between my right forefinger and thumb. "Oh, I cannot believe how stupid I am. Your stage name is Destiny, but your name is Starr correct? What is your last name?"

"Yes honey, Starr. Starr Stewart, with EW as opposed to a U."

I look at her puzzled, so she spells it out, "S, T, E, W, A, R, T. That's how you spell Stewart. As opposed to Stuart with a U."

"Ah, I see. Also, I hate to ask, but could I get your birthdate, too. We always have to log the birthdate with our reports to differentiate people. You know in case there is another Starr Stewart in the system."

She gives me her birthdate and then I ask one final question. "May I get your phone number too, in case I need to get in touch with you again? It would save me a drive. Oh, and not a burn number, please?"

She gives me her number and follows up with, "Oh sweety, you definitely get my real number."

"Let me guess. That was just habit again."

This garners a smile and a wink from my new friend.

As I get into my vehicle, I get a text message from Brown: Officers stormed Wohler's address, but it was fake. They scared the crap out of an elderly couple having tea!

Well, that is disappointing.

Chapter 3.26 – Interviewing Jessie

Jessie lives with her mother, just around the corner from the Magic Stick and since she did not want to alarm her mother, we agree to meet at the bar again. Jessie assures me that Cindy Mason is not working today, so the coast is clear for me. After the media leaks playing havoc with her business, I am certain that I am not too welcome, by the Magic Stick owner and manager.

I park out front in my usual spot and head inside. Jessie is sitting at the bar, so I ask her if she would mind moving to a booth in order to have some privacy.

While we are walking, she surprises me when she asks, "Do we need to go over this again? I talked with an officer last night and Stefan is supposed to be arrested today for drugging me and," she pauses and then finishes the sentence shyly with, "you know."

"Yes, unfortunately, we do have to revisit some items. Being assaulted is awful and I am sorry you went through that. However, I will be focussing on the possible murder of David Stone."

She nods while her eyes water slightly. "I guess Stefan is the person of interest everyone is talking about."

I say, "No," but I nod my head and she gets the message. Try it. It actually takes practice to do this.

She giggles and then says, "Oh, I am sorry that I laughed. It is not about Stefan that I am laughin'."

"Understood. First of all, I am not sure if I got your information before. I can be a little scattered, you know. Anyway, could I get your full name and birthday for my notes?"

"Sure, it is Jessica Parker Williams. Yeah, I know my mom was a big fan of Sex and the City. And, my birthday is actually tomorrow and I turn twenty-one."

"You *turn* twenty-one tomorrow?" I ask as that *is* the drinking age in Michigan. That is an issue that I am not too worried about right now.

"Yes, I do."

"Well, happy birthday! Perhaps you should go out and celebrate, tomorrow."

"I plan to! It's a big day."

"Getting back to the case, can we go back in time and talk about the night you met David Stone and Jimmy Greyson? How did you meet?"

"Jenny and I were just standing over there and we just got our first drink. Bloody Marys. I saw Dave and he gave me a smile. I wanted to go over there, but Jenny didn't want to. She thought that Jimmy was kinda old and all. It's funny how that turned out, eh?"

"Okay, so you approached them?"

"Yeah, I just went over and asked, 'Can we join you guys on the table?' We can play a decent game of pool. Well, good enough to not look foolish anyway."

"Go on."

"There isn't much to tell. We played pool. Jenny and I finished our Bloody Marys about the same time the guys finished their first pitcher, so Jimmy went to get another pitcher."

"Do you recall anything unusual about the beer?"

"Jimmy came back with a darker beer. Dave thought it tasted funny and so did I, but I never had it before, so."

"Can you describe the taste?"

"Dave said it tasted chalky and Jimmy gave him a hard time about. I thought it did too. Kinda like, dry I guess."

"Okay. Continue."

"Well in light of all the rumors about Stefan spiking drinks, I am guessing that is why it hit me so hard."

"I wish I would have talked to you sooner about this."

"Why is that? Well, if this case goes to court, it is better if I had your interview done prior to you hearing any rumors. But it is okay. Try to think of what you saw, heard, and felt as opposed to bringing in outside information."

"Ah, I see. Well, like I said, the drink tasted funny and Dave and I both thought so, but then Jimmy called Dave a candy ass, so Dave drank up and so did I. We played pool for a while and then unfortunately, I blacked out for a bit. Next thing I knew, I was sitting over there," and she points to a corner table. "Jenny and Stefan gave me a glass of water and I felt better, but then I blacked out again. Next thing I knew, I was laying next to Dave in Jimmy's apartment and my phone blew up."

"Sorry, can I back up a little before we talk about the text messages?" That was rhetorical, so I continued, "What happened to you was awful, but I need to know what the extent of your relationship was with Stefan. My apologies if it is too sensitive to talk about."

"Oh no, that's fine. I admit I flirted with him, but all the girls do."

"To get more liquor in their drinks?"

"No, no, no, not me. I am underage, remember. If I flirt with the bartenders, they don't hassle me about my ID."

"Well, I cannot condone that. And of course, flirting is no invitation to what Stefan did that night. So, do you think he misunderstood your flirting?"

"Oh, most definitely. I actually backed off a couple weeks earlier, because I could see that he was getting jealous whenever Frankie was around. From that point, Jenny always went to get our drinks. I was getting a bit freaked out with Stefan. It bothered me when I woke up and Stefan was there. But, thankfully, Jenny was there, too."

"But then right after Stefan and Jenny gave you water, you blacked out again, right?" Jessie nodded. "And then you woke up again when the text messages came in. You still have them, right? Can you take screenshots and send them to this number?" I place my phone on the table.

"Oh, I will just airdrop them to ya. Yep, I see your phone here. There they are," and she taps my screen to accept the photos into my phone.

"Thank you. Now on the night that Dave died, he texted you around midnight. Can you tell me about that?"

"Sure, it surprised me a little. I hadn't heard from him really and I thought that Frankie scared him off."

"What do you mean when you say that you had not heard from him really?"

"Well, we exchanged a few text messages. I apologized for giving him a hickey and passing out. He apologized for anything he

203

might have done when he was drunk. That kind of stuff. No phone calls, just texting."

"Ah, I see. While you are in your phone there, can you take screen shots of those text messages and drop those to me as well?"

Jessie does as requested and as she finishes, my phone starts buzzing and ringing, so I pick it up and instinctively turn away from the conversation. No idea why actually.

After less than a minute, I disconnect and apologize to Jessie, "I am sorry, I have to go. There has been a stabbing right around the corner. It looks like Stefan is being taken to hospital and Frankie is in custody. I have to go. Please do text me if anything else relevant comes to mind."

Chapter 3.27 – 48 Hours

I jump into my rental vehicle and head around the corner, even though I probably could have walked there just as fast. I see an officer talking with someone who looks like a jogger and then I recognize the jogger to be none other than Officer Hodgson.

"Hey Hodge, what are you doing here?"

The uniformed officer interjects, "Hello, I am Officer Murray. And you are?"

I pull out my badge and reply, "I am Detective Finn Gaines. I am working the David Stone case and your two guys are witnesses, or possibly more."

"Well hello, Detective. Officer Hodgson here came upon two guys in an altercation while she was out for a run. Her quick reactions may have saved the one guy's life and ensured we caught the other, who is going to lockup, as soon as possible."

I turn to Hodgson and give her an affirming nod and say, "Good work, Hodge. I really do like your work."

Officer Murray jumps back in again, "The victim appears to be your *person of interest* and he is right down the street at Harper Hospital. I will take this Frances Ticklewood into the station. Are you going to need to talk to him too? I have read him his rights, so we will have to see how long it takes for a lawyer to show up for him."

I say, "Yes, I will. Thank you Officers, keep up the great work."

I get back into the Rav4, drive another short distance to the hospital, and pull up to the parking spots marked for police. They are all full, probably with officers assisting on mental health crises, so I pull into a space with a parking meter. I would put some change in the meter, but I literally have none in my pockets and well, I am driving a rental, so I do not have a stash of loose change built up yet. I would not have to worry about the meter had I arrived in a cruiser, but instead, I put my business card on the dashboard. That should keep the parking police away. I hope anyway.

With my badge leading the way, I walk briskly into the Emergency Room entrance and say, "I need to see a patient that was just brought in. His name is Stefan Johnson. Multiple stab wounds."

A startled nurse points me down the hall and says, "Bay Eight. They are working on him, now, but I am not sure if he is conscious or not."

As I approach Bay Eight, a doctor who is pulling off his gloves, comes out from behind a curtain. I identify myself and ask, "Is he going to make it?"

"We have him stabilized and they are moving him to surgery as soon as possible, but he has lost a lot of blood. If he survives the surgery, it will be touch and go for some time. The first 48 hours will be critical. We will know more after that."

I think to myself, seriously, does this guy watch all of the medical shows on television? It seems like for every person who has a major injury, they give the same line, "Well, it is too early to tell. The first 48 hours will be critical. We will know more after that."

My thoughts are interrupted by loud beeping and the doctor runs back into Bay Eight. Then, I hear someone yell, "Clear!"

After two attempts with the paddles, I hear the doctor say, "Time of death is 4:16 p.m. and you can cancel that operating room."

Chapter 3.28 – Another 48 Hours

I am sitting in Sergeant Brown's office after returning to the station from Harper Hospital and I start with, "Well, it looks like Ticklewood will be booked for the murder of our *person of interest*, Stefan Johnson."

"Ticklewood is an open and shut case isn't it?"

"Yes, absolutely. Officer Roberta Hodgson was out for a run and came upon the altercation. She witnessed the stabbing, stayed with Johnson and called in Ticklewood's description. An arrest was made within minutes by Officer Murray and she also retrieved the weapon. Frankie is dead to rights on this one. Both officers did outstanding work."

"Good, so run me through the Stone case and where you are with that."

"Okay, I will start with motive. Jessica Parker Williams, aka Jessie has an on again, off again relationship with Frances Ticklewood, aka Frankie. Jessie is an attractive young girl who flirts with the bartenders, to continue getting served while underage. Stefan Johnson misinterprets the flirting as more, resulting in a love triangle. Things culminate on the Home Opener Night when David Stone comes into the picture. The girls are playing pool with Stone and Greyson, leading to Jessie and Stone getting to know each other."

Brown interjects, "The love triangle becomes a love square."

"Right, or rectangle or quadrilateral. Johnson gets jealous of Stone and puts some kind of drug into both Stone's and Jessie's glasses before he brings the glasses to the pool table. Both feel the effects to the point where Greyson takes Stone back to his place to sleep it off. Meanwhile, Johnson takes a break and assaults Jessie in the storage room."

"And that is on the video surveillance?"

"No, the camera got moved into the storage room *after* this assault. The bar owner was suspecting Johnson was up to no good and put a video camera in there, but later."

"I see. Did Jessie have any recollection of the event?"

"The other detective looking into the assault on Jessie has indicated that her memory of the night is starting to come back in patches. I understand there is some physical evidence that should be able to tie the assault to Johnson, as well."

"Okay, that is good. And what about the drugging of the glasses of beer?"

"Oh yes, that is on video. Back to my story here. So, Jessie regains consciousness a while after the sexual assault with Jenny and Johnson tending to her. They give her water and I suspect that Johnson spiked her water too. The girls then go to Greyson's apartment."

"That is Jenny and Jessie, right? So why did Jenny not just take Jessie home?"

"Yes, correct. Jenny and Jessie. I can only assume that Jessie was feeling better until Stefan spiked her water, but I can follow up with her on that. Maybe no one was at her home and she was keeping her nearby."

"Makes sense."

"So, Jenny and Greyson do their thing while Jessie passes out on top of Stone. Both all drugged up. Meanwhile, Frankie must have blown a gasket when Jessie disappeared. I am sure there was gossip at the bar. Next thing you know, he shows up at the apartment."

"How did he know she was there?"

"I guess he pays the bills on Jessie's phone and he felt entitled to activate the Find My iPhone feature, for his own use. He followed her signal and started blasting text messages at her. There were all kinds of threats against her and Stone. He must have known somehow which vehicle was Stone's, so he scratched another threat into the back window."

"And you have pictures of the threats and the window, right?"

I nod and continue, "So the barrage of text messages wakes up the four lovebirds and the girls sneak out the back of the parking garage. With Jessie's phone powered off, of course."

"The way I see it, both Frankie and Johnson had motive to kill Stone."

"Yes, true. Potentially they could have been working together and then today was a *falling out*, but I doubt it. I lean towards Johnson for Stone's death."

"Okay, and then of course, Frankie clearly had motive to kill Johnson."

"Correct, there is jealousy, plus the drugging and sexual assault that somehow got leaked to the media."

Brown's face turns red and he says, "If I ever find out who leaked that, well, I don't know what I'll do, but it better not be anyone in the DPD!"

"I am baffled by that, too."

Brown composes himself and then continues, "So, you have motive on the Stone murder. What about opportunity and means?"

"You believe I have a murder now, eh? That is progress. Okay, both Johnson and his date, Starr Stewart aka Stripper Destiny are in Mexican Village at the same time as Stone and Greyson. They are at different restaurants, but they are both on the same block from 10 p.m. until midnight."

"Quite the coincidence."

"Yeah, and as you know, I do not believe in coincidences. Greyson and Stone leave their table at midnight. Stone gets in his vehicle and goes for a drive, apparently awaiting a booty call response from Jessie. Meanwhile, Greyson sticks around for one more drink with an adoring fan. Cell phone tower pings verify that chain of events for both of them."

"How about Johnson and the Destiny girl?"

"Not so much. They both say that they left the other restaurant at midnight. Johnson claims they went for a drive to a dark location and she gave him, well, fellatio. Meanwhile, I talked with Starr Stewart with an *EW*, as opposed to a *U*, aka Riv stripper Destiny. She says that they parted ways at midnight. The cell phone tower pings put him on that dark street, but not her. She made a phone call to her sister, who is having marital issues in the parking lot and they talked for about half an hour."

"So, he is lying?"

"Appears so! And, that puts Johnson and Stone at the same location just a few miles east of the crash site. Minutes later, Stone goes off the road and hangs upside down for hours."

"So, that looks like opportunity to me."

"It appears so and it appears that Johnson left Stone for dead."

"But, how did he get Stone to crash?"

"I do not know, yet. I still need to figure that out."

Brown recaps, "The way I see it, you have a motive and opportunity for Johnson, but the means is still a little loose. Looser than my first wife."

"I thought that was your second wife," I say with a smile. "But right, Sarge. We are close. Unfortunately, our number one suspect is dead and I cannot squeeze him to find out how he pulled it off. However, I will figure it out. Give me 48 hours and I promise that I will have it solved."

Sarge looks at me puzzled and says, "What?"

"I have just always wanted to say that. It is another TV thing."

"I don't watch TV," Brown says dryly and then continues, "I am just being devil's advocate here, but are there any other suspects?"

"Yes, possibly. We have Frankie of course who threatened Stone. There is potential that it could be someone in the organization, perhaps connected to the PEDs, but I really do not know. There is also the guy we came across by accident. This Wohlers character that Greyson got fired at the Whiskey Bar. As you know, he is a career criminal, but his beef would be with Greyson and not Stone. Mistaken identity maybe. But nah, that does not make any sense."

"What if he was trying to set up Greyson?"

"But Greyson is not even a suspect here. If it was a setup, it was not a very good one. I think we can scratch Wohlers, unless somehow he was working with Johnson and/or maybe one of the others."

I run my fingers through my hair as if to stimulate my brain and then I continue, "Oh boss, I forgot one other piece of evidence. Remember that we found a Tic Tac container in Stone's vehicle. It only had Stone's fingerprints on it and pain killer residue inside it."

"Yeah, I remember. You made that out to be the smoking gun!"

"Well, we found a Tic Tac container in Johnson's apartment and it had the same painkillers in it. I really do like Stefan Johnson for this. Give me those 48 hours and I will have the actual method nailed down."

"You better. The press is going to be all over my ass when it gets out that Johnson is dead."

Chapter 3.29 – Frances Ticklewood

I head back to my office to check on messages and I do have a few phone messages on my desk phone. I cannot believe I still have that thing and I wonder when we will run on cell phones only.

One message is of interest. It is from the lab and I am puzzled. There was no evidence of anything foreign in either the Jack Daniels or water bottles. Specifically, there were no drugs in either bottle. However, Stone's DNA was in the Jack Daniels bottle, but not in the water bottle. Clearly, Stone did not drink out of the water bottle. I shake my head, because this makes no sense to me, right now. If Stone did not drink out of the water bottle, then the million dollar question is: Why would a partially filled water bottle be in Stone's vehicle? I will have to figure that puzzling question out later, as now, I need to speak with Frankie.

I go down the hall with a notepad in hand to find Frances Ticklewood, who of course, has his lawyer with him. His attorney is a guy who looks like he is 20 years old and when I walk in, he slides up his large dark framed glasses up the bridge of his nose. I suspect this guy got beat up often in high school.

Pointdexter reaches out his right hand and says, "Hello Detective Gaines. I am Lorenzo Donatello and I am representing Mr. Ticklewood. He is agreeable to talking with you regarding the Stone matter, but he will not engage in any discussion pertaining to the death of one Stefan Johnson."

"Well, they are somewhat intertwined, so I am not sure how that is possible, but let us see how this goes."

I seat myself across from the pair and I adjust until I am comfortable in the chair. In the matter of a few seconds, I decide to change my tact with Mr. Ticklewood.

I start with, "Okay Frankie, I need to understand your interactions with the late David Stone. When did you first meet him?"

"I never actually met the guy. I have only seen him from a distance at the Stick."

"The Magic Stick, right?"

"Yes, sir."

"Now, the night after you went to Stone's apartment building, did you and Jessie talk?"

"Yes, we did."

I pause for the count of ten and then I fix my eyes on his. "Did she tell you that nothing happened between her and Stone?"

"Yes, she did."

Again, I pause. This time for the count of 5 with my eyes still locked on his. "Did you believe her?"

"Yes, I did."

"Mr. Donatello, we are done here. Thank you."

Ticklewood may go to prison for the murder of Stefan Johnson, but I believe he had nothing to do with the death of David Stone.

I head back to my office and check my email once again. I see a new email that I have been anticipating and I open it. Somewhere I have heard the expression *follow the money* and I wonder if this is good advice in this case, too.

Chapter 3.30 – Ahah Moment

I walk up the stairs at Xochimilco at 11:30 p.m. and ask for a Corona at the bar.

The bartender asks if I want a lime and I say, "Yes, please." I hand him a ten dollar bill and tell him, "Keep the change."

I look around and take my time drinking the beer. I look at the bottle and wonder to myself, if you put a Bud Light in a clear bottle with a lime, would anyone know the difference? It really just tastes like lime as opposed to beer. I think it has a bit less fizz, but maybe it is my imagination. Anyway, I sip at the beer, because I want it to last another 22 minutes.

I look at my phone and I see the time change from 11:58 to 11:59, so I down the last half inch of beer, leaving only the lime in the bottle. I discard the bottle onto the bar and I head down the stairs. I stop on the stairs for about 30 seconds and then continue. I walk casually around the corner to where Greyson had indicated that Stone had parked on the night he died.

I get into my rental Rav4 and head to Clark Street. As I am heading southbound, I engage the cruise control while driving 30mph. Once I am approaching the corner where Clark turns into West Jefferson, I hit the Cancel button in order to suspend the cruise control temporarily. As I coast, I look around trying to picture where Johnson's car would have been parked. This is the general location where he claimed that Destiny/Starr went down on him. I slow to just a roll, in fact, slow enough that I think I could open the door and exit the vehicle without being injured. Next, I hit the Resume button on the steering wheel and hit the Plus Sign button repeatedly until I see the cruise speed set to 56 mph on the digital display.

Sure enough, the SUV steadily picks up speed and levels out at 56mph. It navigates the road smoothly, even making gradual turns as necessary. Of course, however, the digital display turns orange and threatens to disengage the lane tracing, because I am not holding the steering wheel. The vehicle continues sailing down West Jefferson Avenue, as long as I give the steering wheel a little nudge every once in a while. I approach the crash site at Rouge River and the Rav4 sails across the bridge without incident.

Then it hits me!

I double back and head towards Mexican Village to find a variety store. I pull in near the door of a 7/11 and head inside. I go directly to the refrigerator section and grab a water bottle. While at the cash register, I notice a Tic Tac tree display, so I grab a pack and put it on the counter with the water bottle. While exiting the store, I crack open the water bottle, take one swig, and get back into my rental. After popping a couple of Tic Tac mints into my mouth, I toss the packet into the console and take another swig of water. It looks about right and I store it in the cup holder, for now.

I make my way back to Xochimilco and once again navigate to Clark Street. While heading southbound, I set the cruise to 56mph and I try my little experiment again. After a minute, the vehicle still has not scolded me for not having my hands on the steering wheel. I cancel the cruise control and I coast into the transition to West Jefferson.

After the curve, I slow the vehicle to a crawl and then hit resume and remove my hands from the steering wheel. As expected, the SUV slowly accelerates to 56mph and navigates the road, curves and all, flawlessly. However, this time, I never touch the steering wheel whatsoever.

I watch in amazement. My experiment modification is working perfectly. After several minutes, I cruise over the bridge once again with no issue.

The pieces are falling into place.

Chapter 3.31 – Mexican Village

With a sense of pride, I make my way back to Mexican Village. I feel I am getting closer to being able to wrap this case up, but there are still some loose ends. I park on the street close to where I believe Johnson had parked on the night in question.

I can see both Mexicantown and Xochimilco restaurants. I can also see part of the parking lot where Stone, Greyson, and Stewart parked, as well. I am trying to run things through my mind about how the sequence of events went down that night.

I imagine scenario one: Johnson and Starr come out of Mexicantown at roughly the same time as Stone coming out of Xochimilco. Stone gets into his Rav4 and heads southwest to his destiny. Speaking of destiny, the happy couple on their first date gets into the Corolla and they head southwest as well. They stop on a dark road and have some fun. Does Stone drive by while they are parked? Or do they get to their location just after he drives by there? Alright, as Stone drives to his death, the couple comes back here, the less than a gentleman Johnson lets Starr get out of the car, and she gets into her own car. They both drive away at about the same time that Greyson comes out of Xochimilco and gets into his vehicle to drive home. If scenario one is true, then maybe Stone drove down that road and passed out and went off the road. Or, perhaps he intentionally drove off the road. He was struggling on the field and he was getting hooked on booze and drugs. But what about the anomalies, like no DNA in the water bottle, the fingerprint issue on the Tic Tac packet, and the phone in the wrong pocket. Okay, scratch suicide or impaired accident from the possibilities. But no, scenario one does not make sense, because Starr was in the parking lot talking on the phone.

I shake my head to clear the thoughts and now I am onto scenario two: Johnson and Starr come out of their restaurant, Johnson heads southwest as the cell phone pings confirm. Starr, on the other hand, heads to her car and calls her sister. At about the same time, Stone comes out of his restaurant, gets in his vehicle, and then heads to the same general location as Johnson. That part just seems like way too much of a coincidence. Anyway, half an hour later, Starr finishes up her phone call, pretty close to the same time that Greyson comes out of his restaurant and gets into his vehicle to drive home. In this scenario, the cell phone data all jive.

It dawns on me that I cannot picture Starr getting into her vehicle, because I do not know what she drives. I cannot picture Greyson getting into his vehicle either, because he has two. It was April 13 and the weather was unseasonably nice, so he likely had his sports car out for the evening.

I shake my head to clear the vision and as my eyes refocus, I see a homeless man walk by pushing a shopping cart. He then finds a spot in a little alcove off of the parking lot and it looks like he is staying there for the duration of the night. He seems familiar to me and then I realize I met him recently. This is Gabby!

I get out of the Rav4, approach Gabby and say in an even tone, hoping not to startle him, "Hey Gabby, it is me, Finn Gaines. Detective Finn Gaines. We met the other day out on West Jefferson."

"Oh, I remember you. I don't think you told me that you were a detective, but I remember that you called me 'sir' and that makes Gabby smile."

Go figure, I gave him five bucks, but he remembers the respect as opposed to the money. My heart melts a little.

"Hey Gabby, I see you are a Tigers fan."

"Oh yes, sir." He tilts the brim of his newly acquired Tigers hat downward and then back up. "I try to find a Tiger game on TV whens ever I can. I get to see maybe a quarter of them. Can't really go to a game. The tickets are too gosh darn expensive, Detective. It's a crime Detective!"

"Well, I will see if I can rectify that for you."

Gabby's face lights up. "Are you serious? I am guessing you are thinking only if I can help you with something."

"I am absolutely serious and that is regardless of whether you can help me. That is a promise from one Tigers fan to another." I am not a huge fan, but I do like to take in a few games each year.

216

Many of the unfortunate souls who live on the streets are often creatures of habit and I am hoping that Gabby is one of those. "Gabby, do you camp out here often?"

"Yeah, pretty much every night. When people gets doggy bags to go, sometimes they give them to me. I'm not a huge fan of Mexican food, but they give big portions here and it doesn't travel good. Gets soggy and all. Customers don't mind givin' it away. They often change their minds and give it to Gabby."

"Ah, I see. Considering you are a Tigers fan, do you know who David Stone and Jimmy Greyson are?"

"I have read about Stone. I get lots of old newspapers out of the trash, so I can keep up on the news and all. Haven't seen him play yet though. And Greyson sure, I know him. I see him here actually once in a while."

"Do you know what Stone looks like?"

"Kinda. He's a brother, right?"

"Yes, he is, or was, black. Unfortunately, he died in a car crash not far from here. He was here that night. April 13. Did you see him here then?"

"Oh, that's terrible, but I'm sorry. I'm terrible with dates. You know I get the newspaper a day or two later, right? And I'm getting fewer and fewer all the time with the stupid online stuff. What does he drive? I'm pretty good with cars."

"He drove an SUV that looks just like mine." I point to it, "A Toyota Rav4. Just like that one, but silver, not black."

"Oh, there are lots of those around."

"Yeah, but it is a hybrid."

"A hybrid?"

"It runs on gas or electric. Oh yeah, and when you back up, it makes this god awful sound like something out of Star Wars."

"Ah yeah, I remember the dude. Yeah, there was a brother that got into this SUV. When it backed up, it sounded like screaming angels!"

"Yes, that is it!"

"Yeah, you know what. I'm not certain, but I do remember that. I was dozing off and that shriek rattled me. I am pretty sure it was a black guy driving. Can't be certain though."

"That is good, Gabby. Thanks so much. Now, would that have been a night that you might have seen Jimmy Greyson as well?"

217

"Yeah, I think I did. A little later, I woke up and I saw him leaning against that wall over there." Gabby points and gets up. "It was funny. I think he was drinking quite a bit."

"Why do you say that?"

Gabby turns around to face the brick wall and demonstrates. "He was standing like this." Gabby puts one arm up above his head, places his palm on the wall and spreads his legs. "It was like he was trying to balance himself while takin' a leak against that there wall."

I wonder why he would not have used the washroom in the restaurant, but then again, he did say that he was on his way out when a fan bought him another beer. I guess it is not unusual for a guy to urinate in public as opposed to going back into the restaurant.

I was wondering earlier; I might as well check with Gabby. "Gabby, do you remember what Greyson was driving?"

"He sometimes drives a pickup and sometimes a fancy black sports car. That night, I seem to remember him getting into the pickup. Yeah, right after he was peeing, he got into the truck over there. I hadn't noticed it earlier."

Gabby goes off on somewhat of a long, convoluted tangent talking about some noisy motorcycles disturbing his sleep and I bring him back by showing him a picture of Stefan Johnson that I pull up on my phone. "Have you seen this guy at all? In particular, that same night?"

"No, can't say I have. He's a pretty average lookin' white dude."

"Yeah, you are right." Gabby is right as he is a very nondescript looking guy. Average height, weight and everything.

"He parked a Toyota Corolla about where my car is at, right about 10 o'clock. Left about midnight too. Oh, and he talked with Stone and Greyson when he got here."

Gabby shakes his head no, "I usually get here around 11 or so."

I pull up Starr Stewart's driver's license photo on my phone. "How about her?"

Gabby just grins, "She is one fine-looking woman. I think I might of seen her."

I get a little excited, because I have differing stories as to her departure time. Although the cell phone records align with her recollection and not Johnson's.

"Did you see her arrive or leave that night?"

"No, that's not what I meaned. I have seen her when I hang out on the East Side. Just east of the stadiums a bit. She works a corner there at times. Use ta be a real regular there. Then, she up and left all of a sudden. Only works there on Mondays, now for some reason now."

"Ah, I see. Tell you what, one last question? Well, I guess two. Is it safe to leave your stuff here if you leave for a bit?"

"Oh, for sure. Nobody wants this crap. Except maybe another homeless guy, but we respect each other's stuff."

"Okay, the second question. Do you want some Mexican food or something else like Nemo's? It is not far."

"Oh Nemo's would be amazing! Are you sure?"

"Yes, I am Gabby. Hop in and we will head over there. I am itching for a burger and fries!"

"Are you sure you want me in your car? I'm not exactly clean and all."

"No worries my friend. It is a rental."

As we are driving to Nemo's, I realize that taking Gabby for dinner is taking me off task, but that is absolutely fine. He has been quite helpful. I make note that once I return Gabby to his alcove, I need to remember to go into Xochimilco to track down the bouncer. Hopefully, the same bouncer is working or they can at least point me in the right direction to find him. Anyway, I have not eaten in a while, so I will enjoy my time tonight with my new friend, Gabby.

Chapter 3.32 – Back to the Scene

I get up in the morning and I am feeling pretty optimistic, although my stomach is rebelling. A burger and fries at one in the morning is not exactly good for my system. I do not know how I used to that in my younger days, along with a half a dozen beers or so.

I text Officer Hodgson and ask her if she will meet me at the Stone accident site and she responds asking for a time. We agree to meet at 10:30.

That gives me enough time to get everything together. After some googling on the web, I go into my kitchen, pull some ingredients together and mix up a pair of concoctions. I feel like a kid again with excitement. I then gather my things and go out to the Rav4 and stop at a local hardware store. A young boy helps me load my vehicle, so I give him a five-dollar tip.

The boy responds with, "You know, I have worked here for two years and that is my first tip."

I respond with, "I am feeling good about today, son."

I make my way to the crash site and I arrive a few minutes early, but Officer Hodgson is already there leaning against her cruiser.

"So, what are you up to, Detective Gaines?"

"A couple of experiments and I need your keen eye! I need you to park on the other side of the road though and then please hop in if you do not mind."

Officer Hodgson moves the cruiser, exits it, and locks it, before getting into the passenger seat of my rental vehicle.

We head eastward back towards downtown and I show her how the cruise control works, although the vehicle gets mad at me if I keep my hands off the steering wheel for too long. We drive until West Jefferson ends and head north on Clark Street. After about a mile, I make a U-turn and head back to the south. I accelerate quickly to 56mph, set the cruise and then cancel it.

As I am coasting to the curve, I take the water bottle from the cup holder and jam it into the steering wheel at the 5:00 position. It fits between the arm coming from the horn and the actual steering wheel.

I brake enough that we are now at a slow crawl and I ask, "Hodge, could you safely exit the vehicle right now if you wanted to?"

She tries the door handle and it is locked, so she unlocks the door and opens the door slightly and says, "Yes, I am sure I could."

"Okay, press the resume button here," and I point to it. "And you can close the door now."

The vehicle accelerates and we are both amazed at how the jiggling of the water in the bottle is enough to fool the car that someone is actually making steering adjustments. The Rav4 hits 56mph and navigates the curves in the road flawlessly. We eventually approach her cruiser by the bridge and as anticipated, we fly by the accident scene at 56 mph.

She asks, "How the heck did you figure that out?"

"I am not too sure, but I kept trying to figure out what was in Stone's vehicle and why. I repeatedly asked myself why there was a water bottle there?"

"Well, to drink the water would be a logical reason! Dah!"

"Yeah, but I had the bottle tested and there was no DNA in the water that remained in the bottle. That is virtually impossible unless you pour the water into your mouth from a distance."

"Ah, I see. Great job, Sherlock. Now how do you get it to crash on demand?"

"Well, it is now time for experiment number two."

I cancel the cruise, make a U-turn and head back to park at the scene.

Once out of the Rav4, I open the rear hatch and show Hodge what I have.

"First, I found online how you can make watercolor paint for kids. It is easy, really. It is just corn starch and stuff. Not rocket science." I pull out two paint rollers and two trays.

"I will take the white and the narrow roller. You take the wider one with black paint. You cover the middle line and the curb line from the bridge to about 20 yards or so back. I will paint new white lines."

In a matter of less than 5 minutes, we finish. We both stand back and admire our artwork. The lane now runs off the road.

I am getting anxious to try this out and shout, "Hop back in and we can try this again."

Hodge yells, "Sure, but I am driving! Hop in, Sherlock! Or should I call you Picasso? Now, I am thinking that I will set the cruise at like 45 mph though. I want to be sure that I can stop this thing before we take a bath."

"How about 50?"

"We will see."

A few minutes later, we are ready to try this again. We have to pull over to wait a minute though, as a car makes its way past us. Hodge waits an extra half of a minute, pulls the vehicle off the shoulder to enter the roadway, and we are on our way once again.

Within a minute, we are barreling down West Jefferson hands free at 48 mph. As we approach our road art, Hodge exclaims, "Hang on!"

The SUV swerves right as anticipated, leaves the roadway and Hodge engages the brakes. The anti-lock brakes are doing everything they can; we narrowly miss the big boulder that Stone had hit, and we skid to a stop in the loose gravel.

Hodge and I turn to each other with stunned looks on our faces and we instinctively raise our hands for a high five.

Hodge then says, "You know, we could have probably done this experiment with like 30 mph!"

"Yeah probably, but man that was exhilarating!"

Hodge responds to that with a punch to my shoulder.

Then, I slap myself in the head, "Oh boy, I forgot I told them at the rental place that no one else was going to drive this vehicle. Good thing you stopped in time!"

Hodge responds with, "You probably didn't get the extra coverage either, eh?" and we both have a good laugh. It is not that funny, but we are both running on adrenaline!

"Hey now, it is time for the final stage of the experiment."

"Yeah, I figured as much."

Hodge puts the Rav4 into reverse and backs her way towards our artwork. Of course, the vehicle makes the high-pitched screaming noise along the way. She opens the back hatch and grabs one of the big jugs of water. I do so as well. These are the type that you put upside down into a water cooler. Four jugs later and we have removed most of the paint from the roadway.

As the water sheds off the roadway, puddles form and I say, "So, I know it is early, but is this what you saw?"

"I suspect it is. You are a genius!"

"Please call my wife and tell her that!" which gets a funny look from Hodge. I continue, "How about I buy you lunch and then we can come back in an hour to check it out?"

"Sure, sounds good, but we have to make it quick and no donut shop!!"

Chapter 3.33 – Tidying Up

Over lunch at Nemo's of all places, we talk about how it might be a good idea for Officer Hodgson to pursue the detective route. She is very smart, has a good sense about her, and can read people well. That is most of the battle.

Just before 1:00, we return to inspect our puddles. When we exit our respective vehicles, Hodge yells to me, "You really nailed it, Gaines. This big one here will probably be the last one to evaporate and it looks just like what I saw that day."

"See what I mean, you have detective instincts."

"Well, if I was a good detective, I would have taken a picture of it."

"I guess that makes me a shitty detective then. I did not even notice it."

"Oh Gaines, I did not mean that."

"I am just pulling your chain, Hodge. No worries."

"You have the method now and you said you have several motives. Can you connect the dots?"

"I am hoping so, but I need to do a few more interviews to address some unanswered questions."

***

Prior to setting up interviews, I put in motion to get banking records from all our suspects, including our deceased suspect.

I meet up with Jenny at a coffee shop near the Magic Stick, as I do not want to push my luck having any further meetings at the bar. Tucked away in a corner, far away from other patrons, we review the events of the Home Opener evening. I clarify what she saw regarding the pills in Greyson's jacket, as well as how things progressed at the apartment. She also knows Frankie decently well, so it is a good opportunity to get her perspective on him. Finally, I run through the night at the Whiskey Bar with her. I already have Greyson's and the owner's take on the events, so Jenny is just presumably confirming what

I already know. Obviously, I have no opportunity to talk with Wohlers, aka Anthony, as he is once again, in the wind.

I move onto the next interview. As much as it would be a delight to go to the Riv strip joint, I opt to call Starr Stewart to review some items with her as well. Doing the interview by phone probably saves me a couple of hours and at least forty bucks! Her responses help me to begin to sort out the discrepancy between her recollection and Johnson's on the night of the murder.

***

I am getting close to calling it a day, but I check my email and I already have most of the banking records. Ironically, there are entries in more than one bank account that raise red flags for me. I have some homework tonight to piece things together.

As I am heading out of my office, I see that Sergeant Brown is still in. I knock on his door jam and say, "Mind if I come in?"

"Sure, have a seat buckaroo."

Buckaroo? Really?

"Oh, I will not be long, Sarge. Are you getting heat from the media about the Stone case?"

"A bit from the media, but more from those above me!"

"I am darn close, Sarge. I can just feel it. You can tell the media that I am ready to change that *person of interest* to *prime suspect* in the near future. I am hoping I will hit that 48-hour target."

"Well, I think you are down to less than 24 now, aren't you?"

I nod to him and say, "Good night, Sarge. I am going to go do my homework."

"Don't let your dog eat it on you."

I really do not understand this guy's sense of humor.

Part Four - The Final Stretch

Chapter 4.1 – Homework With Danica

Despite objections from his wife, Detective Finn Gaines takes over the dining area of the kitchen. Stacks of paper are scattered about the dining room table in disarray. However, where the detective's organizational skills shine is on the patio door out to the back deck. Using erasable markers, Gaines has created a massive diagram of the Detroit core on the glass. He stands in front of the diagram, with both hands on his hips and a marker hanging from his mouth, like a cigarette.

It is obvious that Gaines' mind is spinning and trying to connect the dots in this complicated case. A seemingly obvious singular car crash has evolved into a complex murder plot, along with a spin-off murder. One murderer is in custody and the prime suspect in the other is deceased.

Gaines' wife, Danica, enters the dining area and asks, "How the heck can you see that drawing with it so dark outside?"

Gaines mumbles, "It is actually getting difficult."

Danica walks to the side of the sliding doors and flicks on the deck light. "Is that better?" The deck light generates enough back lighting that the makeshift drawing board comes to life.

"Ah yes, thanks so much, hon."

"No problem. Just make sure that I get credit for solving the crime you already solved. I do not get why you are pouring over all this. The media is reporting that the Detroit Police Department has already determined that the murderer is dead."

"Yes, I know dear. It is sure looking that way. But I need to be one hundred percent positive before I finalize my report. Brownie is taking heat for me to wrap this up A-SAP."

"Well, you always tell me that you need to nail down motive, opportunity, and means. Do you have a motive?"

"Yes, there is this girl named Jessie. Johnson and Ticklewood both thought that Stone slept with her, meanwhile, he did not.

Ticklewood ended up killing Johnson because he sexually assaulted Jessie. We assume anyway; he has clammed right up in custody."

"So, this shit show moved from a love triangle to a square, back to a triangle, then to a line. And now, it is a love dot," Danica pauses, then adds, "for at least the next 10 to 20 years."

"Correct. You summed that up well!"

"Did this Johnson guy have the opportunity?"

Finn points to the Clark Street – West Jefferson transition point, which is marked with a star and says, "Yes, cell phone data puts both Johnson and Stone at this location minutes prior to the crash. In fact, Johnson claims that he was there. However, he claims that his date was performing, uh, ah."

"Just say it dear. We are adults."

Finn turns red and finishes his sentence, "She was performing oral sex on him."

"You're so cute when you blush." She continues, "Okay, so there is opportunity and perhaps this quote, date, unquote was in on it with Johnson. Let's move on to means."

"Yes, I figured out how the murder was accomplished," and Finn then points to the star. "This is where the murderer launched the vehicle with an incapacitated Stone in the vehicle." Then, he draws a big arrow pointing to the accident scene that is marked by an asterisk.

"How was Stone incapacitated?"

"A mixture of drugs and alcohol. It appears that Stone may have had a drug and alcohol dependency issue. The murderer managed to get him to consume more, but I am not sure if the murderer forced him or tricked him into it."

"That Johnson guy seems like a slam dunk to me. And, the oral sex thing is just a really lame alibi."

"Yes, I know. In fact, the date," Finn makes air quotes and continues, "claims she was not there. She was still up by the restaurant, up there where it says MT, on the phone with her sister."

Danica asks, "What do her cell phone records say?"

"The phone records agree with her."

"Johnson sounds guilty to me! Slam dunk!"

"Possibly" He pauses and then moves to means, "Like I said, I am pretty sure I know how the murderer overrode the car's safety features. However, I am not sure the late Mr. Johnson was that savvy. The guy who is, is in the wind. I cannot find him."

"Who's that?"

"Anthony, a guy who was a waiter at a Whiskey Bar. He got fired recently and is plenty smart enough to do it and it looks like he has killed before. But we have no idea where he is."

"Could the two of them have worked together?"

"Good question. It is quite possible, because this Anthony guy gave Greyson and Stone a beer at the restaurant. I suspect that Anthony laced Stone's beer. We cannot talk with either suspect and we cannot find any electronic communication between them."

Danica adds, "But then again, if they were smart, they would not call or text each other."

"Correct, and if they were working together, I just cannot see how they ever got connected in the first place."

"What kind of businesses are they involved in?"

"Oh, that might be it. Johnson and Wohlers were both fired from serving jobs, but Johnson was rumored to be dealing prescription medication on the side. Perhaps Wohlers was a customer."

"You really do sound like you are close to nailing this down." As she shows some leg through the opening of her satin housecoat, she says, "I am tired hon, so I am heading to bed. You joining me?"

"Yeah, I will, but do not wait up."

"So much for trying to take your mind off work. You sure know how to make a girl feel sexy."

Gaines just grins at his wife as an email arrives on his phone. He reads the email and realizes that he is not joining Danica tonight.

Chapter 4.2 – Request for Help

Greyson is on his back in bed, staring at his bedroom ceiling, running plays through his head. Meanwhile, Jenny is snuggled in on his left shoulder. Her eyes open and she gives him a wet kiss on his chest.

Greyson says, "Oh, good morning, sweetheart."

She slowly slides her left hand up his chest and reaches up to his neck to pull them tighter together. Things are just getting intimate and Greyson's phone begins to ring on the nightstand.

He reaches over and hits a button to silence the ringing, but by the time he turns back to Jenny, the phone rings again. This time, he checks to see who is calling and the display says that it is the Detroit Police Department. "Oh shit, I better take this."

"Jimmy Greyson here."

"Jimmy, it is Detective Finn Gaines calling. I hope I did not wake you up."

"Oh no, I am good. I have been up for a while." To that, Jenny smiles and Greyson continues, "Hey, congratulations Detective. I hear you nailed Stefan for Dave's murder. His family is going to be very relieved that this nightmare has come to a conclusion."

"Well Jimmy, we are not quite there, but I think I am really close to officially declaring that Johnson murdered Dave. He may have had some help and I still need to tie up a couple of loose ends. I think you are probably the one that can help me do that."

"Is that right? How can I help?"

"I was actually hoping that you could come into the station to help me. I have all kinds of documents and drawings, here. It would just work better if you were here in person. I hate to ask, but I really do need your help to get justice for your friend's death."

"Okay Detective, when are you thinking?"

"In a half-hour? Does that work?"

Greyson looks at Jenny who is staring up at him and he says, "I will be there in an hour."

Chapter 4.3 – Welcome to the War Room

Jimmy Greyson is in the shower a half-hour later and out the door forty-five minutes from the time that Detective Gaines had called him. As Greyson rides the elevator, he ponders what kind of help Gaines needs. Because it is a nice sunny day, the Challenger keys are in his pocket and he admits that he gets a little adrenaline flowing as he walks up to the car.

Pulling out of his space, he giggles as he thinks of Amp goosing the accelerator and chirping the tires in the garage. Greyson is more controlled in his driving and with five minutes to spare, he pulls into the visitor parking space at the police station. He exits the vehicle and heads to the front door, but he looks back, just for about two seconds.

A young officer coming out of the building holds the door open for him and says, "You know, if you don't look back and admire it, you bought the wrong car. I like it."

"I agree whole-heartedly. And, thank you, I like it too."

He approaches the front desk and says, "Hi, it is Jimmy Greyson and I am here to assist Detective Finn Gaines. He is expecting me."

The front desk officer says, "Correct, he told me you were coming. It's not often we get a celebrity, well at least a positive celebrity, in here. Gaines is just off to the left here in the War Room. Can I get you a water?" Before hearing a response, he pulls out two water bottles and puts them on the counter.

"Oh, that would be nice. Thank you. You must be expecting us to be a while."

Before the desk officer can respond, Gaines says, "Oh, thank you for coming here so quickly, Jimmy. Come on in here. Welcome to…"

Jimmy interjects, "The War Room, I understand it is called. No problem. My pleasure to help you, sir."

"Please just call me Finn."

"Okay, Finn. Thanks."

    "I see the old geyser at the desk loaded you up with water. I can get you black coffee too if you want. You take it black if I remember correctly."

    "Water is good right now, but thanks."

Chapter 4.4 – Demons

Jimmy looks around the room and sees stacks of papers on a large table in the middle of the room and a laptop computer on a small desk in the corner diagonally across from the door. And then on the wall to the left of the door, there is a whiteboard. Finn's elaborate diagram that he redrew from a cell phone photo this morning, fills most of the board.

"So, where do we start, Finn? I cannot believe all the documents you have. And cool map."

"I think I need to get inside David Stone's mind and who would be better to help me with that, than you? I need to understand some of the demons that he faced. You knew him fairly well and you also know what it would be like to come into the major leagues at a young age with everyone thinking you are going to save the team. What kind of pressure was Dave under?"

"You're right. The team has been in the dumps for the last couple of years and VanBuskirk was brought in to rebuild the team. Rebuilding takes time and VanB is aiming for a contender in five years, but the fans and the media want immediate results."

"Oh, I can relate. I am sure the mayor wanted this case solved the day after the accident."

"Exactly. A rebuild takes time to get the team into contention. Frankly, I will not likely be a part of the team, by the time we do contend. I know in public, I say otherwise, but we need to give everyone hope. Anyway, in the long run, the team is, well was, being built around Dave. The pressure would have been immense."

"Do you think Dave was up to that challenge?"

"Truthfully, yes." Jimmy pauses and adds, "He probably had more talent right out of the gate than I did, but I think I understood the game a little better than him when I was his age. I am a student of the game, whereas Dave is a natural talent. He was smart and he was just starting the process of understanding the game. I hope that makes sense.

Studying the game can accelerate your trajectory and for guys like me, I hope it will eke out an extra few years, compared to others with comparable talent."

"I saw your first game back and I think I saw a lot of talent. I loved that first hit and the final play of the game."

"Nah, I have a base amount of talent left, but my first hit was me knowing what pitch was coming and where to put the ball to get maximum impact in the situation. And, that final play, again, I knew what to expect and I could cheat a little to make it look like I cover more ground than I really do."

"That is interesting. So much for the dumb jock theory."

Jimmy just smiles.

Finn asks to clarify, "So, what kind of combination of talent and smarts do you think Dave had? Would he surpass your numbers?"

"Yeah, I think he would've. I think I was faster out of the gate, but he had the potential to become more than I ever was. I think he would've been a franchise player."

"Interesting. Anyway, let us cycle back to the pressure angle. Our analysis of his protein powder in his apartment indicates it had PEDs, performance enhancement drugs in it. Another division of DPD will follow up on that angle, but what is your take? Would he be taking a PED on his own or would someone be helping him? Or other?"

"What do you mean by other?"

"Like someone spiking his protein powder."

"Hmm, good questions. Considering the pressure he was under, I could see him juicing, but it is just so risky. It is a great way to tank a promising career. It is not the eighties or nineties anymore. Nowadays, it is more the guys trying to hang onto their career that take the risk, as opposed to those starting out. NCAA has strict rules and drug testing, so it is not like he could get to the *show* if he was juicing along the way."

Finn laughs and says, "The *show*? Bull Durham right? I promise I will not call you Crash!"

"I appreciate that, Finn. That joke is getting old."

"How about sabotage, Jimmy?"

"I guess that would be a possibility, but then it would have to be one of our Trainers."

"Or someone who has been in his apartment."

Jimmy is taken aback by that comment. "As far as I know, I was the only one who has been in his apartment. That was when I babysat his SUV when he was getting the back window replaced. And where would I get that stuff? That could end my career and Hall of Fame Induction if word got out that I secured a PED. If I were going to risk buying a PED, I would be better off using it myself. At least I might get a benefit from it."

"Oh, trust me Jimmy, I am not insinuating anything. I was wondering if Dave ever took women back to his place? Maybe a setup."

"Nah, he was pretty straight-laced actually. That booty call talk on the night he died surprised me, actually. It seemed out of character for him."

"I do not think this PED thing is even relevant to his murder. Call it a hunch, but I think I am going to let someone else pursue that and let it run where it takes them. I have to warn you that it may take someone down in the organization."

"Shoot, they are all like family. I would be surprised if it came from one of ours."

Gaines emphasizes the first word when he says, "Everyone is like family?"

"Well, mostly. That raises a good point. We had an Assistant Coach quit during Spring Training: Wayne Bedard. He blew a gasket on me and Dave one night because we smoked some cigars. He might be someone to track down. It was so strange."

"Okay, worth noting. Thanks. Would he still have access to any of the facilities?"

"Unbelievably yes. VanBuskirk brought him back, in some kind of lower capacity. I am not sure what he's doing, 'cause he steers clear of me. I really don't understand where the tension came from."

"Hmm. That is really interesting, so that is Wayne Bedard, right?"

Jimmy nods to confirm and continues, "Yes, that is Bedard spelled B, E, D, A, R, D. I just have no idea where a PED would come from though and I hope that the DPD can track that down. We need to nip that crap in the bud. Maybe Bedard is mixed up in that, I really don't know."

"I completely agree, Jimmy."

Gaines goes over to the table and picks up several pieces of paper.

"We need to talk painkillers, Jimmy."

"I have told you before; I think Dave had a problem. I told you about him taking pills from my jacket at the Magic Stick, right?"

"Yeah, you did and Jenny confirmed that suspicion, too. Now, think about the Home Opener Night and how Dave got really tired, really fast. Come and look over here." Finn leads Jimmy over to the computer in the corner and pulls up a video. "This is when you ordered the second pitcher of beer. You carried over the pitcher, but watch Stefan the bartender, get your glasses. It appears that he puts something into two of the glasses. We are speculating ground-up painkillers."

"I heard about this, but seeing it with my own eyes is disturbing. He had a thing for Jessie and he saw Dave as competition. He drugged Jessie to take advantage of her in the Storage Room. Pure scum. I hate to say it, but Frankie did the world a favor."

"Officially, I cannot agree with you, Jimmy."

Finn goes back to the table and picks up two documents. "The Tic Tac containers bother me, Jimmy."

"Containers? As opposed to one?"

"Yes, right. You said there was one in the Rav4, but you cannot remember when, right?"

"Correct."

"And you picked it up, right?"

"Yes, correct again. And then, Dave got protective of it. It was strange."

"Well, there were painkillers in that Tic Tac packet at some point, before we found it in the vehicle after the accident. The strange thing is that there were only Dave's fingerprints on it. I thought it was odd, because I found the receipt from when he bought the Tic Tacs. I went to the gas station and the Tic Tac packets are displayed in a tree. I imagine you have seen the displays by the register. The gas station attendants load the tree one by one, so there should have been more fingerprints. That is why I got very suspicious, as there should have been at least one more set of prints. Then, when you said you handled it, it got even stranger. Either someone switched the packets or wiped the packet clean. Any thoughts?"

"I have no idea, Finn. Is that why you said containers plural?"

"No, actually. He points to the other document. This packet was found in Stefan Johnson's apartment and it had painkillers in it, too. So, why would both Dave and Stefan carry painkillers in Tic Tac packets? I guess you are the only one using pill bottles, Jimmy."

Both laugh briefly and Jimmy says, "You got me, Finn. Any theories?"

"Not a one. How about you? Can you theorize something?"

"Well, I think Dave was skimming my pills and maybe he was just storing the pills in his container. As for Stefan, he makes a habit of drugging women, not to mention Dave! So, maybe he uses the container because it is inconspicuous."

"Huge coincidence though, is it not? Homicide detectives do not believe in coincidences."

"Good point. That would be a huge coincidence."

"After what we have talked about, do you still feel that Dave had his own demons?"

"Yeah, I do. I don't think he would intentionally take the PEDs, but he was drinking a fair amount and I do believe he took some of my pills."

"Did you call him on it? I mean taking the pills."

"Yes, I did, but he denied it. But, it's obvious that he did have painkillers. I think he was hooked. And, his work on the field was certainly suffering. He was off his game."

"That is true. So, suppose he was fighting some demons, but not doing PEDs, at least not intentionally."

"We need to talk about the Jessie connection, but do you want a coffee now?"

"Yes, please, Finn."

"I will be right back. Give me five. Oh, and there is a washroom just across the hall if you need it."

Jimmy stays in the room and moves over to the whiteboard. He is amazed at how much Finn has pieced together. Jimmy is fascinated by the detail in the parking lot by Xochimilco and understands most of it; however, he sees the initials GB and wonders what that represents.

Chapter 4.5 – "Anthony"

Jimmy is still looking at the whiteboard when Finn returns with two cups of black coffee.

"Here you go, Jimmy. Sorry, I do not have any donuts."

"Geez, you beat me to it! I am just admiring your artwork here, Finn. This is good."

"Ah thanks, but can we hold off on that for a bit? I want to talk to you about this Anthony character first."

"You gave me your account of his actions at the Whiskey Bar. He seemed quite slimy. I talked to Gord and his recollection is right in line with yours for the events that night."

"Gord is a straight shooter."

"Oh yeah, and Jenny's recollection is bang on with both of you."

"Well, that is comforting that I didn't lead you astray," Jimmy says with a smile.

Finn grabs another piece of paper from the center table and hands it to Jimmy. "Look at the rap sheet on this guy. Real name is Norbert Andrew Wohlers. There is a warrant out for him as he is the prime suspect in his wife's death down in Toledo."

"Holy shit!"

"And get this, he is some sort of computer whiz. He hacked into a car's computer somehow to cause an accident involving his wife. He got nailed on insurance fraud, but then disappeared, allegedly after severely beating his wife and leaving her for dead in a ditch."

"Oh man, I pissed off the wrong guy! Do you think he is involved here?"

"Possibly. It would not be too far out of his wheelhouse."

Jimmy smiles as he says, "Hey, you got the expression right."

Finn smiles briefly too and then gets back on task with, "Fill me in more about the night at Xochomilco and running into Anthony there."

"Sure, I just saw him a few tables over and I felt like he was staring us down. I was getting a little nervous. Knowing what I know

now, I should've been scared. We were close to being ready to leave and he shows up at the table with two beers. He apologized for what he did at the Whiskey Bar and he left. It was sure an about face."

"Was there anything left to chance as to who drank which beer?"

"Actually, no. He initially placed them between us, but then he placed one in front of Dave and one in front of me."

"You know Jimmy. You have an eye for detail. I like working with you. If you ever decide to leave baseball and earn a salary that is only a fraction of what you make now, …"

Jimmy finishes the sentence, "I know where to find you. This stuff does fascinate me though. To me, it's like running plays through my head."

"But it is so important to get details. For example, if Wohlers placed the beers one in front of the other and they were both equidistant from you two, that is completely different. If he was trying to drug Dave, he would not leave things up to chance as to who took which beer."

"I see what you mean. So, you think Anthony, I mean Wohlers drugged Dave."

"It is possible. Dave was not stumbling down the stairs, was he?"

"No, he was tired and all, but I didn't think he was tired enough to fall asleep while driving. Then again, that is what I thought after the Magic Stick, too."

"Okay, let us move on to the next topic."

"And what is that?"

Finn rubs both of his temples with his thumbs and pauses. Then, he says, "Hang on, let us assume that Wohlers and Johnson *were* working together. What kind of beer was it?"

Jimmy is taken aback by the change in direction and the seemingly random question, but he responds quickly, "Sol, double limed."

"There you go. That is good detail and important. If Wohlers put ground up pills in the beer, Dave would not likely taste it over two wedges of lime. It stands to reason that Dave was drugged both at the Magic Stick and Xochimilco by Johnson and Wohlers, respectively."

"So, maybe they *were* working together. That makes sense."

Chapter 4.6 – The Run Down

Finn points at the whiteboard and says, "Okay, Jimmy we can move over to the whiteboard, now. I can tell you are a visual learner and you will like this. As you can guess, this is the Detroit core. The river along the bottom, of course. Do you like my little blue waves?"

"Cute."

"There is the Renaissance Center, which of course, anchors the downtown and provides a beautiful silhouette for the Detroit skyline."

"From the Windsor side, anyway."

"True," Finn replies and then continues, "There is Comerica Park. I forgot to identify your apartment building, but it is close to these, right?"

Jimmy points to the approximate location and Finn prints a JG where Jimmy's finger is indicating.

Finn says, "You will know this area well, but maybe not the west side so much."

"I know it fairly well too, as that is where Tiger Stadium stood."

"Ah, true. I actually usually refer to the new park as the *New Tiger Stadium*. It pains me to say *Comerica Park,* like I just did."

"I hear ya, but it is finance. Naming rights are big business. The park names are falling like crazy. Look at the NHL. Now that Joe Louis Arena is gone, I think there are only one or two non-sponsored arenas left."

"Madison Square Gardens would be one," and without even a pause, Finn segues to, "okay, so the MT is Mexicantown Restaurant and the X is Xochimilco."

"I was wondering what the GB is."

"Oh, that is Gabby. He is a homeless guy that I met in the parking lot. He can confirm some pieces of information and time stamps for us."

"Ah good, is he reliable? Being homeless and all?"

"Actually yes, he is good. The funny thing about homeless people is that to many, they just blend into the pavement. I am amazed how many so-called regular people do not even notice the homeless."

"I suppose that is true. If he was there that night, I certainly didn't see him. I hope that doesn't make me a bad person."

"So, let us get into the run down here."

"Rundown? That is an odd description. In baseball terms, a rundown is what we used to call *hot box* as a kid. It is when a runner is caught between two bases and the runner has to try to get to either base without being tagged by one of the fielders."

"Oh, I see what you mean. No, I mean that we are going to rundown or run through the timeline. There is no one caught between bases here, except maybe the murderer or murderers, as the case may be."

"Okay boss, how about we go through the run down then?"

"Alright, bear with me, but please do jump in if you want to add anything."

Jimmy replies, "Absolutely, I will if I can."

"On April 1st, Starr Stewart visits the Magic Stick, MS on our map up here on Woodward Avenue. She is there with her girlfriend and she hits it off with Stefan, the bartender. Apparently, she likes it when guys look down her top. Almost two weeks later, they make a date for Mexican food. Their plan is to meet at the restaurant and she arrives slightly before 10 and gets a table."

"That is when we arrive, as well. Dave parks here."

"Okay, good. Dave drove a Toyota Rav4, so put a TR there."

Jimmy continues, "And, I park here." Jimmy prints CS.

"Chevy Silverado?"

"Correct."

Finn says, "Hang on a second," and he paces, while running his ten fingers through his hair from front to back. After three or four seconds, he continues, "Sorry about the tangent. I am a pretty simple guy and just have one car. It is an old Dodge Journey. How do you decide which vehicle to drive?"

Again, Jimmy is taken aback, but he is starting to get accustomed to Finn's odd mannerisms and random questions. "Normally, it depends on the weather. The Challenger does not like rain or snow, obviously. And, I guess it depends on the area I am going to drive, as well."

"Really, it does not like rain?"

"Truthfully, no. The ass end will kick quite a bit."

"Hm, that is strange, but okay."

"Why is that strange, Detective?"

"From what I have read, the Challenger and Charger are mechanically very similar. Meanwhile, we drive our Charger cruisers all year round, rain or shine and in the snow, too."

"If I am not mistaken Finn, the Police get the Pursuit Package and I believe that many of those are all-wheel drive. My SRT is rear wheel drive and with summer tires. I am sure even if you do have a rear wheel drive version, it will have at least all-season tires, until it snows. And of course, you'll run winter tires in the winter. There really is no comparison."

Detective Gaines plows ahead, "Ah, that makes sense. The weather was great that night, so I guess you were more worried about the neighbourhood than the weather, right?"

"Don't remember exactly, but yeah, probably."

"Okay, sorry to interrupt the flow, but as you have probably noticed, if a question pops into my head, I ask it! Where was Johnson parked?"

"Oh, I *have* noticed! Anyway, Johnson was parked on the road, I will put a TC there for Toyota Corolla. I have no idea where Wohlers, aka Anthony or Starr parked, let alone what they drove." Jimmy pauses in thought and then adds, "Ah, now I think I know why it is relevant what kind of vehicle each person drove that night."

Finn rubs his chin and then says, "Oh, do not get ahead of yourself too much." He continues with his train of thought, "Starr said she parked in the parking lot as opposed to on the street, but maybe I should follow up with her if I see her again. As for Anthony, we may never see the guy again, although hopefully he gets scooped up on his previous warrant."

Jimmy chimes in, "Dave, Stefan, and I all arrive at basically the same time, right around 10 o'clock. This is where we talk with Stefan. I will put an exclamation mark there. Dave was good and tried to break the ice with him, by talking about his car. Then, Dave made a comment about Jessie, something like she is not for him and Stefan got all pissed. That is when I used my cane to put a stop to the festivities."

Finn rubs his temples and then says, "That cane can come in handy!"

Jimmy continues, "We part ways and Stefan heads to MT and we go to X."

"Tell me about the dinner."

"It was uneventful really, other than Anthony showing up. Dave and I talked a bit about girls, namely Jessie. It is not like I wanted to double date or anything, but she is not a bad girl. She needs to cut away from Stefan and Frankie though. Well, I guess mission accomplished on both fronts."

"But your exit is when some events happened, correct?"

"Yes, there was a loudmouth Tigers fan who was harassing us, me for being old and Dave for not coming out too strong in his rookie season. The bouncer took care of him. Unfortunately, if he hung around outside, Dave may have run into him. I didn't really think of it at the time, but I can't picture that guy being involved in this."

"Then, you said that when you were going down the stairs, another guy handed you a beer and insisted that you stay for a drink, right?"

"Yes, exactly. That is not uncommon."

"What kind of beer was it?"

"Oh geez, I am not sure. Oh yeah, it was a Corona. I remember seeing the lime. Just one wedge though."

"Okay. What did you talk about? Get a name from the guy?"

"I may have, but I never remember names of the random autograph seekers. As for what we talked about, he just kept asking me to review plays. Now, that is what I have a photographic memory for!"

"Random question here, sorry. When you went to leave, you had another beer, so did you use the washroom before leaving?"

Jimmy pauses and thinks. "I doubt it. I would not go back up the stairs to use it and I really don't know if there is a washroom on the ground floor. You know what, I know it is not exactly the right thing to do, but I actually went pee outside in the parking lot. Is it okay to admit that to a sworn peace officer of the law? And you're right; that was a random question."

Jimmy thinks to himself that he would bet that none of Detective Gaines' questions are actually random. He may have a convoluted plan, but he is sure there is always a plan.

Finn says, "I will explain the peeing question later. Let us rewind to midnight."

"Sure."

Finn points to the MT and says, "Starr Stewart and Stefan Johnson leave the Mexicantown restaurant. Johnson claims that the two of them went for a drive down to around here, where she performed oral sex on him. Cell tower pings confirm that he *did* go down there. However, Stewart indicated that she sat in her car and talked to her sister for half an hour. The cell phone records and tower pings support her version of the events."

Jimmy jumps in, "So, Johnson lied about the reason he drove down to that location?"

"That is what the evidence indicates."

"Interesting. It is not even just *he said – she said*, you have electronic proof. Well done, Finn."

"Well, they do say that cell phones are the key to investigations now! Oh yeah, that reminds me, when Dave left the restaurant, where was his phone?"

"It was in his hands when he told me that he was going to text Jessie."

"Did you see him put it away?"

"No, can't say I did."

"Okay, that is fair. And, did I tell you that his phone was found in his left front pocket at the scene?"

Jimmy shrugs his head to the side and replies, "Not in so many words, but I gathered there was some kind of discrepancy about the phone location."

"Ah, I bet you would love to play poker with me, eh?"

"Not sure about that, Finn. I have a feeling that you have an ability to reel in the big fish."

Finn shrugs that off and says, "Alright, back to the timeline."

Jimmy decides to serve up Finn with some of his own medicine. Jimmy says, "Hang on a second," and then rubs his temples with his thumbs. Then he asks, "So Finn, how did you know which pocket David carried his cell phone in?"

Finn smiles and replies, "Well, you actually told me!"

"Me, how so?"

"The health app you showed me. It is buried in your health app. Dig deeper into the walking asymmetry and you will find that the app tells you the Device Placement. For example, *Left Side of the Body* or in Dave's case, the right side."

"Well, I will be damned. Really?"

"Yes," Finn says and jumps right to the next point. "While you were having one more beer, Dave and Stefan both got down to here," and he points to where Clark Street transitions into West Jefferson Avenue.

"They both drove down there? Or did Johnson go in Dave's SUV? And then maybe Wohlers picked him up?"

"Well, we do not know that for sure. Johnson said he did drive there, but to get oral sex though. Regardless, he did go there, that is for certain."

"I am sorry, Finn, but why does this even matter? How did Johnson and/or Wohlers cause the accident? Oh right, you said this Wohlers guy is a big-time hacker."

"Well, yes, but no. I have a theory that is much lower tech." Finn tosses a full water bottle to Jimmy. "Put your arm out straight," like this and Finn holds his arm straight out in front of himself.

"No, the other arm you fool, the one with the water bottle." They both laugh, "Now, turn it on its side and watch the water."

"The water vibrates a bit. So?"

Finn walks around the table and approaches Jimmy. "You drove the Rav4 and it has these Safety Sense features. The adaptive cruise, blindspot monitoring, and lane tracing assist. I believe the reason they call it lane tracing *assist* is because they do not want the driver to rely upon it consistently. They built in a feature where the lane tracing shuts itself off, if the driver is not holding the steering wheel."

"That is correct. Dave told me that. It is not actually sensing your hands, it is sensing steering adjustments. Ah, I see where you're going with this."

"Yes, exactly. There was a water bottle found in Dave's car and it was maybe 90% full. An interesting fact though, is that there was no DNA in the water bottle."

"Let me guess. When people drink out of a bottle, they backwash a bit."

"Absolutely. See, I am going to make a detective out of you. That water bottle had to be there for a reason and it was not for Dave to take a drink from it."

Jimmy opens the water bottle, puts it in the air above his tilted back head and pours a couple of ounces into his mouth. After wiping his mouth, he says, "Unless he drank like that. Not likely."

Finn grins and says, "Exactly. Now, I will give you ten seconds to solve this puzzle."

"Don't need ten. Can you wedge the water bottle into the steering wheel somehow? And that is why it was important to know what everyone was driving that night. Stefan's Toyota Corolla must have the same Safety Sense features."

"Bingo!"

Jimmy surmises, "Now, this Wohlers character, if he can hijack a car's computer, he can certainly figure out your water bottle trick. Did you try it? Did it work?"

"Yes and no."

"What do you mean?"

"It worked well. The car stays in the middle of the lane perfectly, even around curves. But It worked too well. It sailed right past the accident site."

"Ah, any theories on that?"

"Well, do you remember as a kid painting on big paper on an easel?"

"Yeah, sure."

"You probably wore an adult dress shirt on backwards to protect your clothes. In reality, that was probably overkill. You would have been using watercolor paint that would have easily washed off your clothes."

"Oh, that stuff that looks like a hockey puck and you put a wet brush in it?"

"Yes, exactly. I did another experiment. I made up some black watercolor paint from an online recipe and painted over the road lines by the bridge. I then painted new white lines that veered off the road."

"Did it work?"

"Yes, too well. Officer Hodgson and I almost put my rental vehicle in the Rouge River!"

"You are a regular McGyver! Let me get this straight. Johnson and Wohlers get Dave down there, presumably passed out." Jimmy points to the road transition. "Then, they put him into the vehicle and engage the cruise control. The SUV drives several miles on its own, follows a hand painted detour and crashes. And of course, when the SUV crashes, the water bottle dislodges from the steering wheel and ends up in a random location inside the vehicle. Is that about right? Well, what happened to the lines. I assume they were not there in the morning."

"That is right Jimmy. As for the fake lines, in my experiment, I had four water cooler jugs that I poured onto the paint and it washed away. I am theorizing that the murderer, or murderers, came by shortly afterwards, while Dave was hanging upside down in his vehicle, probably still alive, and they poured water on the road."

Jimmy, visibly shaken by that depiction, puts one hand on the table and sits in a chair. "Oh my god, really? Would he have still been alive?"

"Yes, he likely died an hour or so later from the effects of gravity on his organs and blood. I am also theorizing that it would have to be a bigger vehicle than a Corolla to carry enough water. My four jugs was not really enough and I am sure the murderer, or murderers, would have wanted enough water to ensure there was no trace of the paint in the morning."

Finn let that sink in for a good thirty seconds, then continued, "The cell phone tower pings put the wreck at 12:19 a.m. give or take a couple of minutes. So, moving back to the northeast, you come out of the restaurant at about 12:30 or 12:40 or so. Johnson appears to be back in that area about that time. And, Starr finishes her conversation with her sister about then, as well."

"That is quite the coincidence."

"I do not believe in coincidences. Tell you what. We need something to eat. I will order in a pizza. I think now would be a good time to take ten."

Chapter 4.7 – The Hustle

Finn goes to his office to order pizza, while Jimmy uses the washroom. When Jimmy returns to the room, he rummages through the documents trying to absorb as much information as he can. He then returns to the whiteboard and pictures the moving parts, just like a baseball play. Baseball plays are much more complicated than what spectators see on television. The cameras only follow the ball; however, with most plays, all nine fielders have a job to do. There are many moving parts. Jimmy envisions all the moving parts in this scenario, just like he has replayed it several times already.

Finn returns to the War Room, and finds Jimmy staring at the whiteboard, in a thinker pose. His left hand is holding his right elbow and his right hand is holding his chin. Jimmy says to Finn, "You know what, I don't think my truck was in this spot. I think it was over here."

"Oh, okay, just fix it on the board."

Jimmy does as he was instructed and he rubs out the CS, to reprint it again in the new location.

Jimmy starts with a summary, "The way I see it, Wohlers, on behalf of Johnson, drugged Dave with painkillers. By the time Dave consumed his fourth beer, which was spiked, he would be well on his way to being incapacitated. Add in some force fed Jack Daniels and he would be over the edge. Then, Johnson goes in the vehicle with Dave to that location where Dave and Johnson's cell phone records intersect."

Finn chimes in, "Correct, where Clark Street turns and becomes West Jefferson. I can take over from here, because I did the dry run with my rental Rav4. Johnson must have been wearing gloves, in order to not leave any prints behind. He set the cruise at a significant speed, put the water bottle in the steering wheel, slowed the vehicle to a crawl, hit the Resume button on the steering wheel, and jumped out the passenger door before the car got moving too fast."

Jimmy continues, "Then the car speeds up to a dangerous speed, but with the water bottle jiggling in the steering wheel, it navigates the road just fine and then when it gets to the painted section of the road, the vehicle gets confused and drives off the road."

"Right, then it hits the rock, the water bottle goes flying, the vehicle overturns and it lands on its roof."

"So, you have it solved, Finn. This is good!"

"Not quite, Jimmy. There are missing pieces. Johnson would have had to be sitting in the passenger seat. How does he get the car into gear without having a foot on the brake? He would have to press the accelerator to get the vehicle moving, too."

"Well, that is not too hard to do. He could just reach over and press the pedals with a hand." Jimmy demonstrates reaching down while holding an imaginary steering wheel and trying to keep his head as high as possible.

"Yeah, maybe. More likely, it would be a pole or a stick I guess. That would be doable."

"So, are you convinced that you have it?"

Just then, Finn pulls out his phone, looks at it for about five seconds and slides it back into his pocket. He then looks confused.

"Problem, Finn?"

"Yeah, kind of. We need to cycle back, because we have some new information here."

"So, what new information? Is there an issue?"

"Well, it appears Stephan Johnson did get a sexual favor from Ms. Starr Stewart. We just had an officer talk to Starr's sister. Starr did call her at about midnight that night, but she was sound asleep and did not answer the phone. In fact, she always has her phone set to Do Not Disturb between 10 at night and 7 in the morning. Starr called and left a 30-minute blank voicemail. I am guessing her phone was just sitting in her car, all by itself. She may very well have gone with Stefan to a quiet road, but her phone did not."

"Wow, that complicates things, just when you think you have it nailed. Any chance Starr and Johnson were working together? But, then she had an exit plan to blame it on Johnson if they caught any heat?"

Finn responds, "Possibly, give me a minute to think," while he holds up his right hand, as if he is calling timeout from an imaginary umpire. He then stares at the diagram on the whiteboard for a solid 20 seconds.

Finn interrupts the silence by saying, "We need to cycle back to Gabby. Gabby sets up camp right here in the parking lot in a little alcove. He got there while you were in the restaurant. He can confirm that Dave left about midnight. He remembers hearing Dave put the Rav4 in reverse. You know how it makes that strange sound. He also recalls seeing you sometime between 12:30 and 1 a.m., urinating in public. He also remembers seeing your vehicle. Unfortunately, he did not see any of the other players in this scenario."

There is a knock on the door and Finn walks towards the computer. "Hey Jimmy, I need to check my email. Can you get the door? It will be the pizza and it is already paid for. Thanks."

Jimmy moves from the whiteboard to open the door. Sure enough, the front desk officer is there holding a pizza box and he says, "No tip necessary."

Behind him, Jimmy sees Officer Hodgson, whom he recognizes from the Lucy Chan segment, walking an attractive woman down the hall in handcuffs. Jimmy turns pale and tries not to make eye contact with either woman. He grabs the pizza quickly and turns back into the War Room. The officer who delivered the pizza raises his eyebrows in response to the abruptness of Jimmy's actions.

When Jimmy sets the pizza on the big center table, Finn is humming while looking at his email. He says, "I will be right there. Eat it while it is hot."

Chapter 4.8 – The Squeeze

Jimmy finishes one piece of pizza, but his stomach is churning. Meanwhile, Finn devours four slices like he has not eaten in a week.

Finn says, "You not hungry, Jimmy? You okay?"

"Yeah, I am fine. However, what you said earlier really shook me up. The part about Dave hanging upside down for hours. You obviously deal with death all the time, being a homicide detective and all, but I do not. Closest I get is a dead ball."

"Understood. Sorry about that."

"We should probably get back to things here." Finn brings out a stack of papers. "We got bank account records for everyone involved in this mess. Here are all the reports. I combed through these reports and it took hours."

"Can you give me the Cole's Notes version?"

"Surely, Starr Stewart gets a regular paycheck from The Riv, but of course, she lives way beyond that salary. She is in a cash-rich business. Her bills get paid out of her account, but she must pay for most other things with cash."

"Sorry Finn, what is the Riv?"

"Oh, I assumed you knew. She is a stripper out in Dearborn at a place called the Riviera. According to Gabby, she also does some street walking, but I have not confirmed that yet. Officer Hodgson is going to look into that, but I am not sure where she is with that."

"I see."

"Johnson has a similar profile. I think Frankie was right when he told us that Johnson supplemented his income with pushing drugs. That Toyota Corolla, it is no Challenger, but it is above his pay grade as a bartender. By the way, he paid cash, even though he told me he got it with low percentage financing."

"Can no one just make an honest living?"

"Well, not everyone is graced with elite abilities, like you Jimmy. Moving to Frankie, he is very straightforward and clean as a whistle. And, of course, I cannot find diddly squat on Wohlers."

"I assume you checked out Dave and me, too."

"Yes, actually. Dave barely spent anything and literally bought nothing with cash. I am actually surprised there was some loose change in his vehicle when we found it. He charged everything he could, but of course, he paid his credit cards off in their entirety every month. He also had an automatic transfer of $3,000 per month to his mother. He was clean as a whistle, and saintly, actually."

"And me?"

"I am impressed how much you make!"

"And how much my ex makes?"

"No doubt! There was one red flag and that is that you do take out exorbitant amounts of cash each month."

"Yes, I do, but if you look back far enough, you will see that I have done so forever, or at least since my marriage fell apart, actually even before that."

"Oh okay, I believe you."

"You see, I eat out a lot, but being a local celebrity, I rarely am able to pay. I often get meals comp'd. It is hard to tip when you don't have a bill to pay. It's not like you are going to ask for the credit card machine to give a tip on a zero balance. For example, you talked to Gord at the Whiskey Bar, right? He covered the bill for the entire night. I put down three bills that night to pay anyway and to leave a tip. He really didn't need to cover our bill for the night."

"Alright, I see. That makes sense. Anyway, I really could not find a smoking gun anywhere in this stack. The expression is *follow the money*, but it led me nowhere in this case."

Jimmy and Finn are both startled when there is a loud rap on the door. Finn jumps up and before he can open the door, Sergeant Brown barges in. "Finn, Officer Hodgson needs to see you A-SAP. She has a breakthrough in the case."

"Awesome, tell her I will be right there. Sorry Jimmy, I will be back as soon as I can. You are welcome to continue combing through things here."

"Will do. I will probably have the entire thing solved before you get back." Jimmy follows that with a forced laugh.

In Finn's absence, Jimmy looks through the documents on the table, but they have already discussed everything there. He moves over to the whiteboard and studies the diagram further, again visualizing the movements.

Fifteen minutes pass and Finn returns to see Jimmy pacing back and forth in front of the whiteboard. "Jimmy, we might have a break. Officer Hodgson picked up Starr Stewart on a solicitation charge, so she definitely has been supplementing her income beyond table dancing. Gabby was correct. He may be homeless, but he is solid. I let Ms. Stewart know that we know about the fake phone call to her sister. Officer Hodgson is letting her stew for a few minutes and then she will go back in, to try and find out with whom she has been working. It will be the good old speech about the first one to talk, gets the better deal."

Jimmy interjects with a smirk, "That is amazing that Officer Hodgson just walked in with Starr Stewart, basically at the same time we were talking about the two of them."

Finn replies, "Yes, quite the coincidence."

Jimmy looks at his feet and says, "I don't believe in coincidences."

"Nor do I Jimmy, nor do I."

Chapter 4.9 – The Goods

Jimmy continues to look at his feet for a solid two minutes, before he breaks the silence, "You didn't just get a text message did you? When did you find out that Starr made a fake call?"

"Oh, I found out late yesterday and thanks to you."

"To me?"

"Yes, I remembered that you would call VanBuskirk when you knew he would not answer and that was when you would leave him your scouting reports. I realized that could have been what Starr did and it was not hard to verify."

Jimmy goes silent as his mind moves onto another aspect of the night. He replays his movements in the parking lot. "I had my truck location right the first time, didn't I? You tricked me into changing it based on what the bum had seen."

"No, you must have just got confused and second guessed yourself. And, he is not a bum. He is unfortunately homeless and his name is Gabby. Gabby was actually very helpful. He knew you were there, because he saw you urinate and then you got into your truck. Ironically, he also noticed that your truck was not in that same spot all evening as there were several motorcycles parked there at one point. Loud ones that interrupted his sleep. He also thought it was odd that you had the truck, as he has seen and heard your muscle car there many times in that parking lot. I asked myself why would you drive the truck on a beautiful night? More troubling though was why the heck would you move your vehicle?"

There is no response from Jimmy.

While Finn points at a spot on the whiteboard, he continues, "Anyway, I am guessing that you parked here at 10:00 in a spot that was just out of Gabby's line of sight. Then, you left in the passenger seat of Dave's SUV, using your cane to drive. Your convenient cane! You launched Dave to his death and then made your way back to the restaurant on a bike or something that you had stashed near where Starr was distracting Johnson. So, you got back to the restaurant, retrieved your truck and returned to the bridge to unload water from the bed of your truck. Perhaps you had jugs like I had or maybe storage bins. Whatever, we will find out eventually. Then, when you returned to the Xochimilco parking lot with your truck, your parking spot must have been taken by a late arriving customer, so you happened to park closer to where you urinated. Ironically, Gabby had only seen where you parked later in the evening and knew you did not park there earlier, because there were loud motorcycles parked there."

Jimmy shrugs.

"If you actually *saw* homeless people, you might have noticed Gabby in the alcove."

Jimmy bows his head.

"You know, I went to the parking lot late last night after finding out about Ms. Stewart's fake phone call. I stood where Gabby said you were urinating. When I raised my left hand, I noticed a window ledge that was just out of my reach. You are slightly taller than me and I assume that is where you left your cell phone, to avoid cell tower pings that could have placed you at the scene of the crime. It was a nice casual way to retrieve your phone. That was actually a very nice move. Again, Gabby saw you though."

"I really do not know what to say."

"You did not tweak your knee on the Home Opener Night either, did you? You wanted to have the cane to reach the brake and gas pedals. You have been planning this for some time."

Jimmy resumes his silence.

"How much did you pay Johnson to drug Dave and Jessie at the Magic Stick? By the way, we did find out that you recently sold an autographed, game-worn World Series jersey. I bet that drew thousands. Johnson was probably willing to take some of your painkillers for payment, too!"

Again, Jimmy remains silent, but he sits down and pulls out his phone.

Jimmy sends a text to Amp: I feel stupid

And another: I come undone

He sees the grey dots come up, disappear and reappear. Amp replies: Mad Season – Rob Thomas

Jimmy: Close enough (Matchbox 20)

Amp: It was Mad Season though right?

Jimmy: Yes, it was, it really was - sorry brother – signing off – turn on CNN in an hour or so – again, I am truly sorry

To that end, Jimmy powers off the phone and sets it aside.

Jimmy returns his attention to Finn and begins to open up. "I had nothing to do with Johnson drugging Jessie and I promise you that I did not intend to kill Dave. I was slipping him painkillers regularly to mess with his performance and it worked. I wanted him to get caught with an impaired driving. That is what I tried to do on the Home Opener Night and that stupid Last Chance guy let him off. I wanted to tarnish Dave's image and hopefully violate his morality clause in his contract. That is all. After failing the first time, I wanted to make sure there was an accident the second time."

"You left him for dead, even though he idolized you. His family worshiped you and you left him for dead, Jimmy!"

Chapter 4.10 – Jimmy's Loose Ends

Finn had most of it figured out, but some loose ends remained.

"So Jimmy, what about the Anthony Wohlers guy? Was he working with you too?"

"Nah, not at all. The Whiskey Bar stuff was all true, but he was not at Xochomilco. I just made that shit up. Got lucky that he was a viable suspect and all."

"That was actually pretty good. You had me on that one. For a while, I really did think it was Johnson and Wohlers working together."

Jimmy smiles a little with pride.

"Loudmouth Tigers fan?"

"All true."

"But no sharing glory day stories with the other fan over a Corona?

"Correct."

"Okay, what was with the Tic Tac packets?"

"Well, that is actually how Stefan carries his pills around. I got the idea from him."

"Ah, so he legitimately panicked when I interviewed him and showed him the Tic Tac packet that we found in his apartment. I thought maybe you planted them there to misdirect me."

"Nah, I got the idea of the packet from him when we met a few months ago, when I got sent back from Florida. We got to chatting when I was out for a beer one night at the Magic Stick. Anyway, I dumped Dave's mints from his packet, put in a few of my pills, and shook it up to leave behind some residue. It was just to support the ruse that Dave was strung out on pills. So were the ziplock bags in his apartment."

"Did you wipe the Tic Tac container down to remove prints?"

"Yeah, because I had brought the packet into my apartment to load it. Before I got to it, the packet was sitting on my kitchen counter and Jenny took a couple of mints. When I put it back into the vehicle, I remembered that, so I wiped it clean. I could not leave behind any evidence that could implicate Jenny to any of this."

"I am guessing you are the one that reached out to Jessie on behalf of Dave, for the booty call."

"Yeah, Dave pulled out his phone for some reason, but he was not really coherent. I took it from him and texted Jessie. That is when I put it into his pocket, and apparently the wrong pocket!"

"How about the water bottle?"

"You had that all correct. It was used to ensure that the lane tracing would not cancel out. I poured out a little bit to make it look more at home in the vehicle. I thought an unopened bottle would look suspicious. I had no idea that the no DNA thing would make it look more suspicious. I forced Dave to take a swig of the Jack Daniels to top things off."

"Ironically, those three things were what made the difference for me. If it was not for the misplaced phone or the wiped Tic Tac container, I may have written the crash off as an accident. Then, the DNA issue with the water bottle got me thinking of why. Why was it there? It could not have been left there by Dave. Those three anomalies were just too much to let go."

Finn switches gears and asks, "As for Ms. Stewart, how much did she know?"

"Nothing whatsoever. She was to leave the restaurant at midnight, fake the phone call, and well, you know the rest. She had no idea why."

"How did you connect with Starr?"

Jimmy looked up with a crooked smile and rolled his eyes.

"Okay, I see. On the street corner?"

To that, Jimmy nodded.

"Man, talk about morality clause and a use for cash. You were playing with fire doing that. And now, you burned up your morality clause, not to mention, your entry into the Hall of Fame. Just ask Pete Rose."

"Yeah, I know."

"Jimmy, what about Frankie and Stefan? Did you pay Frankie to kill Stefan?"

"Absolutely not! The plan was for Stefan to leave town once the dust settled a bit. I gave him a grand and some pills for spiking Dave's drink, only Dave's drink, I swear. Frankie stabbed him before he got a chance to leave. Since he was going to be gone anyway, I figured I might as well use him as the patsy."

Finn desperately wanted to say, "The patsy for what Jimmy? For an impaired driving? So much for the *I did not mean to kill him* story," but he bit his lip and that will be a conversation for the District Attorney. Finn also noted that Greyson activated Stewart back on April 1st when she *happened* to meet Johnson. This was prior to the first failed attempt at a drunk driving charge. Finn is certain that this was a premeditated crime with long-term planning. However, now is not the time to engage in that conversation.

Finn winces and it is obvious that hundreds of things are firing around in his brain, then he blurts out, "Oh, you were the one that leaked that there was a *person of interest* connected to the Magic Stick. That is probably what made Frankie snap. I really do not know how you sleep at night Greyson. Well, Jimmy, just when I started to like you, now I have to place you under arrest for the murder of one David Stone and there may be several other charges by the time things shake out. You have the right to remain silent…"

Chapter 4.11 - Finn's Loose Ends

The day after arresting Jimmy Greyson on murder, Finn takes his Rav4 back to the rental office and the total bill is substantial considering the number of days he had the vehicle. Thankfully, there was no damage to it from the near disaster simulation. He gets the paperwork and stuffs it into his breast pocket of his jacket.

Finn walks into the station and knocks on Sergeant Brown's door. He hears, "Come on in Finn. What say you?"

Gaines gives an odd look at that question.

Brown continues, "Congratulations man! To get a confession for something that didn't even look like a crime, is amazing. You are a rock star! What was the tipping point for you?"

Gaines clears his throat and says, "Like I said, there were some anomalies that kept me pursuing the case. However, the tipping point was getting some dumb luck. When Antaya happened to see Destiny on my screen in the office, that led me to identify Starr Stewart. I am sure Greyson was not expecting me to track her down, let alone discredit her supposed call to her sister. At that point, I knew I had an accomplice. The thing is she set the time and place for her date with Johnson in order to frame Johnson. Similarly, Greyson set the time and place for his meeting with Stone. Way too much of a coincidence!"

Brown jumps in with, "And frankly my dear, you do not believe in coincidences, so she had to be working with Greyson then. Good reasoning!"

Gaines laughs and responds, "I would not say it like that, but correct. Anyway, once Greyson was arrested and he consulted with his lawyer, he sang like a bird. I guess they are hoping for leniency for cooperation."

"So, what are you doing here? Looking for praise? Well, you've got it. Great job!"

"Ah, thanks Sarge, but my main reason for being here, is this." Gaines pulls out the rental paperwork, places it on Brown's desk, turns, and then exits the office.

Brown yells after him, "You have to at least fill out the expense report."

Finn replies without turning, "Nah, they invoiced you personally, Sarge!"

***

Finn flags a taxi outside of the police station and hops in. After a short drive, the taxi pulls into the Toyota Dealership. Finn exits the taxi and approaches Hugh, who is in the lot, just saying goodbye to a potential customer.

Hugh exclaims, "Detective Gaines! Welcome back! What can I do for you?"

"You can sell me a car. It has to be something on the lot, because I plan on leaving with it today."

"Oh, I have a deal for you."

***

Detective Paul Antaya is sitting at his desk in the station when the front desk officer calls to let him know that there is a package waiting for him. Antaya walks to the front desk and looks at the box quizzically. It is six inches square and about twelve inches tall with UPS stickers on it, that indicate it came from Florida.

The officer working the front desk asks, "Do you think it is safe? You are not expecting an explosive device today, are you?"

"Well, there is only one way to find out. Here, you open it."

"Oh geez, if anyone is going to blow up today, it's going to be you."

"Do you have a knife? Or Scissors?"

"Here you go. Please don't hurt yourself. I don't want to have to fill out the paperwork."

After conducting surgery on the box and removing half of its contents, Antaya begins a deep belly laugh and says, "Gaines, that is a good one!"

Antaya raises a bottle and turns it towards the other officer. It is one of two large bottles of Destin Blonde Ale and there is a black magic marker Y added to form the name, Destiny."

The desk officer says, "Clearly, this is an inside joke. Get out of my area with that Antaya. Oh yeah, by the way, Gaines asked me to remind everyone about this poster over here."

The desk jockey points to a crudely designed flier that was clearly designed by someone with limited computer skills. On it, there is a message, "Come out to celebrate the weekend at the Magic Stick on Friday at 4 p.m.! Everyone is welcome. Wings and nachos are being supplied from a private donation to the DPD. Drinks are your own responsibility. Rumour has it, there will be a number of Detroit Tigers present to sign autographs, as well."

Antaya replies, "Can you give me that poster? I will scan it and send it out by email to everyone. We need to pack that place after the damage we've done to its reputation."

***

Finn pulls into the parking lot by Xochomilco and looks around to see if Gabby is there. Sure enough, he is tucked into his little alcove.

As he exits his vehicle, Gabby shouts, "Yo detective, is that a new vehicle?"

"Yes, it is. The salesman at the Toyota dealership did me a solid during my investigation, so I bought a hybrid Venza off him. I think he actually gave me a pretty good deal."

"Sweet."

"And Gabby, you did me a solid as well. Not sure if you have heard, but I solved the case."

"Well, not yet. Remember newspapers are slow at reporting news and plus I get mine a day or two later than that!"

"Ah, good point. Anyway, when people do me a solid, I repay the favor."

"Oh detective, you do not need to do that."

"Well, I do not want you waiting for news. You know Xochi's Gift Shop over there. They will give you a newspaper free of charge, every day for as long as you can still get newspapers. I cannot promise that they will continue printing newspapers forever, though."

"Oh, thank you, detective. That is very kind of you."

"Also, keep an eye out for the first Tigers home game of every month. If you go to the Will Call gate, they will have two tickets for you. It will be a different pair of seats every game, so you will get to see the entire park."

"The entire season? That's so kind."

"Actually no, that is a lifetime commitment."

Gabby is in awe and asks, "Really?"

The Tigers organization actually gave those tickets to Finn, but he was not able to accept the gift, according to department policies. He asked the organization to pass them on to someone who is more in need.

"Yes, enjoy them, buddy."

"I do not know how I can ever repay you."

Finn replies, "Well, I know how. Every once in a while, I want to be able to take you out for dinner at Nemo's. I hope that is okay."

"Of course. And if you ever need any street info, you know where to find me."

Chapter 4.12 – Mrs. Stone

As Gaines drives directly north of the city to Romeo, Michigan, he has mixed emotions. On one hand, he is excited to inform Mrs. Stone that he has secured a confession for the killing of her son, but he is also nervous about how she will react. After all, her son David idolized Jimmy Greyson and David wanted to emulate his career after the famed Tigers infielder.

Gaines parks his cruiser in front of the modest home and takes a deep breath before exiting the vehicle. Since Mrs. Stone is expecting the detective's arrival, she is standing in the front doorway looking grim.

Gaines walks slowly up the sidewalk, trying not to meet her eyes until he reaches the 4-step front porch. As he raises his left foot onto the first stair, he tilts his head upward and realizes she has both arms out, inviting him in for a hug. Gaines obliges and they embrace for several minutes while both shed tears.

They separate still holding hands and she says, "Come on in, Mr. Gaines. I have some tea and cookies ready for you."

She leads him by one hand through the front door and into the living room where the local news is on the television, at inaudibly low volume. They sit at opposite ends of the couch and Mrs. Stone pours tea into two cups on the coffee table.

"Thank you for seeing me, Mrs. Stone."

"Oh, I am thankful to you. It has been all over the news about you arresting Mr. Greyson for my son's murder. God bless you and thank you."

"I was hoping to tell you personally first, but you know how the media is so fast these days."

"I understand sir. That is not a problem. I can only assume that Mr. Greyson was perceiving David as a threat to his position."

"Yes, and he blamed David for his injury."

Mrs. Stone clarifies, "Which was clearly accidental, but he must have perceived it was intentional."

Finn says, "I suspect so and perception can be people's reality," as he takes a sip of tea.

"Can you share details with me, sir?"

Gaines shares a skeletal version of the events leading up to David's death, being careful not to divulge details which could upset the grieving mother. As he is finishing up, the newscast on television switches to coverage of the arrest.

A still photo of Jimmy Greyson in the cemetery, that must have been taken by a paparazzi at a distance, is displayed next to a newscaster who is speaking, presumably giving details of the arrest. Jimmy is dressed in a suit, along with designer sunglasses and he is holding Jenny's hand. In the background are Jessie and Amp, but their faces are not in focus.

Gaines looks at the picture of Jimmy and company, shakes his head, reaches for the remote control, and asks, "Would you like me to turn it off?"

Mrs. Stone looks at the picture intently and she squints to get a better look. She whispers, "No, Detective Gaines, no."

Gaines asks, "Mrs. Stone? Are you okay?"

She continues to stare at the picture and her hands are visibly shaking, so she carefully places the cup and saucer onto the coffee table.

Gaines again attempts to get her attention, "Mrs. Stone?"

She slowly replies, "I think, I think I know that girl. The one holding Jimmy's hand. She looks a little older now and she used to have darker, longer hair. She lived down the street and her brother *was* Ken, David's best friend in high school. They played ball together and were both considered rising stars and destined for the major leagues."

"What became of Ken?"

Mrs. Stone continues to stare at the television even though it is now displaying a commercial for a laundry detergent. She mumbles, "Ken died when they were in high school. David and he were out one night and there was a tragic accident. Ken's sister, Jennifer withdrew completely after that and I have not seen or heard from her since Ken's funeral. I am almost certain that is her."

About the Author

Phil Warner grew up in Windsor, Ontario, Canada, where of course, he played a significant amount of baseball and hockey. After graduating from the University of Windsor and then the University of Western Ontario (now known as Western University), he relocated to Sarnia, Ontario where he began his teaching career. Phil taught secondary school mathematics and computer science prior to moving into administration.

While teaching in Sarnia, Phil met his wife Wendy and together they began their *million dollar family* raising two outstanding humans! Coaching athletes, as well as coaching professionals through mentoring, has been a passion throughout Phil's personal life and his career. In retirement, Phil has taken up hobbies such as pickleball, renovations, teaching part-time at a university, and writing, but most importantly becoming a proud grandpa.

With significant time on his hands during the 2020/2021 pandemic, *Undone* came to fruition and he hopes to share his love for baseball and the City of Detroit through this novel.

Phil.Warner@mail.com

9 798731 350228